K. L. Loveley is the author of three works of contemporary fiction, a collection of poetry and a series of children's books written under her maiden name.

She lives in Nottinghamshire with her family and enjoys gardening, sewing, travelling and of course reading and writing.

As a retired nurse, who has dealt with a wide range of medical, social and family drama, she uses her life experience to create fascinating characters and intriguing scenarios within her books.

In memory of my parents, Gordon and Dorothy Oliver, who gave me life and taught me to love.

K. L. Loveley

UNION BLUES

AUSTIN MACAULEY PUBLISHERS™

LONDON · CAMBRIDGE · NEW YORK · SHARJAH

A CIP catalogue record for this title is available from the British Library.

ISBN 9781398422797 (Paperback)
ISBN 9781398422803 (ePub e-book)

www.austinmacauley.com

First Published 2022
Austin Macauley Publishers Ltd®
1 Canada Square
Canary Wharf
London
E14 5AA

I wish to thank Austin Macauley Publishers and their hard-working, dedicated team for bringing *Union Blues* to publication.

To my husband and children for their continued love and support throughout the writing process.

My biggest and most heartfelt thanks of all, though is to you the reader for choosing this book and to all of the bloggers and everyone who has helped promote *Union Blues*, *Alice* and *Love, Secrets and Absolution*.

Thank you.

Other Books by K. L. Loveley

Alice

Also published by Austin Macauley, this was Katie's debut novel and the first of her **social voice series.**

Alice is near breaking point; her life is slowly spiralling out of control. When her daughter Anne-Marie repeatedly falls victim to aggressive vandals and her husband offers no support, she decides to take control of the mess that has become her life. Freeing herself from the chaos in her own home, she discovers that freedom isn't as sweet as she thought.

5.0 out of 5 stars: Captivating read.
Reviewed in the United Kingdom on 1 July 2019

Verified Purchase

A very gripping read that kept my interest throughout. Easy to lose yourself in the characters' lives. Feel most women would be able to relate to various aspects of Alice's journey. Cleverly written, well done.

Love, Secrets and Absolution

Set in an early eighties' Midlands Town during the miners' strike, we meet Alfie, the longed-for son of Grace and Paul. However, young Alfie is not like other boys and people in the village gossip about him.

He is a lonely boy full of secrets, lies and obsessive thoughts.

How far can a mother's love go?

REVIEWER LADY

It's been a long time since I have **pondered over a book** as much as I have this one. **It's more than a story** – it could easily be a true story and that is all credited to the author's style of writing. I have no hesitation in giving *Love, Secrets and Absolution* the **very highest recommendation**.

In addition to three works of contemporary fiction, Katie has published a collection of poetry.

Chameleon Days is a collection of poems from *The Changing Emotions of a Woman Unleashed.*

Reviewed in the United Kingdom on 27 December 2019

Verified Purchase

I decided to purchase *Chameleon Days* after seeing a local promotion. The quirky front cover and title drew my attention. There is a range of poetry that clearly reflects the changing emotions of the poet, cleverly written using modern technology to describe emotion. For example, 'humming down the diamond line'. Also, the physical world, using magnetism to reinforce the strength of feelings. I enjoyed reading about the changing emotions of a woman unleashed.

Also by K. L. Loveley:

A series of illustrated children's books written under her maiden name of Alyson Oliver.

Morning Mystery, the first of her children's *Coop Chaos* series, published 2020.

5.0 out of 5 stars: Our children loved this book
Reviewed in the United Kingdom on 7 June 2020

Verified Purchase

What a wonderful book! The author has captured the personality of each hen perfectly and has great illustrations throughout! We look forward to reading all about Daisy, Lily, Rose, Buttercup, Bluebell and Poppy's next adventure.

Chapter One

Ascending the warm and comforting road towards the place of new beginnings; laying closer to the security and physical satisfaction of the familiar. A tiny hand brushed against her face, as she wrapped her leg around soft, tender flesh. Floating in a sea of exquisite beauty – weightless and free from torment.

Echoing through the gentle pulsing fluid, she heard a distant sound.

Willow, Willow. Can you hear me?

The booming sound of base and the shrillness of Janet's voice drew Willow back to the here and now.

'What did you say?' she called above the sound that was threatening to burst her fragile eardrums.

Shaking her head in frustration, Janet beckoned Willow towards the exit sign, the only decent light in the hazy room.

'I've been looking all over for you. What's happened to your dress? Are you aware that it is totally transparent? The guys are in their element?'

Willow quickly placed both hands over her breasts, wishing she had put her bra on. This was the first and last time that she would risk going bra-less even if her straps did show.

'Some crazy guy spilt a whole pint of beer down me when I was on the way to the loo. Can you believe it, Jan? The hand dryer was broken and the paper towels scattered on the floor?'

'Where's Susan?'

Janet pointed to the dance floor where their friend was attempting to shake her ting to a reggae number.

'Let's rescue her and get in the taxi queue before everyone else, I can't stand here all night with my hands on my chest,' laughed Willow.

The girls kept watching one person at a time getting into taxis and felt frustrated that the queue was hardly reducing. Suddenly, a black cab pulled up beside them.

'Fancy a ride?' shouted one of the passengers. He winked at Willow, 'I can help you out of that dress if you like.'

Sudden realisation that this was the guy who had spilt his beer down her and had made a number of innuendoes. This time, she was more prepared for the banter and decided to give him a taste of his own medicine.

'Are you sure you won't have any premature accidents this time?' she asked.

'Wow! Gabriel, mate, she got you good,' said a ginger haired lad next to him.

'Fair play, I like a feisty girl,' Gabriel said. 'Anyhow, I want to apologise about that and offer you our taxi.'

Willow was shocked, however, didn't want to *look a gift horse in the mouth.*

'Thanks,' she said, 'that would be brilliant.'

Gabriel passed some cash to the taxi driver to compensate him for the delay and turned to his friends and said, 'Come on lads, let's get a kebab.'

The other two guys dutifully climbed out of the taxi, making way for Willow and her friends. Gabriel deliberately brushed by Willow and pressed a beer mat into her hand. She was surprised, however, quickly slipped in into her handbag. The girls sat together in the taxi and began to laugh hysterically.

'Willow, can you keep getting drinks spilt on you as we might be able to get home quicker again?' said Susan.

She was deep in thought and then said, 'Is it me, or does this guy have a big ego?'

'You know what they say about huge egos,' said Susan, 'anyhow, I personally thought his mate was better looking.'

'The tall guy was gorgeous,' said Janet, 'I wouldn't mind bumping into him.'

'What do you say girls – should we go clubbing again next weekend?' asked Susan.

'Oh yeah,' they replied in unison and started laughing again much to the taxi driver's annoyance. He had a cracking headache after the nightshift and wanted to go home to bed, however, he had to endure more *girls talk* for a further ten minutes.

'I think I'm going to treat myself to a new dress,' said Willow, as she looked down at the stain, 'what style should I get?'

'Something which doesn't end up see through if another drink gets spilled,' replied Janet, 'though, maybe this fella will like that.'

'He did stare at my breasts, though it's my fault for not wearing a bra,' Willow said. 'I best add some nice underwear to my shopping list, just in case.'

They began talking about what outfits they would wear for next time and made plans where and when they would meet. However, soon it was Janet's drop off, then Susan, and finally Willow was the only one left. She hated the last part of the journey; she was scared in case the taxi driver turned out to be a psychopath. She knew she shouldn't judge all men the same, however, she tensed up and was on guard just in case. The taxi had an unpleasant smell, until she realised it was the stale beer on her dress.

She dug into her handbag to find a mint to help freshen her mouth which still tasted of cheap wine. However, instead she found the beer mat which she pulled out and examined using the light from her mobile phone. She read the appalling handwriting, and tried to decipher the name, 'Gabriel,' she said out loud and thought, *Where will this lead?*

She suddenly looked up and realised that the taxi driver had made a wrong turn, causing her to feel uneasy. Fidgeting around on the seat, crossing and uncrossing her legs and frantically staring out of the steamy window she felt a rising panic. Her imagination playing all kinds of scenarios. The driver seemed to sense her discomfort and started small talk.

'Don't worry, love, this is a shortcut I know,' he said in a friendly voice. 'I was born and raised around here, so I know it like the back of my hand.'

'No worries,' replied Willow, even though she was still on guard.

'Had a good night then?' he asked.

'Good, thanks,' Willow replied, 'How about you? Is your shift nearly over?'

'Yep, you are my last ride then I am off home to my wife and kids.'

He pulled into her street and slowed down.

She took out her purse and paid the driver, thanked him, then got out holding her high heels and bag. *Seriously, why did I wear these?* She tiptoed barefoot towards the front door trying to be as quiet as possible so as not wake her parents. Unfortunately, Sandy her little Jack Russel terrier began to bark loudly and scratch at the front door.

'Is that you, love?' called her father.

'No, it's a burglar! Of course, it's me,' she replied and then quickly added. 'Sorry, if I've disturbed you.'

Sandy jumped up and down in front of her, excited and wanting to play. She bent down and stroked his back, smoothing down his short hair. She loved his black and tan markings and his fiery nature. As small as he was, Sandy behaved as though he was as brave as a lion.

'Come on, boy, back to your basket; it's sleep time not play time. There's a good boy.'

Tail between his legs and head down, Sandy reluctantly returned to his basket.

Once in her bedroom, Willow decided to read the contents of the beer mat in a better light. In addition to his name and number, he had also scrawled, *same place – same time?*

A huge smile crept across her face. *Actually, he is rather cute,* she thought. Perhaps I might make a very special effort next Saturday.

Chapter Two

Gabriel was smitten. He had never felt so instantly attracted to a woman before. How could this be? He didn't believe in the fancy notion of "love at first sight" and yet here he was, unable to get the image of Willow from his mind. Sure, he understood the concept of chemistry, the effect of pheromones on his psyche.

The visual messages sending love chemicals soaring around his highly aroused body. Those breasts of hers, firm beneath the beer-soaked blouse she was wearing. He was tempted to lick the beer right off those delicious, pert breasts. Her expression was electric. Just feisty enough without being aggressive and her eyes the colour of dark chocolate, framed with deliciously long black lashes. *She is a stunner,* he thought and hoped, that Willow was feeling the same about him. Though he doubted it.

He considered himself vaguely attractive in a manly kind of way but compared to his mates Leo and Adnan, he was no heart-throb. His auburn, curly hair was most difficult to manage, and he always felt that his unruly hair prevented him from being conventionally handsome. Broad-shouldered and with a hint of a sportsman's build did help to catch the eye of some young women and for that, he was grateful. One thing he knew for sure, he would be at the nightclub, the following Saturday, holding his breath in the hope of seeing Willow again.

The week passed slowly. He was enjoying his final year at medical school and looking forwards to spending time on placement at the *Queens Medical Centre*. Although distracted with thoughts of Willow, he managed to knuckle down and get on with some serious revision. There were a number of research articles piled up on the desk in his room that he needed to go through and make notes. He very much enjoyed being a medical student and felt that in many ways it was his vocation in life. Even as a child, he was fascinated by how his body worked and was always asking questions about life and how each body system worked. While his school friends were fascinated by the workings of a car engine or how an aeroplane could fly, he wanted to know how his heart managed to keep on pumping day and night, year after year. He was fascinated by the way his own body healed itself after being wounded. He couldn't understand why it was more important to know about a car engine than the fascinating piece of machinery that the human body was.

Looking around his bedroom, he realised it needed a good clean and tidy before he could even consider bringing someone as special as Willow back to his place. There wasn't much light entering through the sky light window, which helped to prevent the observation of dust. The ragged sofa was stained from the many takeaways he'd consumed over the past few years and truthfully, it smelled like a curry house sofa. Perhaps some of that fabric deodoriser would do the trick, he thought. Now, what was it called, *Fabreezee* or something? Perhaps if he changed the bedsheets and threw a few cushions on the bed, it may look more appealing. Gabriel decided that it might be a good investment to pop into the pound shop or a bargain shop of some kind and buy a couple of cheap scatter cushions. Women seemed to like such things. From his previous experience with ladies, on the occasion he was invited back to theirs, he noticed the ridiculous number of cushions they had on their bed. All of which, need to be removed before any kind of serious romance could take place.

This is crazy, he thought to himself, *she probably won't even be interested in me. No rush, I'll see how things develop before making any effort with the room.* Besides, none of the other girls seemed to complain. Some of the student nurses he'd enticed back to his room, who he expected to be very particular about cleanliness, had not seemed fazed at all.

It was a totally different matter at work. On the occasions that he was on placement on the hospital wards, he was very up to speed with hygiene and cleanliness. Hadn't his parents always drummed it into him? *Cleanliness is next to godliness.* Perhaps they were right in that respect he mused.

He shared a rented terraced house in West Bridgeford with Leo and Adnan. Two of his closest friends. Both on the same course as himself, which was very helpful in terms of having shared interests. They met as first year medical students and bonded while working on a joint assignment in the morgue department. An experience neither of them will ever forget. It was the first time they'd attended a post-mortem examination to reveal the cause of death of a patient. The bright lights reflecting off the stainless-steel tables and the smell of formaldehyde was overwhelming. The senior pathologist was very slow at the procedure and went into great detail to explain each part of the body, organ by organ. The scalpel so sharp slicing through the skin was like an invisible opening already in place. Nausea, revulsion and fascination were rolled into a huge bundle of emotions surging through their impressionable minds.

It was a necessary part of their training and most unpleasant; they were all glad when it was over. So much so, that they all rushed off to the student union bar to have a few drinks together, to get the taste of death from their mouths and the smell of chemicals from their system. That was over four years ago when they were all living in the halls of residence. It was a natural progression that they rented a house together until their studies were completed. During that time, neither of them had been involved in a serious relationship. Sure, they'd all had their flings and one-night stands, but nothing to distract them from their studies or their friendship.

Despite being close friends, he chose not to share his feelings about Willow. Even when the guys laughed at him for giving up their taxi to the girls, he denied having a crush on one of them. Truth be known, Leo and Adnan were both the worse for wear and were not too impressed that they'd to wait in a taxi queue for forty minutes when they already had a perfectly good taxi.

Leo definitely the most intelligent among them; nothing seemed to faze him, apart from the post-mortem incident. He just got on with his studies and was always the first to complete his assignments. Generally, though not always, he got the highest grades. His family lived just outside of Birmingham. His mother ran her own publishing company, which by all accounts was very successful. His father was the manager of a well-known car manufacturer. Leo had his feet firmly on the ground when it came to his future and although he enjoyed a night out with the lads, he had his sights set firmly on making his parents proud and passing his medical degree.

Adnan, despite being a refugee following the war in the Balkans, had succeeded to build a new life for himself. He was very lucky to have escaped from his hometown in Bosnia. A time when young men of his age were being persecuted and killed. He was rescued by the Red Cross volunteers who were doing sterling work in the Balkans. Later, he was offered an opportunity to go to England where he won a well-deserved scholarship to a school in Manchester. He became their star pupil and was offered a place at Cambridge University.

Adnan's father had been a surgeon in Bosnia. While helping out at a field hospital during the war, he lost his life as a result of an explosion that ripped through the operating theatres, killing the whole surgical team. Determined to carry on the family tradition, Adnan finally decided to attend Nottingham University to study medicine, based on the high reputation of medical studies. He was an ace student and seriously dedicated to becoming a surgeon. His mother and sister had remained in Bosnia to help with the war effort, both independent, strong women. He was very proud of his family and intended to return to his country when he was a fully qualified surgeon and a member of the faculty.

They made a diverse group of loyal friends. Each one of them with their own private agenda.

Gabriel is not a big drinker. Sure, he enjoys a couple of pints when out with the lads, but he very rarely drinks the strong stuff. His parents are both tea total and very pious in their attitudes. He was raised to avoid the sins of man and to concentrate on his all-important life vocation, working in medicine and helping others. To some extent, this ethos was ingrained in him, and yet at times, his passion for pursuits that would be considered inappropriate, by his parents and the church overruled his common sense.

Long ago, he'd allowed himself to take a path that he should not have taken. Despite being strong with other matters in his life, somehow this one flaw in his otherwise impeccable personality was difficult to overcome. He knew with time and patience that he would one day win this battle. He was certain of this. Now, though, wasn't the right time.

If only they knew the truth. His parents would never understand.

Coming from a privileged background, he and his younger sister, Victoria, had attended a private school. Their two years age difference meant that throughout their schooling, at some point, they were in the same school. They both went to *The Nottingham High School* where they enjoyed an excellent education, enabling them both to go to university. Victoria was a brilliant mathematician and had a natural ability with chemistry. She was offered places at a number of universities, finally settling on a course at Warwick University to study chemistry to be close to her friends of which she had many. She planned to work in research for one of the major pharmaceutical companies.

Victoria and he knew how fortunate they were to enjoy the fruits of their parent's success, which was against all odds, according to his parents who had both come from humble backgrounds. They had achieved their ambitions of setting up a small newsagent business and a number of other retail businesses. Including one of the first video rental shops in the small village of Mansfield Woodhouse on the outskirts of

Nottingham where they lived. So successful was the video shop that his parents were able to invest in stocks and shares that proved to be very lucrative. Their mother, Joan, was the brains behind the investments. She had a natural ability with maths and science that she passed on to her children. Their father, Sam, was a natural entrepreneur and the brains behind the business. Together, they formed an awesome team.

Until quite recently, Gabriel had not thought about what they meant by the term *against all odds*. As a child, he just accepted that his parents had worked hard to achieve their success and their respect within the church community. He never questioned any of his parent's ideas, neither did Victoria. They just muddled along enjoying life. However, now he began to think about it, they very rarely spoke about his grandparents or other family members and he remembers nothing about any of them, something that he needed to address. One very important lesson that he'd learnt at medical school, was that certain conditions can be genetically linked and that family history of some conditions, such as diabetes and heart disease were very relevant. He decided to find out a little more about his family history when the opportunity arose.

He had a lot to live up to, in terms of maintaining his family's reputation. They were stalwarts of society and highly respected in the church community, always generous with their money and their time. So much emphasis was put on their education and religious upbringing when they were young that Gabriel and his sister very rarely had much fun on the weekends and during the school holidays.

Victoria didn't appear to mind. When she was young, she seemed to enjoy her own company, spending hours reading stories and playing with her chemistry set. Victoria could spend hours curled up on the beach during their annual two weeks summer holiday at Skegness in Lincolnshire reading every Enid Blyton book she could get her hands on. She lost herself in the adventures of *five on a Treasure Island* imagining that she was like George, a fearless tomboy.

Both she and Gabriel wanted a dog when they were children, they had the name already in their minds. Timmy, just like in the Enid Blyton stories. Sadly, it wasn't to be. A dog wasn't allowed in the household for fear of it being a distraction from their school work. This saddened them very much, but their parents were strict about the rules and decisions they made. Nothing would change their minds.

Victoria enjoyed her reading, while he was drawn to the bright lights of the fun fairs and the penny arcades when they went to the seaside during the school summer holiday. He loved the sound of the machines as the metal reels rolled round and round and the penny drop machine, pushing the coins over the edge. The bright lights mesmerised him. So did the sound of the winning coins, as they fell into the tray ready for him to scoop up and put directly back into the machine. The possibility of winning some money became irresistible to him.

Gabriel, set up a betting system on the table football game in the school common room when he was thirteen years old. Just small amounts of pocket money, but enough to intrigue him. The teachers appeared to have no idea, what was happening. Encouraged by the secrecy of it all, he ventured into the local betting shop when he was sixteen. Already six feet tall he managed to mingle amongst the men, without drawing attention to himself. Taking an interest in the different betting systems without actually placing a bet. Having become a regular face at the bookmakers, the staff turned a blind eye when he eventually placed his first bet on the horses at age sixteen.

As he became older, most evenings after school, Gabriel was involved with Rugby training and played scrum-half for his team. He enjoyed sports. The competitiveness intrigued him. He often set up a syndicate to bet on the winning team. This way, he made a little extra money of his own. Sometimes enough to pop into the bookies on the way home from school.

Chapter Three

Willow loved her job at the garden centre on the outskirts of Nottingham. It suited her perfectly. Fed her need to be close to the land. The smell of the garden composts, the peat and the fragrant herbs was like nectar to her soul. She was part of a team of ten staff. Most worked part-time, unlike Willow, who was employed as a full-time nursery adviser.

She'd gained a qualification in agriculture at the local college, during which time she was given a placement at Ollies Garden Centre. After completing her diploma, she was offered a full-time contract at Ollies and never looked back. Despite her studies in animal, rural and environmental science, Willow took to the science of horticulture with a passion. Her experience with crop production and soil types helped her to understand the practical side of the work. She also studied farm management, something that she hoped may help with future promotion in the company.

The manager, Dorothy, a brilliant horticulturist is a pleasure to work for, she shares the same passion as Willow in terms of her love of the land. They work well together and despite the age difference of only twelve years, Dorothy treats Willow as a daughter. Nothing much escaped her notice, so it was no surprise on Monday morning that she noticed the glint in Willow's eyes.

'Well, someone looks like they have had a good weekend if the glint in your eyes is anything to go by,' said Dorothy.

'I'll put the kettle on and then you can tell all,' she said while making her way in the direction of the kitchen; situated close to the office.

Willow watched her manager, as she walked away. She smiled to herself, as the more than ample bottom of her manager wobbled beneath her tight dungarees. Her long, auburn, curly hair caught the early morning sunshine enhancing the beauty of her best asset. She followed her into the kitchen and while Dorothy filled the kettle, she reached up to the dresser to get a couple of china floral mugs that were hanging neatly in a row. Dorothy insisted that they should not drop their standards just because it was a work environment. After all, we spend most of our day here at work, so why should we not enjoy a little luxury was her ethos. Consequently, the dresser contained china plates, cream and milk jugs, none of which you would expect to see in a staff kitchen. The garden centre also sold homemade produce including cakes and cookies, some of which ended up in the biscuit tin for the staff.

They sat together at the small pine table chatting about the order of work that needed to be completed that day. Willow preferred to keep her private life, just that. But Dorothy had a way of wheedling information from people, so it wasn't long before Willow was telling her about Gabriel and how they'd met.

'Is he good-looking, is he tall and strong, what does he do for a living?'

The questions came thick and fast, from Dorothy, as Willow knew they would do. She tried to think back to Saturday, hoping to remember every detail about his face.

'Well, he is quite tall, at least six foot and has broad shoulders, I remember that much,' said Willow.

'Oh, and he has a mass of light auburn hair, not dissimilar to your own, Dorothy. In fact, I would go as far as to say it's even curlier than yours. You don't happen to have a younger brother, do you?' laughed Willow.

'I have no idea what he does for a living, but looking at his physique, it's probably something manual I would guess.'

'Are you planning to meet up with him next Saturday?' Dorothy inquired.

'Yes,' replied Willow.

Looking down at her hands, she added, 'Don't be surprised if I turn up at work next week with fabulous nails. I intend to have a French manicure next Saturday after work. I don't suppose I could finish an hour earlier could I please, just this once?'

Dorothy nodded. 'No problem at all,' she replied.

Saturday was the busiest day at the garden centre. Families often came together to choose new plants and garden accessories. Children ran frantically around the garden swings and wheelbarrows and some customers just came for a day out, with no intention of purchasing anything. Usually, Willow enjoyed working on Saturdays and was in no hurry to leave, but that particular Saturday was the exception. It was to be marked with a manicure and a long soak in the bath.

She took a long time getting ready and after trying on a number of outfits decided to wear an emerald-green Lycra shift dress and black patent kitten heel shoes that enhanced the shape of her legs. The dress hugged her figure in all the right places, she felt fabulous. Generally, Willow wore very little makeup. She had good skin that required just a touch of blusher to highlight her cheekbones and a thin layer of mascara to her already long dark lashes. On this occasion, she decided to go a step further. She applied a light foundation before her blusher and a line of black eyeliner to her upper lid, giving it a gentle flick at the ends. Instead of her usual lip gloss, she applied a coral lipstick that enhanced her full lips.

When she came downstairs and into the lounge, the fragrance of her perfume wafted gently around. The sweet smell of floral notes that suited her so well. Her mum smiled approvingly.

'Oh, Willow, you look wonderful, I hope that you have a nice time, luv. Just keep safe and have fun with your friends, give them my love, they are such nice girls. Perhaps you should invite them around for a meal one evening, it's a long time since us girls had a nice chat.'

Her dad offered her a lift into town where she planned to meet up with her friends Janet and Susan. Before leaving her, he reminded his daughter to be wary of the wolves in sheep's clothing. Willow loved her father and his quirky sayings. This one was one of his favourites and yet she understood the implications of what he was saying. Her parents loved her dearly, she knew this for certain. They were very protective of her at all times and had found it difficult to let go and allow her the freedom, to enjoy her independence.

Willow was born a twin. Sadly, her identical sister, Molly, died shortly after birth and her mother nearly died following the emergency caesarean section. Complications meant that there would be no more children. Willow felt a great responsibility of being the twin that survived. Survivor's guilt weighed heavily upon her conscience at times, resulting in an empty hollow feeling inside. Sometimes, she felt as though part of her was missing, she felt somehow incomplete and at odds with herself. She felt the need to reassure her parents of her safety and tonight was no exception. Willow hugged her father tightly, unaware that over the other side of the road, a certain young man witnessed this act of parental affection.

The three friends were all in good spirits. Janet and Susan complimented Willow on her choice of outfit and couldn't believe that she had a manicure. They were so used to seeing her broken nails and ragged cuticles that indicated she was working in a manual job. Unlike themselves who both worked in retail.

'You should wear that eyeliner more often, Willow, it really suits you,' said Susan.

Working in retail, both of her friends were always up to date with the latest fashion trends, they got staff discount on the clothes they purchased and occasionally passed on this perk to Willow. They were similar in size, so Willow tried the clothes on in advance and the girls purchased as their own. This enabled her to afford a few nice outfits that she otherwise wouldn't have purchased. Willow was sensible with her wages and after paying towards her keep, she put a substantial amount into her savings. During her working week, she wore dungarees. Not very glamorous, but suitable for the work she was involved in.

It was pointless going to the nightclub too early, the dance floor would be empty and they would look conspicuous at the empty bar. No! That wouldn't do. In any case, Willow did not want to appear too eager or indeed needy. Susan and Janet were both hoping to grab the attention of Gabriel's two friends and rather hoped that the three of them could hang out for the night.

They were not disappointed. When eventually they arrived at the club, the moment they made their way to the bar, the trio of guys made their way to join them, introduced themselves and bought the first round of drinks. The girls decided on a glass of white wine each, so Leo suggested that perhaps a bottle of wine to share would be the better option. He duly carried a tray of wine and glasses across to a booth that was vacant close to the bar area. Gabriel and Adnan followed with three pints of lager, which they promptly put on the small glass-topped table; that was set between the six lounge chairs of a dubious brown colour. Whether naturally or not, the girls left a chair either side of themselves, allowing Gabriel to sit beside Willow, Leo beside Janet and Adnan beside Susan. The dynamics were right, and the conversation flowed along with the wine and lager. As the night drew to a close, and the music slowed down, Gabriel asked Willow to dance with him.

The moment that Willow was in the arms of Gabriel, she knew that she'd found her fit, it felt so right, so perfect it was as though he was the lock and she the key, each the perfect shape and size. The warmth of his body pressed against her own slim frame, felt like a huge comfort blanket enveloping her uncertainty, her vulnerability. She rested naturally on the curve of his shoulder. They danced as if they'd danced together countless times before. She didn't want the music to end. But end it did. As the final notes played out, Gabriel held Willow's hand and led her over to a quiet corner. He gently wrapped his arms around her tiny waist and drew her body close to his. She did not resist. She was powerless against him. His aftershave manly with a hint of musk was deliciously alluring. As if under a spell, Willow lifted her face upwards towards Gabriel, who responded with the gentlest of kisses. She felt intoxicated with the moment, returning his kisses with a passion she did not know she possessed.

Meanwhile, her friends had noticed the coupling up of Willow and Gabriel, so decided they would make themselves scarce. Leo and Adnan although kind and polite to the girls, were not interested in taking things any further. They had excused themselves after Gabriel and Willow took to the dance floor. Although Janet and Susan were disappointed, they were happy for their friend. They agreed earlier in the evening that it would be acceptable for them to make their own way home by taxi if the need should arise.

Gabriel and Willow sat down in a quiet area of the club in a chill out room. They learnt about each other's lives. Willow was surprised to discover that Gabriel was a medical student at Nottingham University. She felt in awe of his achievements and was reluctant to discuss her own work. When she eventually told Gabriel that she worked at a garden centre, he did not appear fazed at all. In fact, he wanted to know more about her work. Willow found herself, explaining her love of the land and nature. She told him of her childhood, how she was surrounded by love and encouraged to follow her heart in all aspects of life. Gabriel appeared to be a good listener. She felt comfortable telling him about her parents and the time she'd spent with them on their humble smallholding, learning about agriculture. He encouraged her to tell him everything.

Locked in each other's arms and joined together at the lips for the remainder of the night, they were surprised when suddenly the whole room was ablaze with light. They had been so engrossed with each other; they'd failed to notice that the club had closed down. The cleaning staff were sweeping up around them.

Laughing, they ran out through the emergency exit doors and into the coolness of the night. Gabriel wrapped his arms around Willow after taking off his jacket and wrapping it around her bare shoulders. He hailed a taxi for them to share, staying with Willow until she was home, before going back to his own place. They swapped mobile numbers, agreeing to meet up very soon.

Chapter Four

'Well,' said Dorothy. As she stood facing Willow on Monday morning, with her arms folded carefully beneath her more than ample breasts.

'Do tell all,' she smiled.

Willow loved Dorothy for her straight talking and frankness and was unable to keep much from her. She knew that Dorothy was always looking out for her and meant well, but some things were private. So, Willow gave a diluted version of events, otherwise, Dorothy might be concerned that things were moving a little too fast. She didn't mention her excitement about the previous day's events and only told her about Saturday evening.

Gabriel rang Willow early Sunday morning with as much excitement in his voice as a young child about to embark on an adventure.

'Willow, I can't get you out of my head, you are so hot. I know this is short notice, but do you fancy a day at the races with me, I can pick you up in an hour. Will that give you enough time to get ready unless you have other plans?'

Without hesitating, she told Gabriel that would be great and yes, she could be ready within the hour. There was no denying the relief in his voice, as he reminded her that he knew where she lived and to expect him within the hour.

Her parents were already out in the garden harvesting the sweetcorn that had provided them with a good crop this year. She ran out into the garden, brushing herself deliberately against the swathes of lavender that filled the borders along the garden path. As the heady scent of lavender filled the air, she felt almost delirious with happiness.

'Mum, Dad,' she called, as she ran towards them.

'Do you mind if I skip Sunday lunch, a friend has invited me to go to the races?'

Her parents simultaneously straightened up their backs from the bending position they were in. Rubbing the back of his neck, her father spoke first. 'Races, hey love. That sounds a bit fancy for a Sunday day out.'

He turned to his wife. 'What do you think love?'

'Bloody marvellous if you ask me. I wish I had such an opportunity when I was younger. You go and have a great time lass and place a bet for me and for your dad.'

She blew both of her parents a kiss and ran back towards the house at breakneck speed. After a quick shower, followed by an even quicker blow dry of her hair, she began to search her wardrobe for something suitable to wear. She had no idea what kind of outfit to wear at the races, in fact, it suddenly occurred to her, which race track she might be going to. In her excitement, she'd forgotten to ask Gabriel that all-important question. She considered phoning him on his mobile but decided against it, for fear of sounding foolish. In the end, she chose a pair of black tailored trousers with a cream satin blouse and a black box style jacket that showed off her slim waist and bottom. The footwear was even more difficult to choose. Would she be stood on the grass beside the race track or inside the area where the betting took place? Decisions, decisions. In the end, she wore black ankle boots, hoping to cover all the odds.

Exactly on time, he pulled up outside of her house, beeped the horn and waved to Willow as she walked down the path. The sound of the horn attracted the attention of her parents, who both watched their daughter looking a million dollars, climb into the battered-looking Ford Fiesta.

'Hi,' said Gabriel. 'Sorry about the car, I'm working on my parents to help me upgrade to a better model, perhaps if we're lucky at the races today I might not have to trouble them.'

'Actually, I have a Fiesta myself, that's probably even older than this one,' she replied.

They both laughed at the coincidence of them having the same car, as he held the passenger side door open for her.

Which race track are we going to, only I've never been to the races before and have no idea what to expect?'

'Southwell Racetrack; it's not far from here at all. I go regularly and know my way around quite well. Don't worry about the betting system, I will teach you to understand,' he reassured her.

True to his word, Gabriel appeared to be very knowledgeable about the races. She was surprised to discover that he was on first-name terms with some of the bookies who had strange stands located close to the track raised above ground level that had display boards outlining the odds for each race. On arrival, he took Willow for a drink in the bar, encouraging her to have a glass of prosecco. While Gabriel was at the bar, Willow glanced around at the other punters who were in the bar area. Satisfied that she didn't look out of place and had dressed appropriately, she began to relax. They looked at the race card together, choosing a horse for the first race. Willow decided on a horse that was tipped as a favourite and wagered the minimum bet of five pounds. Gabriel mentioned something about spread betting that she didn't understand, so was unsure exactly which horse he'd chosen. She never did get to know. He always went alone to place the bets, which suited Willow, allowing her to savour the surroundings and avoid the rough and tumble of the crowds around the betting stands.

Spurred on by backing the winner of the first race, Willow tried her luck at two more races. However, she was not so lucky with these and decided against any more bets. It was all very exciting, and she was really enjoying the day.

Gabriel looked so handsome in his jeans and Oxford-blue shirt. He had a navy, red and white striped tie, hung loosely around his neck. A university tie perhaps thought Willow, or maybe an old school tie. Either way, he looked sexy and difficult to resist. She felt unusually aroused by his closeness, a feeling that surprised her, considering they'd spent such a short time together.

It had taken her six months to feel anything like this with her one and only serious boyfriend. Charles was a young farmer she'd met at one of the annual Farmers' events. Their relationship had been a slow burn, then a fast fizzle out following the one and the only intimate moment they'd shared when she lost her virginity to him. In a haystack of all places. It hadn't been a very satisfying coupling up for her and she guessed that Charles probably felt the same. It wasn't many weeks later that they called a mutual end to their relationship.

When the last race had been won, Gabriel bought Willow another glass of Prosecco and asked if she was okay for a moment while he went to collect his winnings. She was a little surprised at this, as Gabriel's excitement from race to race seemed to decline, so she assumed that he'd lost his money, an amount that she had no idea of.

On his return, Gabriel appeared a little more optimistic as he gently held her hand and thanked her for joining him in one of his favourite pastimes.

'Have you had a good day, Willow?' he asked, as they made their way back to the car. Before she could answer, he swung her around to him and gently kissed her on the lips. A feeling spread through her body, creating a longing she'd never felt before. The ache between her legs was giving her thoughts she wouldn't dare admit to anyone.

'Just as I suspected,' said a breathless Gabriel. 'Your lips taste even better than they look.' He gave her a sheepish grin and reached for her hand.

'Let's get inside the car, before we attract a crowd.'

On the journey home, Gabriel spoke of his family and how upset his parents would be if they knew that he'd been to a race meeting on a Sunday. He told Willow that his parents were self-made millionaires who had worked hard to achieve their success. He was very proud of them and of his sister, but he didn't necessarily share their views on how he should lead his life. They had hoped that he'd study theology and go into the priesthood. When it became clear that wasn't going to happen, his parents accepted his choice of a career in medicine as a good second best. He told Willow that his sister Victoria was very studious and much more serious about life than he was. He spoke of her with great admiration and pride.

He also doubted that Victoria would get romantically involved with anyone outside of the church as she tried too hard to please their parents. Willow felt somewhat uncomfortable about this statement, as though somehow, she would be accused of leading their son astray. The term Scarlet woman sprang to mind. Gabriel interrupted her thoughts.

'Willow, I wasn't expecting to be saying this so soon, but you are constantly on my mind and I can't stop thinking of you...'

Willow put her hand on his shoulder reassuringly.

'There is no rush, Gabriel, we can take our time and get to know each other. I'm not going anywhere and I guess that you have lots of work to be done before the year is out. Concentrate on your studies, we can spend as much or as little time together as you need. Promise that you will put your studies first. It is your whole future. Make your parents proud.'

Gabriel appeared to look relieved with her response. His shoulders slackened and relaxed and he appeared more at ease. He gave her the impression that he was living a life that was at odds with his parents. The more Willow thought about this, the deeper her worry became, for fear of meeting them and not being accepted. She knew that she was prone to worrying too much and overthinking things. Willow chided herself for her unhealthy thought processes and tried to focus on the moment. She'd enjoyed a great day with Gabriel, enjoyed a whole new experience of a day out at the races and even managed to back a winner. She couldn't wait to tell Janet and Susan. They had arranged to go to the cinema midweek to watch the new "Jason Bourne" movie. She loved going to the cinema and the theatre, perhaps she could book some tickets to a show at the Theatre Royal. Maybe treat Gabriel as a thank you for a lovely day out. Yes! That is what she would do.

Gabriel took Willow home, gently kissing her on the lips before she opened the car door. The gentle kiss left her wanting more, but she knew that it wouldn't be appropriate to embrace him outside of her family home. Instead, she blew him a kiss and told him that she hoped they could meet up soon. She walked up the garden path looking up at the inky blue night sky, which was filled with the twinkling light from stars, many million miles away. She took in a deep breath, allowing the lavender scented air to fill her lungs with life. The opaque shadows of the surrounding landscape, which she'd seen many times, appeared even more magical this evening. Willow felt as light as air, as she opened the door and quietly entered her home.

The following week, Willow told Dorothy about her Saturday night out with her friends and that she had indeed hooked up again with Gabriel, who of all things was training to be a doctor. Dorothy was suitably impressed and happy for Willow.

'Do you have another date arranged?' she inquired.

For reasons unknown to herself, Willow did not mention the day at the races. Although it was indeed a great day out, it was a rather unusual place for a first date and she did not wish to put him in a bad light. So she told her that they were hoping to get together the following weekend; providing Gabriel had completed a very important thesis he was working on, towards his finals. Dorothy seemed satisfied with her reply and said no more on the subject.

Willow knew that Dorothy was content when her team of staff were happy. She nurtured a friendly workplace and tried her best to maintain a good working environment. In return, her staff were loyal and hard-working. By the end of the day, despite being careful, Willow was aware that her nails were showing evidence of the manual work she did, but for some reason, this did not faze her at all. Gabriel had not been surprised or put off by the fact that she worked at a garden centre. He told her that he found it endearing that she was true to herself and followed a career path that suited her. However, she couldn't help worrying about what his parents and sister might think about her background and her choice of employment. It seemed to Willow, that Gabriel did not care a hoot about what they may think, in any case, she was probably getting ahead of herself.

Chapter Five

Over the next six weeks, they met up every weekend. Sometimes just for a drink in town where they met with Leo and Adnan and sometimes Janet and Susan. They returned to the races twice, on one occasion going to York races. Gabriel taught her about betting and how to set up an accumulator. Although she enjoyed the races, it wasn't high on her list of favourite activities, but Gabriel appeared to thrive in the environment and was always at his most joyful when among the crowds of punters.

Willow decided to take back a little control of their days out together and purchased some tickets to see *Sister Act* that was on at the Theatre Royal in the centre of town. She thought it would be light-hearted and fun. Gabriel was not as enthusiastic as she was, but he went along with her and appeared to enjoy the evening. Willow enjoyed the whole production, remembering the gospel songs and singing along quietly. After the show, they called at the *Stage Door* pub for a drink. Finding a quiet corner, they sat holding hands, content to be with one another while soaking in the vibrant atmosphere of the theatre bar.

It was quite a surprise when Gabriel turned the conversation around to a more serious matter. Apparently, his parents had invited them both for Sunday lunch the following day.

Willow felt that it was rather too soon to be meeting his parents. She'd not yet considered taking him to her humble family home to meet her own. Her parents were well aware of their daughter developing a relationship with Gabriel but never pressed her for details for which she was grateful. She now felt a certain amount of pressure to introduce him to her own family. These feelings made her feel uncomfortable, although she wasn't quite sure why.

Over breakfast the following morning, she confided her concerns to her mum. As usual, her mum looked on the positive side of the invitation.

'Try not to look into it too much, Willow. Do you know, I met your dad's parents following our second date? He told me afterwards that he was so proud of me that he wanted to share his happiness with them.'

Willow considered this and thought that maybe her mum was right, perhaps she was once again worrying unnecessarily. Willow thought carefully about what she should wear. From the little that she knew about his family, she guessed that they probably dressed up for church on Sundays. With this in mind, she wore a modern take on a tea dress, with neutral ballerina pumps. She wore a single row of pearls with matching earrings. A gift from her parents for her twenty-first birthday two years previous. Dorothy gave her a huge bouquet of mixed flowers to take along as a gift. *Such a lovely gesture*, thought Willow.

As usual, Gabriel was on time, but this time instead of beeping his horn, he came to the door to collect her. Willow was a bit thrown by this. Put on the spot, she had no alternative than to ask him inside her modest home and introduce him to her parents. They were still in their garden clothes after digging up some potatoes and carrots for their own Sunday lunch. Her dad held out his grubby hand to shake Gabriel's, who willingly accepted and shook it heartily. Not fazed at all. Gabriel then offered his hand to her mum, who thank goodness did not have her curlers in that morning. It was a brief introduction, but none the less, a good start of sorts.

'Fancy a Sunday dinner at ours next week, Gabriel,' called Mum, as they walked down the path.

Gabriel stopped, turned around, and said, 'Thank you; that sounds great. See you next Sunday,' he replied.

During the journey to his family home Gabriel told Willow that he loved the quiet serenity of her parents' cottage and smallholding.

'I get why you're the woman you are and your love of the countryside, Willow. You are so lucky that your parents are unpretentious. They are everything I imagined them to be. I know I've only met them briefly, there is a warmth about them, salt of the earth kind of people. Do you know, I don't remember the last time I saw my parents laugh together or cuddle, never mind a peck on the cheek. They are so bound up in their pious behaviour, I'm surprised that they managed to have two children.'

Willow felt more unsure than ever about meeting them. She asked Gabriel if her outfit was suitable.

'Truthfully, Willow, you look amazing, as always.'

For some reason, she was expecting the house to have a long sweeping drive, so was a little surprised at the modest drive and forecourt, where two identical Ford Mondeo cars were parked. The semi-detached house was built from local red brick; it was quite large with three stories. The third being the roof space which had four Velux windows set in the roof.

She couldn't hide her surprise from Gabriel.

'Not what you expected I see. My parents were raised having nothing, their childhood was sparse, and they were classed as poor. But don't be fooled, it is not a mansion, but their income is better than most peoples. They tend to be more generous with the church than with themselves or their family. I'm not sure what they are trying to prove, but I suspect that the elders of the church probably benefit from my parent's money more than my parents themselves.'

Gabriel let himself in the house, calling as he did so. Willow stood shyly at his side. She could smell roast lamb cooking. Her favourite Sunday roast. Things were looking up. On hearing their son call out, his parents came into the hallway. Neither of them was smiling. If anything, they looked quite serious and stern. They were tall and slim to the point of looking as though they could do with a good steak and kidney pudding inside of them. Willow handed the bouquet of flowers to his mum, who said a curt 'thank you'. Gabriel's father nodded his head to Willow as a form of communication and beckoned them both to follow him into the lounge. She looked around, taking in the utilitarian furnishings in the lounge. It was not very welcoming, to say the least.

There were two, brown leather, three-seater sofas facing each other with an oak coffee table between them on which lay a bible and a book of psalms. In one corner of the room, there was a writing bureau and along the main wall a matching sideboard that held a huge brass cross in the centre. There were no family photographs, ornaments or mirrors. The only print on the wall was of the crucifixion. Willow found it hard to believe that Gabriel had been raised by parents that appeared to be so different from him. If it wasn't for the evidence of his father's auburn, curly hair scattered with wisps of grey, she would have questioned his parentage.

Gabriel wore a simple smile that she couldn't read. He sat on the opposite sofa to her and gave her a wink. His father sat next to him and inquired if they'd had a good journey. Gesturing towards Willow, Gabriel said, 'Father, I would like to introduce my girlfriend, Willow.'

Finally, his father looked at Willow directly, with an expression that she was unable to fathom.

'Nice to meet you. Are you also training to be a doctor?'

Willow decided to take a leaf from her own parents' book, she intended to be true to herself. No hairs and graces, no pretence, just honest and friendly.

'Actually, no,' she replied.

'My interests lie elsewhere. I studied agriculture, I currently work in a garden centre, something that I enjoy very much.'

'I see,' came the curt reply.

She read the disappointment in his voice but was not at all surprised. These were cool people that she was dealing with. They seemed to have no heart and lacked any kind of joy. Checking out their body language, Willow came to the conclusion that they were not pleased to meet her.

Gabriel's mother came in with a tray of china cups. Moving the bible to one side, she placed the tray on the coffee table with absolute precision. As if talking to herself, she mumbled something about the bible being the greatest book of all times. The first cup of tea she poured and passed to her husband followed by Gabriel's tea. She then looked at Willow. 'Young lady, do you take milk and sugar?' she inquired.

'Mum, I would like you to meet my girlfriend, Willow,' interrupted Gabriel.

'I see,' said his mum.

'I do hope that you're not a distraction to his studies, Willow, we have great expectations for our son. We are hoping that one day, he will represent the church and go to Africa to use his medical skills there.'

Willow was unsure how to respond to this. Gabriel's parents' rhetoric was like something from an old movie, stoic and old fashioned. Before she had the opportunity, Gabriel stood up and replied for her.

'Mother, Willow is well aware of what is right and wrong and as for your plans for me, don't you think that I should have a say in my own future?'

His mother excused herself to attend the dinner. Willow inquired if she could use the bathroom, at which point, Gabriel said that he'd show her the way. Glad of the respite, Willow reached for Gabriel's hand. Just like the lounge, the bathroom, although very nice, was plainly decorated and lacked any evidence of female luxury items. It was as if they were in denial of having worked hard to achieve their success. Gabriel was quite the opposite and spent his money freely. Too freely at times, but rather that way than to live so frugally, she thought.

She just about managed to get through dinner, such was the dullness of the conversation. Thank goodness they'd been to see *Sister Act* the night before. At least that held his parents' interests to a small degree. Apparently, they'd both watched the film on DVD when it first came out and had enjoyed it in parts. For a short while, they spoke of when they opened their first video rental shop in the village where they still lived. For a brief moment, Willow thought that she saw a smile creep over their faces as they reminisced but it was so fleeting, she decided that it was wishful thinking on her part.

Thinking they might want to reminisce about the early years of their marriage and the success of their business, she inquired if it had been difficult to start up a new business. With all the pitfalls of tax and VAT, not to mention the fact that they had two young children. Gabriel's father said that he dealt with that side of the business and the ordering of the stock. His wife mainly dealt directly with the customers. It was hard to imagine them ordering in some of the racier video titles, perhaps they were different in the early years of their marriage. She couldn't help but wonder if that was a remote possibility.

Willow was glad to say goodbye and was surprised when his father shook her hand. The formality was underwhelming. Both of his parents stood at the door and watched as they made their way towards Gabriel's car. Neither of them had hugged their son.

It was some time before Gabriel spoke.

'I'm glad that's over with. Don't worry, Willow, I won't be expecting you to go through that experience again.'

On the way home, Gabriel pulled up outside of a Newsagent shop, telling Willow that he needed to check his Euro lottery ticket that he'd purchased earlier in the week. On his return, he presented her with a large box of chocolates.

'For you Willow, I need to apologise for my parent's rude behaviour. They can be intimidating. I'm afraid the older they get, the more I notice it. When I was a child, I just accepted that they were hard-working and stricter than my friend's parents. Victoria and I were encouraged with our studies, which I'm grateful for. I guess that somehow they lost sight of the joy that life can bring.'

The following day, Gabriel was due to start a placement at the Queens Medical Centre. He was spending some time on the Paediatric wards and needed to refresh his memory about the most common paediatric conditions and some of the more obscure diseases. He apologised to Willow, for taking her straight back home, despite there being absolutely no need to do so. That's what she liked about Gabriel, he had such good manners and was always a perfect gentleman. She knew from the way that his body betrayed him that he wanted her as much as she wanted him, and yet he'd taken their relationship no further than a passionate embrace and kiss. She guessed that he was showing her respect, but truthfully, she didn't know how much longer she could wait to feel him skin to skin. She longed for him to make love to her and need her as much as she needed him.

Chapter Six

Willow was unable to get Gabriel out of her mind. Even when she was doing her favourite tasks at work; ordering the next season's plants and making decisions about which would be the healthiest and sturdiest of seedlings for her to nurture.

He totally consumed her thoughts. She had a niggling worry that Gabriel could potentially meet a gorgeous nurse, or a doctor while working at the hospital. He was surrounded by smart, intelligent medical professionals. If she was so wildly attracted to him, surely, she couldn't be the only one. Willow had never been prone to any kind of jealousy or possessiveness in the past. These were new feelings. Feelings that worried her immensely. Such was her worry that midweek instead of going to work in her dungarees, she dressed smartly and changed at work, with the full intention of calling in at the hospital to check out the paediatric ward staff. Just out of interest, of course!

Dorothy noticed but didn't pass any comment. She thought that perhaps Gabriel was picking her up straight from work and taking her out. Actually, she was intrigued at the thought of meeting him and was surprised when Willow finished work and drove off herself.

By the time Willow found a parking place in the hospital car park and realised the size of the hospital, she decided against the charade and eventually drove home. Feeling foolish at her own insecurity her thoughts turned inwards towards the little corner in her mind, far out of reach of the day-to-day activities of living. An archived area of distant memories where a little voice in her ear was advising her against such an action. The little voice that had put in an appearance a number of times during her lifetime. Usually, when she needed to make an important decision. She liked to think that it was her twin sister guiding her in the right direction. She realised that it was a fanciful thought and that others would consider her quite insane. Willow never told her parents for fear of upsetting them. They may be distressed if she told them that she felt as though she had to live her life for herself and her lost sister. A task that she was willing to do.

'You are later than usual, love, have you been somewhere nice after work?' questioned her mum, who was busy in the kitchen preparing the evening meal.

Willow felt foolish explaining her insecurities, despite their very open relationship with each other. Neither did she want to lie to her mum, so she dismissed the question and offered to help in the kitchen. She adored her. They were a good team in the kitchen, her mum always encouraging and teaching her new skills. From a very young age, Willow enjoyed the warmth and nurturing her mum provided.

'What shall I cook for that lovely young man of yours, this coming Sunday?' inquired her mum. Willow thought about the tough lamb that she'd struggled to chew the previous week at Gabriel's parents.

'How about a nice piece of brisket, mum, it makes tasty gravy and is always so tender. Besides, there will be no need to hover around the oven to keep basting it, giving you more time to get to know Gabriel a little better'

'I like the sound of that, Willow,' answered her mum.

The remainder of the week dragged by for Willow such was her pleasure in the thoughts of Gabriel joining them all for Sunday lunch. She knew it would be a significant day for her parents too as this was the first boyfriend she had invited to her home.

She need not have worried. On Sunday, Gabriel arrived in plenty of time, he bought flowers and chocolates for the ladies and some beer for her dad, who on gratefully receiving it, ushered Gabriel into their conservatory that overlooked the gardens at the back. Willow popped her head around the French doors leading into the large conservatory. She was happy to see her father was relaxed and enjoying the company of Gabriel.

Returning to the kitchen to help her mum with the dinner Willow felt as though walking on air, such was her happiness.

'What can I do to help mum?'

'You could rinse the cabbage and pop it in the large pan on the stove, the kettle has just boiled, pour it over the cabbage and put a light under the pan then would you mind setting the table?'

Willow went into the dining room to attend to the table. As this was a special occasion in terms of it being the first time, she had formally invited Gabriel, she set the table with care. When her mum entered the dining room carrying the steaming dishes of home-grown vegetables, she gave a huge loving and knowing smile to her daughter. Without speaking a single word, her mum acknowledged the importance of this day for her daughter.

'Go and call the men,' said Emma.

'Hey, you two,' she called. 'I see that you've made yourselves comfortable. Dinner will be ready in about five minutes, so come through when you can drag yourselves away from man talk.'

Her dad nodded his head in polite response. Gabriel winked at her and gave her a huge grin.

Back in the kitchen, her mum was busy making the gravy, so Willow returned to the dining room to join the men.

'They are both excellent cooks,' said Tom to Gabriel, as they sat down at the table, 'and my Emma the best wife and mother a man could wish for.'

'Do you know, we've been married for twenty-five years next month and never a day goes by without me telling her how much she means to me?'

Gabriel smiled at the way Tom said, 'My Emma.' There was no denying the love that Tom felt for his family.

Emma blushed. 'Is it that long, Tom, how time flies when I'm happy?'

'Twenty-five years, Mum, I hope you and Dad are doing something special?'

Her dad touched the side of his nose and told Willow that it was all in hand.

As expected, the meal was delicious, followed by apple crumble that melted in the mouth.

'Are these apples from your orchard?' asked Gabriel.

'They are indeed, lad, in fact, the next time you visit, how about you and I go and pick a few baskets. You can take some to your parents?'

'Great,' replied Gabriel with tongue in cheek. He could not imagine his own mothers' response if he arrived at their house with a basket of apples.

Throughout dinner, the conversation flowed. Emma and Tom took a great interest in everything that Gabriel spoke of. They hung on to every word and appeared to be enjoying the stimulating conversation.

'Does your family live in these parts?' inquired Emma.

Gabriel said that they lived about thirty minutes away, north of Nottingham. He told them a little about his family but spoke mostly of his sister, Victoria, whom he held in high regard.

By all accounts, they all had a pleasant afternoon. After helping her mum with the dinner pots, Willow suggested that they perhaps have a drive out to one of her favourite spots in the countryside. After thanking her parents for a wonderful dinner and agreeing to return the following Sunday, Gabriel waved them goodbye.

'I'll drive,' said an excited Willow.

She drove for quite a long way before pulling up outside of a pub and parking in the car park. Throughout the journey, Gabriel couldn't bear to take his eyes off her. He praised her mum's cooking and told Willow that she was so fortunate to have parents as loving and kind as Emma and Tom.

'Your home is so relaxing and free from tension,' he said.

Of course, Willow was aware of the contrast between her own parents and his. She did not remark on this. It wasn't her place. Perhaps they were having a bad day when she went for dinner, thought Willow.

After parking her car, she held out her hand to Gabriel.

'Come on Gabriel, let me show you the wonders of nature so close to the towns and cities. I love this stretch of the canal.'

The car park sloped down towards a grassy bank. Towards the side of the bank were a set of concrete steps leading down towards the canal.

'Welcome to the Grand Union Canal, Gabriel,' she said, as she spread out her arms before her.

Just at that moment, a brightly coloured narrow boat sailed by. Willow waved to the occupants who were standing at the back of the boat. They returned the wave heartily.

'This is my favourite place to walk, Gabriel. Besides the tranquil water. I can watch the swans, ducks and moorhens glide gracefully by. Sometimes I'm lucky enough to witness their new born chicks swim in a little line behind the mother. It is such a sweet sight to see.'

Willow bent down, pointing towards the hedgerow. 'Look! Rose-bay Willowherb and over there, Red Campion,' she called out in delight. 'Isn't it wonderful here, Gabriel?'

'It's you that's wonderful, Willow,' Gabriel replied.

Willow flushed with delight and reached out her hand towards him. For a second, she allowed her gaze to drop below his waist then gradually and shyly she looked up towards his face.

'You are very special too, Gabriel. Our time together means so much to me. I think about you all the time, in fact, I think about you most of the time. I've never felt this way before.'

Gabriel felt a warm flush spread across his neck and face. He felt his throat tighten and a shudder travel down his spine. He felt his penis stir and thicken as his arousal became evident, such was the effect she had upon him when she lowered her gaze.

He drew her into his arms. 'I love you, Willow, I've never felt this way about anyone before and so soon. I can't believe this is happening to me. You are my first thought when I wake and my head swims all night just thinking about you. I can't get you out of my head. I feel crazy at times, almost drunk with emotion. It's so weird and yet unbelievably satisfying.'

Then he kissed her with such tenderness and love that she felt herself melt into his arms, returning his kiss with equal measure.

'I love you too,' she whispered.

They walked a little further along the towpath hand in hand. Willow noticed a Heron on the opposite side of the bank and pointed it out to Gabriel. But his mind was not on the wonders of nature that surrounded the Grand Union Canal. He was more interested in Willow and how he could take their relationship to a more intimate level.

With his arm slung loosely around her waist, they made their way back to the car. Both of them filled with surprise at the easy, comfortable way they shared their feelings of love.

Neither of them wanted to break the magic spell that was surrounding them. It was as though some kind of sorcery had occurred. Gabriel was unsure how to proceed with the day. Oh, he knew that his body was willing him to take Willow and make him his, in the carnal sense. He was relieved when Willow suggested that perhaps it might be nice to go back to Gabriel's house for a coffee. They both knew that it wasn't coffee, but something more special that Willow had in mind.

Chapter Seven

He directed Willow to his home in West Bridgeford, hoping that Leo and Adnan were both out, which was often the case on Sunday afternoons. Unfamiliar with the area, Willow was pleasantly surprised when he advised her to pull up ahead on the left side just after a Rowan tree that was one of many that lined the delightful street. She parked outside of a very nice suburban type house, noticing the many expensive cars parked on the impressive sweeping driveways of the houses close by. As they walked along the blocked pavement pathway leading to Gabriel's house, she couldn't help noticing the number of weeds pushing through the cracks and joints.

Willow made a mental note to give the guys a helping hand with garden maintenance should she revisit.

They entered via a traditional style oak door which led into a large hallway that smelled of trainers and damp coats. Willow twitched her nose.

'Sorry about the manly smell,' grinned Gabriel. 'It doesn't get any better further in.'

Willow laughed. It broke the ice that was threatening to build and spoil the moment.

In all honesty, she was only interested in one room of the house, a room that she hoped Gabriel would take her as soon as he could before any of his friends arrived home. He reached for her hand and led her up two flights of stairs. Such was their haste, they were both breathless on reaching the landing, which was in fact just a small area at the top of the stairs, leaving very little room to manoeuvre. They were quite squashed, as they practically fell into the room giggling.

'I chose this room in the attic because it reminds me of my room back home. Although there are fewer windows. It is still the best room in my opinion and very private, he grinned.

Willow guessed that he'd probably kept his room somewhat tidy, in anticipation of such a moment as this. She glanced nervously over to the bed. The bedding looked clean enough, although it was a strange shade of blue, or maybe it was meant to be grey. Either way, it didn't matter. She smiled to herself at the sight of a collection of cheap scatter cushions piled against the headboard. Gabriel went over to a small drinks fridge and brought out a bottle of white wine. He collected two glasses that were on a shelf above the fridge and passed one to Willow.

'I know you're driving, but please, just a very small measure to toast the moment.'

Mesmerised, Willow took the glass with the least in. They clinked glasses and made a toast. 'To us.'

Sitting side by side on the bed, after only two sips of the drink, Gabriel took her glass and placed it next to his on the bedside table. She kicked her shoes off, as he unbuttoned her blouse, revealing the breasts that he'd longed to touch since the very first night he'd met her. He unclipped her front fastening lacy black bra and shuddered with the most intense

57

of feelings, as he cupped her breast in his hand. And then, he kissed her. A deep, passionate kiss that left her wanting more. Much more.

They made love, in the way that lovers do who have been waiting for this moment all of their lives. Willow totally abandoned herself to Gabriel, who in return gave everything of himself to her in a slow and controlled way. He had plenty of sexual experience but had never made love to a woman who he loved so deeply. It was a whole new experience for him, and he did not want it to end.

They lay quietly in each other's arms, both savouring the moment of their love being sealed in such a profound way. Gabriel was the first to speak.

'Thank you, Willow, that was amazing. I love you and never want to lose you. Please tell me, that no matter what, we will always be together.'

She turned to face him, her face still flushed from their love-making, her shiny dark hair forming little damp tendrils around her face. Despite the heat of the moment, she felt confused with his pleading… 'No matter what.'

'I love you too, Gabriel, I will not give you any reason to stop loving me, not intentionally anyway. Why are you so worried?'

'No reason,' he swiftly replied.

Satisfied with his answer, they once more ignited their passion and made love again. This time knowing each other's body and what pleased them, they reached orgasm together in a breath-taking finale of love, lust and passion that was immeasurable.

They slept in each other's arms until disturbed by loud music coming from the floor below. Gabriel sat up in bed and pulled a pillow behind his head. Willow did the same. All the while she was looking at Gabriel, her heart felt so full of love, she didn't want the day to end. But end it must.

'Time to leave our cosy love nest, my darling girl,' he sighed.

Together, they made their way down the stairs where they were greeted by Leo with a huge knowing grin on his face.

'Hi, Willow, he has talked about nothing else but you for the past few weeks, it's good to see you again,' said Leo. Gabriel gave Leo a friendly, but gentle push in the shoulder. He grinned at his friend, who got the subliminal message and grinned back. Willow blushed, she wasn't used to being surrounded by all of this testosterone and manly banter. Adnan, who was in the lounge, gave a thumbs up sign causing the colour of her cheeks to a rosy heated blush. While Willow sat in the lounge that was nowhere near as tidy as Gabriel's room, he went to make them both a coffee.

'You're going to need that mate tonight to keep yourself awake,' said Adnan, as he joined them in the lounge.

'Shit! I forgot about my night shift, still, it was worth it,' said Gabriel.

Willow looked towards Gabriel.

'Are you at work tonight?' she asked.

Gabriel nodded and told her that it was his turn to do the on-call shift for the next eight nights. He explained that it was part of their placement and compulsory. He told her that as part of his paediatric placement, he had to do eight on-call duty shifts, but the good news was, that he had four days off.

'Perhaps you and I can go away together, Willow, do you have any time off work due to you?'

She thought for a moment. It had been a long time since she'd requested any leave from work and she knew that Dorothy would have no objections.

Besides, how exciting to have the chance to spend a few days together. 'I will check the duty rota at work when I go in tomorrow, I'm ready for a holiday.' Do you have anywhere in mind?'

'Nope,' he replied. 'You decide.'

It was getting late and Gabriel needed to sleep before going on night duty. Adnan offered to drive him to work and fetch him back in the morning when they planned to call at Willow's home for Gabriel's car.

'Please tell your mum I'm sorry about dinner at your home next Sunday Willow, I will probably be in bed exhausted, having completed seven-night shifts.'

Willow said that was fine. Besides, she had lots of things to think about and a whole week to plan a potential holiday.

Willow drove home in a loved-up daze. She had so much on her mind in addition to planning a four-day break. First thing Monday morning, Willow planned to speak with Dorothy about having the following week off work.

On arrival home, her parents were sitting comfortably together on the sofa in front of the fire. Although they had gas central heating, her parents sometimes enjoyed putting a few logs on their open fire grate that was set in an Inglenook. The sound of the crackling logs and the smell of wood burning created an atmosphere of love and warmth. *Hearth and home,* thought Willow, *nothing to beat it*. Sandy lay in his little basket close to the hearth, fast asleep. The lounge was homely and inviting, a tranquil place…sanctuary. Willow knew how happy her parents were together, enjoying the simple pleasures of life. It warmed her heart to see them so content.

'What a nice polite young man Gabriel is,' said her mum.

'Strong and not bad looking either,' remarked her father.

'Is that his car out there on the road, Willow?'

She told him about the on-call night shifts that were expected of Gabriel as part of his training.

'He sends his apologies, Mum, sadly he can't make dinner next Sunday. But he'd love to come some other time.'

'The car will be gone tomorrow after he has finished work,' she told them.

Monday morning, Willow's first thought was to ask Dorothy about the time off. Dorothy, as Willow knew she would, was beyond happy to hear that her best worker, finally wanted some well-earned leave.

'Going anywhere nice?' she inquired.

Willow shook her head.

'The thing is, Dorothy, he has asked me to arrange it. Gabriel promises to pay, whatever it costs and has left me to decide. Now I'm not sure what to do. I'm at a complete loss.'

'Tell you what,' Dorothy replied. 'You go and start with the cuttings in the greenhouse and I will look online to check out a few ideas.'

By lunchtime, Dorothy had done everything except make a booking. She showed Willow a few four days breaks up and down the country. The one that appealed to her the most was a mini cruise on a liner to Zeebrugge in Belgium with the option of visiting the medieval town of Bruges. The ship was sailing from Southampton on Monday morning and returning Thursday afternoon. *Perfect*, she thought. *I will drive us down to Southampton, Gabriel will be shattered, so he can sleep on the journey.*

Excited beyond belief, she texted Gabriel with her idea. As expected, he didn't reply until late afternoon.

'Sorry I have only just seen the text message, I'm knackered. I have never done a night shift before and believe me there is no chance I will be volunteering for any in the future. When I've completed my training, it will be sociable hours only.'

'Yes right! In your dreams, Gabriel, you know very well it is a part of your work. So, what do you think of my idea to go on a mini cruise?'

'Brilliant idea, can't wait.'

'You do have a passport I hope?' she inquired.

'I have, yes and it is in date, how do you think I got to visit Amsterdam with the lads?' he joked.

So that was it. The following day, Willow booked online for a last-minute booking. The only double stateroom available was an inside cabin, so she booked it, hoping that Gabriel didn't suffer from claustrophobia.

For Willow, the week flew by in a flurry of excitement. Planning her wardrobe just for a few days was a challenge in itself. There was to be one formal night on board when the ladies wore a ball gown or a cocktail dress and the men a tuxedo. Not owning either a cocktail dress or a ball gown, that evening she rang her friends, to ask for help. They arranged to meet at Willow's home the following night for a few nibbles and wine.

The girls had lots to catch up on, especially the progress of their friend's developing relationship. Without giving too much away, she told them how fast the relationship was going and that Gabriel had already said that he loved her. They didn't need to ask about her love life, after all, the fact they were going away together on holiday told them everything they needed to know. Her parents were in the same frame of mind and did not pry in any way. That evening, Janet and Susan bought a suitcase of clothes for Willow to choose from. They both had a variety of evening dresses. Together, they did their own fashion show in the lounge. Willow tried on a number of dresses, finally choosing a long black sequined cocktail dress that flattered her perfect curves. It was just the formal night that she needed an outfit for. The other nights she had covered from her own wardrobe of clothes. The girls giggled the night away and made plans to meet for coffee during the week.

Just before going to bed a sudden thought occurred to her so she rang Gabriel, forgetting it was already late and he was probably on duty. The phone went to voicemail. She left a message telling him of the formal night and the appropriate dress wear. She hoped he had a tuxedo or dinner suit, and if not, perhaps he could borrow one. As a backup, she sent a text message. No way was she risking any embarrassment for Gabriel on board their first cruise together. She wanted everything to be perfect.

Chapter Eight

Gabriel was finding working on the children's ward emotionally draining. The night shifts were difficult to cope with because of his lack of sleep. He was not a nocturnal creature and suffered great difficulty in finding sleep during daylight hours. Despite his mother calling to his home during the week and bringing him a blackout blind, the room was still, either too hot, too light or there was too much noise going on outside.

He heard every noise, from the postman to the refuse workers. He even heard the family's comings and goings to the local primary school. Consequently, four days into his eight-night rota, he was not only exhausted but vulnerable due to sleep deprivation. Such was his vulnerability, that when his mum came with the blackout blind, he confided to her that he was finding the emotional side of his work, difficult to deal with.

The death of the first child on the ward while he was on duty hit him hard. The young girl, Sally, was only five years old and had died from a rare form of leukaemia. Gabriel had got to know Sally and her family while he was working the day shift.

'I cannot believe it, Mother, that God would take such a beautiful, young creature and give her all of that pain and suffering. Life is so unfair for some. Sally was an innocent child, why should God want to take her away from her wonderful and loving family? I am finding it hard to accept.'

She told him to *pull his self together* and stop looking for blame.

'Life can be hard and at times cruel, such was nature,' she harshly replied.

Pull myself together? he thought. *What kind of advice is that?* But he didn't say as much to his mum. He knew that his words would fall on deaf ears.

The day he'd sealed his love with Willow, Gabriel thanked God for sending her to him. Yet, days later, he questions the will of God in his actions against Sally.

Despite his obvious distress, his mother did not reach out and hold him or comfort him as he would have liked. When he was a child, the only affection he received from his parents was a good-night kiss after saying his prayers. He knew that they loved him and Victoria, but they seemed to be stuck in some kind of time warp when it was classed as distasteful to show any kind of affection publicly.

His mother half-listened though and allowed him to pour out his sadness and grief that he was experiencing while caring for sick children. After a while, she steered the conversation in a different direction.

'How are things going with you and Willow?' She inquired.

As tired and stressed as he was, Gabriel did not miss the undertones of her voice or the rigid stance of her body language. He wasn't about to give too much away.

'Yes, things are good, thank you. We are both very busy with work, so our time together is limited,' he informed her.

'Well, just concentrate on your studies, please, your father and I have enough to worry about with Victoria.'

That got his attention. 'Is Victoria all right mother?' he inquired.

She walked over to the sofa and flopped down in an unusual ungainly manner.

'The thing is, Gabriel, she is getting engaged. Your sister has informed us that she is getting engaged, and we didn't even know that she had a boyfriend. We know nothing about him or his family, she has kept this a secret from all of us. How could she?'

Gabriel sat down next to her and in an unusual gesture, held her hand. She looked up, startled, but did not pull her hand away.

'Perhaps she was afraid that you might try to spoil things for her. Would you have encouraged her to concentrate on her studies and to forget about pursuing a loving relationship? Or would you have welcomed him into our family with open arms mum? Which one?'

She knew that there was more to the questions than just responding on his sister's behalf. She let this slide. For now, anyway.

'It doesn't matter now, Gabriel, she is getting engaged in a few weeks' time apparently, so it's out of mine and your father's hands. We have been invited to meet him and his family in two weeks' time, somewhere neutral apparently.'

'Does he have a name, Mother?' asked Gabriel.

'Duncan, he is from somewhere in Scotland,' she replied.

The name Duncan seemed to stick in her mouth as though the name itself tasted bitter.

'You are invited too, Gabriel. Just you, no mention of a plus one.'

He ignored the slight from her but got the message loud and clear. Willow was not welcome. Victoria was not aware of Willow, why should she be. Just as he wasn't aware of Duncan. *There are some serious psychological issues in this family,* he thought to himself.

How can I get Willow involved with all of this antagonism? The families were so far apart in terms of values and beliefs. Willow and her parents were free spirits as opposed to the bigoted behaviour of his own family.

'Are you and father going?' he asked.

'Well, I suppose that we must go if only to show Duncan and his family that Victoria comes from a good family with manners.'

Gabriel should not have been surprised at the answer, but he was because he remembered how they forgot their manners when he first introduced Willow.

That night at work, he had even more to mull over. Thankfully, the night was uneventful, no admissions or transfers to the high dependency unit. The night sister was more than capable and encouraged him to close his eyes during his long break.

She noticed how tired Gabriel looked. These young doctors had a tough time of it, she knew the long hours they worked and the amount of study they had to cram into the same length day as everyone else. Sister Clay had seen many student doctors and junior house men come and go over the years. Most of them, she liked and respected. Gabriel was one such doctor.

Sister Clay found him to be very dedicated to his work and if anything, she noticed that perhaps he allowed himself to become a little too emotionally involved. Although that was a good thing and nurtured good relationships with the children and their families, it put undue stress upon him, at a time when already under pressure to pass his medical exams. She was old enough to be his mother and as such, her instincts were to keep a close eye on him.

It was the end of the shift before he had the opportunity to switch his mobile phone on. He was pleasantly surprised to see that he'd received a voice mail message. The sweet voice of Willow lifted his spirits. She seemed to have a way of relaxing him and making him happy, it was as though she wove a magic spell around him. He hoped that she could weave her magic in a number of useful ways that would help him to remain focused on the important aspects of his life. He had a hidden fear that he had the potential to drift from the path that he was raised to follow, by his parents.

Willow, bless her, was making sure that he had a tuxedo for the formal night aboard. Thankfully, he did own one that he'd purchased for the first summer ball at the university. Whether it still fit him, was another matter.

Feeling exhausted, Gabriel went straight to bed. The house was very quiet. Adnan and Leo were both on the early day shift, he guessed that they would arrive home mid-afternoon, giving him the opportunity to sleep undisturbed. He slept soundly for six perfect hours, waking only to attend to his bathroom needs.

'Fancy a cuppa, mate,' called Leo up the stairs.

Gabriel's mouth felt dry and his throat sore when he tried to shout his answer, the noise that came out was more like a bark than a yes.

'Was that a yes or do you have a dog upstairs?' Laughed Leo.

Gabriel made his way downstairs, still wearing his boxers and nothing else.

'Gosh, Gabriel you look a little rough mate, was it a tough night shift?'

Gabriel forced a smile. 'Where's that tea?' he croaked.

'Coming up,' said Leo.

They sat together at the table sipping the tea, both glad of the comfort it gave them.

'It's been a tough day on the medical unit,' said Leo. 'We have had twelve admissions and two deaths in one morning. It's been manic, I tell you. The ward is full, despite transferring two of our elderly stroke patients to the stroke rehabilitation ward. The paperwork was never-ending. I feel sorry for the afternoon shift picking up where we left off. The nurses have been working their socks off. Do you know, they never get a break? The only chance for a cup of tea was during the morning report and the afternoon hand-over. I don't know how they keep it up.'

Gabriel was listening and thinking about his own challenges on the paediatric ward.

'It's tough, that's for sure, Leo. Which makes it all the more important to wind down on our days off. Willow and I are off on a mini cruise to Belgium for a few days,' croaked Gabriel, while holding his throat.

'Sounds like you've picked up a virus from one of the children, mate, hang on a minute, I've got some antiseptic mouthwash in my room for you to gargle with.'

Leo fetched the mouthwash and a pack of paracetamol.

'Best dose yourself up tonight, otherwise, it's going to be a long one,' said Leo.

Gabriel nodded his head and made his way back to bed. He swallowed the tablets and gargled his throat, then set his alarm, just in case.

He slept a further two hours, waking to the sound of his alarm. Feeling no better, he was tempted to roll over and go back to sleep. He knew that was impossible, slowly he dragged himself out of bed and into the shower. The warm water and the steamy room eased his aching joints and scratchy throat. He had no appetite, but common sense told him to eat something. Looking through the kitchen cupboards, he came across a packet of instant porridge. *That will do*, he decided.

Sister Clay knew almost instantly that Gabriel was not well. She made him a black-currant tea drink, before handing him the new admission notes. As he read the notes, Gabriel told himself, that what he was feeling was minuscule compared to the young boy who had been admitted with pneumonia. The poor child had cystic fibrosis, which was bad enough and had now developed viral pneumonia. He pulled himself together and found his inner reserves to push himself through the night shift, knowing full well that within a few days he'd be well again. Whereas, some of the youngsters on the ward will never fully recover.

It was the next to the last night shift when he suddenly remembered the tuxedo that he meant to be trying on. He needed to pack his holdall bag before leaving for work the next evening, as Willow was meeting him at the hospital, so they could head straight to Southampton.

Before going to bed, the following morning, he looked for his tuxedo suit. Thankfully, his mother had it dry cleaned after the ball, apparently, it smelled of stale beer. He found it still in the dry-cleaning cellophane carrier at the back of his wardrobe. Quickly trying it on, he began to feel an excited anticipation of the coming holiday with Willow.

His work had consumed him so much over the past few days. He hadn't allowed himself the joy of the anticipated reunion with Willow. Fortunately, the suit fitted, albeit a little loose around the waist. Snatching food here and there and working long hours was not an ideal lifestyle, he must be burning more energy than he thought. The tuxedo suit and a double cuff white shirt, he placed in a suit bag. The black bow tie and his cufflinks were a little more difficult to put his hands on. Despite the exhaustion, he hunted for the accessories. Adnan heard the commotion as drawers and cupboards were opened and closed.

'Want any help?' he shouted.

Gabriel told Adnan about his predicament.

'No problem, mate, you can borrow mine, I know exactly where to find them,' he told Gabriel.

Thankfully, Adnan's accessories were black. Gabriel was half expecting a brightly coloured bowtie and obscure cufflinks, so was relieved to discover they were perfectly acceptable.

'Phew! Thanks, mate, you have saved me from embarrassment.'

'Best get some shut eye, Gabriel, you are going to need all your energy to keep that girl of yours happy. 'Don't do anything I wouldn't do, mate,' he laughed.

Exhausted beyond belief and still recovering from the virus, he literally flopped onto his bed and within minutes was asleep.

Chapter Nine

Willow must have tried every garment on in her wardrobe before deciding which day clothes and shoes to pack. The cocktail dress, she packed with extra care to avoid any creases. It was unlikely that an iron would be available and besides she hoped to be doing better things than ironing creases from her clothes. During the week, she called into a Debenhams department store to purchase new underwear. Willow spent a long time choosing these. She wanted sophistication, not sleaze. She purchased one set of navy lace and one set of black lace. Both colours flattered her skin tone. After washing them through, she placed a sprig of lavender from her parent's garden between the sets.

While packing her suitcase, Willow's mum entered the room. She passed a gift bag to her daughter.

'For you, sweetheart. I know how much this holiday means to you. Both your dad and I like Gabriel. He has fine manners and integrity, not to mention a worthwhile career in front of him. This is a good time to get to know him even better. Spending a few full days and nights together can make or break a relationship. Have fun and be very careful. Just one more thing, Willow. You are both still young, it's too soon to be having babies, so I hope that you have got that side of your relationship sorted.'

Willow opened the gift bag, inside was a small bottle of Coco Chanel perfume.

'Thanks, Mum. Please don't worry. I've been to the family planning clinic and had a Depo contraception injection. Do you know, I only need it to be repeated every twelve weeks, isn't that a step in the right direction. No worry about me forgetting a contraceptive pill, and apparently, my periods might stop as well. What more could a woman ask for? Other than a man like Gabriel, she smiled.'

Her parents waved her off. They stood at the end of the garden path, holding hands and smiling. She caught sight of them in her rear mirror. After all of these years together, they are still in love, she noted. This is what Willow aspired to. Her parents were such good role models. They taught Willow the value of mutual love and respect.

The drive to the hospital was not good. Despite the early morning start, the road was busy with commuters and heavy haulage lorries. The sky was gun-metal grey and looked heavy with rain; very soon, the clouds released their content. Even with the wipers on full speed, she had poor visibility and was relieved when she pulled up outside the main hospital entrance.

She saw Gabriel, sheltering under the entrance canopy and pressed the horn. As he came running over, she opened the passenger door ready. He looked so happy but very tired. She suddenly felt guilty for arranging a holiday that entailed a very early start. Sat on the front seat, dripping wet, with his holdall and suit bag across his lap, he looked like a lost little boy. Willow leaned across and kissed him gently.

'There's a blanket and a pillow on the back seat, Gabriel, please go and lie down.'

She flipped a lever, and the boot sprung open. Gabriel climbed out and after putting his luggage in the boot, climbed into the back of the car and gratefully, laid his head down.

He slept the entire way to Southampton as she hoped he would. Sleep sounds escaped from Gabriel's lips now and then, but otherwise, he was a quiet sleeper. So as not to disturb his sleep, she refrained from turning on the radio or the travel information. Thankfully, there were no disruptions on the route; she was content to drive in silence, making for a quiet journey. The background hum of the engine, purred away, taking her closer and closer to what she hoped, was to be the perfect holiday.

Willow had never spent an entire night in bed with anyone before. Her bedroom had originally been furnished for two but had long since been converted into an individual room.

When she was small and felt a little lonely in bed, she made up stories in her head about her twin sister and how they would have played together. Sometimes, when she read out loud, she pretended to be reading to her sister, Molly. Willow tried to include Molly in most of her pretend games. As Willow grew older, so did Molly. Her childish conversations with her sister changed over the years. Although Willow spoke infrequently to Molly now, on the odd occasion she still confided in her sister.

Tonight, she was to spend the whole night in Gabriel's arms. Her face flushed with joy, just thinking of the intimacy they were about to share. Willow considered his current sleep pattern; after all, he'd been working the night shift for a while now. Having slept for the entire journey it might be an issue.

After the long drive, it was likely that she'd be tired and Gabriel well rested. Willow smiled to herself and thought, *Why I'm overthinking things. Gabriel wouldn't concern himself about such matters, I'm sure he has other things on his mind.*

She woke Gabriel when they arrived at the dock gate. Then drove towards a designated parking spot, as per the instructions on the car sticker in her window; which she'd downloaded along with the confirmation of booking forms and embarkation instructions.

Once in the parking spot, the attendants took their luggage, attached labels and directed them to the check-in. Holding hands, they walked to the check-in building. Hundreds of people of all ages were milling about and forming queues.

'I'm desperate for a coffee, do you want one?' croaked Gabriel.

Grateful for the offer, she nodded her head and watched as Gabriel went over to a table that contained large flasks and what looked like disposable mugs. She noticed how smart he looked in his navy jeans and white shirt. He had a navy suit jacket on that was casually open, emphasising the swing of his hips. Her heart began to race, and she felt her face flush. Just looking at Gabriel sent a rush of love, throughout her body. She could hardly believe that he loved her. She felt afraid and in fear of ever losing his love; she knew that her heart wouldn't recover from such a loss.

Clutching two large paper mugs of coffee, Gabriel sauntered over to Willow, all the while looking straight at her and grinning. He handed the coffee to her.

'You look great, Willow, that flush to your cheeks is a dead giveaway. If you're feeling half of what I'm feeling, then we're going to make sparks fly over the next few days. Believe me when I say I love you to the moon and the stars and back. In my eyes, you are perfection.'

Willow sighed a deep longing sigh. She knew they had to wait a while longer before their stateroom was ready. The wait would be unbearable, to say the least. They handed their passports to the desk clerk and signed a declaration that they were healthy, with no risk of having a transferable disease. After having a photo taken, they were handed a stateroom card and told this was the key to their room and also acted as identification for boarding and for payment. Gabriel provided his credit card details, telling Willow that he wanted to take care of the bill.

Willow made a mental note, to be careful in terms of the drinks. From what she understood, they were quite pricey, made even more expensive by the added gratuities.

Together, they made their way up the gangplank and into the lower deck of the ship where once again, they had their identities checked. A group of the ship's officers mingled among the crowds as they entered the ship. Although smart and handsome, Willow only had eyes for one man, as she walked beside Gabriel, arm in arm. A member of staff offered them a drink. Despite it being early in the day, they both chose a flute of prosecco, clinked glasses, and grinned contently as they surveyed the outstanding décor of the ship.

The lift that took the passengers to the upper deck had glass sides, allowing a panoramic view of each deck as they made their way up the atrium of the ship. Gabriel looked at the deck map on the inside of the lift.

'Let's get off at deck five and check out the casino first,' he excitedly announced.

Willow, still mesmerised by the vastness of the ship and the décor, was willing to start exploring any one of the decks.

'Deck five sounds a good place to start,' she replied.

Gabriel was like an excited child as he made his way towards the casino. Willow looked at him in wonder. She was unable to decide if the obvious joy on his face, was related to the fact that the ship had such a huge casino or if it was the whole package that made his face light up.

Gabriel suddenly picked Willow up and twirled her around in excitement.

'You are brilliant, Willow. I would never have thought of booking this kind of holiday. It is perfect.'

The first thing that Willow observed, was the rows of one arm bandits. *Such an appropriate name*, thought Willow, as she gazed at the multitude of bright lights emitted from the machines. Bandits were certainly what the machines were. She couldn't fathom out, how people could be drawn into gambling. Amusement arcades, with the penny slots and fruit machines never really appealed to her nature, either as a child or adult.

Walking over to the far side of the casino, she noticed a number of Black Jack and roulette tables. Gabriel pointed to a very long table with high-back chairs placed around. She did not recognise the gaming table and not wishing to show her ignorance of such matters, just nodded her head in agreement. Gabriel then went into great detail about the game of craps or was it crops. Either way, truthfully, she wasn't in the least bit interested.

Due to still being in port, the casino was closed. However, the bar was open, so they made themselves comfortable on a high stool, close to the bar itself. Gabriel ordered himself a neat Irish whisky and a Prosecco for Willow. Not wishing to mix her drinks, she told Gabriel that she'd stick with the same drink all evening. After all, it was still only two o'clock. It was three hours before the ship was to set sail.

An announcement over the tannoy advised all passengers that the staterooms were ready, and the luggage had been taken to the rooms. She finished the last dregs of her drink and stood up. Gabriel appeared not to notice either the message that had been relayed or the fact that Willow was making to move.

Surprisingly, Gabriel ordered another whisky and a prosecco then sat comfortably, surveying the entire casino. Reluctantly she sat back on the bar stool. Every now and again, Gabriel pointed out the special features of the room, such as the magnificent chandeliers that hung over the bar area. As interesting as it was, there were other areas of the ship, that Willow was interested in visiting. For example, she wished to see the indoor swimming pool and the Solarium. She'd packed her favourite swimming costume, hoping to catch a swim at least once a day while on holiday. In addition, she'd packed her bikini, which was just for lying around the solarium in. Any serious swimming involved a proper costume.

Lost in his own world, it wasn't until Willow's stomach gave out a gentle growl that Gabriel came back to the present moment.

'Sounds like someone is hungry, come on, let's go check out the restaurant.'

As they left the casino, Willow noted that a few more passengers had started to explore the area too. She had no intention of spending any time gambling, but understood that Gabriel was quite taken back by the place and would likely return when they were at sea.

Scattered throughout the ship were maps and directions. A model of the ship was placed at intervals along the corridors advising which way was forward or aft. They got lost many times before finally finding the restaurant, by which time they were both ravenous. Having settled down at their designated table, the waiter introduced himself as Toni and proceeded to take their order. The wine waiter introduced himself as Gregor, then discussed in great detail the wine that was available. Having had three prosecco drinks, Willow requested water on this occasion. Gabriel ordered a glass of red wine. *He was certainly chilling out*, thought Willow. She was pleased of course especially as he had a tough week.

The meal was delicious. Having eaten three good courses, followed by coffee and mints, Willow was struggling to keep awake. The long drive down was now taking its toll, her eyes felt heavy from the strain of driving and she was struggling to quell the yawn that was threatening to escape.

Sensing her tiredness, Gabriel winked at her, held out his hand and guided her out of the restaurant. Their stateroom was on Deck eight, they couldn't decide if it was on the port or starboard side, aft or forward. Together they wandered along the many corridors of the ship; laughing together as they recognised the absurdity of their geographical skills. Eventually, they managed to find the room, which was very fortunate for Gabriel, as the call of nature was imminent.

The stateroom door was very heavy to push open. Willow guessed that it was built that way to keep it airtight or perhaps something even more disturbing. "*Titanic*" sprang to mind. Gabriel having rushed into the en-suite bathroom, Willow found she was momentarily alone, to view the room that she was to be sharing over the next few days. It was very nice. Her eyes were drawn towards the main feature of the room. The huge, super queen-sized bed that took up the entire width of the cabin, except for a small bedside table either side. The crisp white bedding was offset with an azure blue satin throw, folded neatly at the bottom of the bed. On each pillow, lay a chocolate. The entire lighting system was of spotlights scattered throughout the room. Along one wall, was a long-fitted unit, comprising wardrobes, dressing table and desk. A huge, brightly lit mirror was fitted over the dressing table, surrounded by mirrors that were concealing a number of slim cupboards. A drinks fridge was set to the side of the dressing table, where stood a silver tray containing a kettle, cups, spoons coffee and an assortment of teas. However, what caught Willow's eye was the wine bucket full of ice and a bottle of white wine cooling inside. *Just perfect*, she thought. While Gabriel checked the suitcases, she poured two glasses. Passing one to Gabriel, she clinked his glass and said cheers, her voice husky with desire.

Before the last of the wine had been drunk, they made love twice. The first time, fast and needy. The second time, slow and full of love.

It was eight o'clock in the evening when they awoke from their loved-up sleep. Willow was the first to wake. She was secretly pleased to see Gabriel was still sleeping. Although tomorrow evening will be the official formal evening, she still wanted to look her best on their first evening aboard.

Quietly, so as not to disturb Gabriel, she showered and washed her hair. The hair dryer would be too noisy for now, so she wrapped her hair in a towel. She carefully chose her outfit. It was an elegant, yet understated black, sheath dress. She attached a small diamante flower to the Bardot style collar and placed matching diamante studs into her ears. While Gabriel continued to sleep, she applied her makeup. Satisfied with her appearance, Willow began to blow dry her hair. Knowing full well that this would disturb Gabriel. In any case, it was time for him to shower and change. Otherwise, they would miss the evening meal.

As anticipated, he woke up. Stretched his arms behind his head and gave out a huge wolf whistle. Willow smiled.

'Come on, sleepy head, there is another three or even four-course meal waiting for us in the restaurant. I thought we might go to the show after dinner. I've been checking out the ship's magazine. There is loads going on, it's so exciting. Do you know there's a cinema on board and an ice rink? Perhaps tomorrow after we've spent some time in Bruges, we can join in some of the fabulous activities on board. Gabriel, I don't think four days are going to be enough time.'

The excitement in her voice was a tonic to Gabriel. Having spent a few tough weeks on the paediatric unit, he desperately needed to chill out. Willow had chosen a perfect way for him to do just that.

It took him less than fifteen minutes to shower, shave and dress. A quick splash of aftershave and he was ready to enjoy the evening. With his beautiful girlfriend, resting her hand gently on his, they made their way to the restaurant.

Most of the guests who were on the second sitting had already arrived and taken their places at their designated table. The maître d' showed Willow and Gabriel to their table. It was a table for six, the other four people had already taken their places and were in the process of ordering their meals. Gabriel nodded his head in acknowledgement to the other diners, Willow smiled sweetly. She would have preferred that it was just them at the table. She wasn't particularly fond of small talk; usually finding it false and tiresome.

While checking the menu, she surreptitiously listened in on the conversation of the other four guests at the table. From the sound of their accents, they were Irish. She smiled when they entered into a conversation about who had been the most "wasted" the previous evening. As the conversation turned into a debate, the term feck was increasingly used which made Willow grin.

Suddenly, one of the Irish contingency banged his drink on the table and began to sing an Irish jig. It was so funny that Willow burst out laughing. Gabriel, also amused began a conversation with the lady seated next to him. She appeared to be a good ten years older than himself, very attractive with her striking red hair. She introduced herself as Colleen, explaining that she was married to the one who thought that he could sing.

Willow never did get to find out, who had been wasted most, on the previous evening. Neither did, Gabriel and herself finish dinner in time to watch the show. Instead, after the meal was finished, they went off with their new-found Irish friends to the late lounge on the ship's promenade deck. Collen introduced her husband, Seamus, and her friends, Eugene and Maeve. Willow was unable to keep up with the drinking habits of the rest of the group, but Gabriel managed perfectly well. By midnight, Willow was flagging and couldn't keep her eyes open.

Gabriel walked back with Willow to the Stateroom. He did not stay with her. Instead, he indicated to her that he was just having a wander around the deck and check out his bearings.

Willow did not object, she was just happy to lay down in the comfortable bed and wait for Gabriel to return. However, the gentle swell of the sea and the subtle rocking of the ship from side to side lulled her into a sweet and much-needed sleep.

Chapter Ten

Gabriel knew that if he waited long enough, his opportunity would come. He knew that Willow was exhausted from the long drive and needed to sleep. He wasn't sure how she'd react to his departure from her company on their first night together, but as luck would have it, she didn't appear to mind. The lure of the casino had been calling him all day. From the very moment that he first stepped foot, onto the plush, deep red carpet and entered the Casino, he felt driven towards addressing his compulsion. For Gabriel, it felt like an itch, that he couldn't scratch. An irritation. Which needed addressing. He just had to return to the Casino, one more time.

He had no intention of getting involved with the lure of the bandits. Although, the bright lights and the spinning wheels, of the fruit machines, were tempting to him. No. Here was an opportunity that he couldn't miss. He drew closer to the Roulette table. His eyes, drawn towards the spinning wheel. He had always trusted certain numbers and colours. The numbers four and two, both even numbers, were calling him.

There was no room around the table, other punters, were standing around, a drink in their hand. Waiting patiently for an opening. Gabriel pushed himself forwards to get a closer view, as the croupier called out, 'Place your bets.'

He watched the roulette wheel, spinning around and the little ball spinning in the opposite direction. He made a bet in his own head. Red number four. Mesmerised, he watched the wheel slow down and the ball bounce over the grids. Finally, it came to a halt. 'Black eight,' called out the smartly dressed croupier. A few low groans could be heard, as two of the punters, left their space at the table. Gabriel quickly moved forwards and sat down on a cream, leather stool, close to where the croupier was standing.

The excitement was building inside of him. That old feeling of "this time, I will be lucky". He reached into his pocket and removed his stateroom card. Handing it over to the croupier, he requested £200 worth of chips. He reasoned with himself, that these would last him, throughout the holiday. In any case, he was expecting to have more than doubled his money by tonight alone. That, he was sure of.

A waiter came to the table to take the drink orders. Gabriel did not want or need a drink. He was having fun. With each spin of the wheel, his excitement rose, in anticipation of choosing the right number, the right colour. When his number did not come up, he was not fazed. He knew, that the next spin of the wheel was going to be his lucky break. The excitement of the occasional win, drove him on to place higher stakes.

When he'd lost all of his original chips. Gabrielle purchased another £200, because this time, he was certain to win. Not only to win his money back but also a substantial amount.

He felt a tap on his shoulder. For a moment, his heart skipped a beat. Surely, Willow had not returned to find him.

It's not that he was embarrassed or ashamed of his losses. No, he didn't want her to worry. She was so very special to him, and besides, there wasn't any need to tell her about this side of his life. After all, a man can have his little secrets.

'Feck, man. How much have you lost tonight?' shouted a familiar voice.

Gabriel spun around and saw Seamus, hovering behind him. He pointed to the bar as Eugene made his way over with some drinks.

'Not much, Seamus,' he replied.

Seamus raised his eyebrows and shrugged his shoulders.

'Then that will be all right, my man,' said Seamus in the tone of voice that suggested otherwise. 'Now here is our Eugene, can we be getting you a drink, while you don't lose much money?'

Gabriel looked at his chips on the table. It was not much of a pile at all. Only two chips lay where before had been a collection of different coloured chips.

'I guess I will call it a night then,' said Gabriel, to Eugene and Seamus, who was already pushing each other out of the way, to get on the stool that Gabriel had just vacated.

'Now you get back to that pretty Colleen of yours, we will be seeing you tomorrow,' called Seamus.

Gabriel hoped that the two Irish men wouldn't be discussing this evening's event in the presence of Willow. Now that wouldn't do.

Very quietly, he entered the stateroom. Willow was sleeping soundly as he'd hoped. She'd left the bathroom light on, giving enough light for him to see her quite clearly, laying in the huge queen size bed. Her hair was splayed out against the pillow, shining dark ebony. He could smell her perfume throughout the room. Gabriel desperately wanted to hold her, to stroke her hair and to make love. He could quite easily have intentionally disturbed her sleep. Guilt and shame prevented him from doing so. Tonight was the first and last visit to the casino; he wouldn't go back. He vowed to himself, that tomorrow evening when Willow was rested, he'd concentrate on giving her the most wonderful evening of her life.

As he gently climbed in beside her, she instinctively rolled over towards him. He moved closer, feeling the softness of her skin. Her beautiful body close to his own was enough to arouse him into submission. Against his earlier intentions of not disturbing her, he caressed her inner thighs; working his way towards what was surely the most heavenly place on earth.

Willow responded as he hoped she would. Sleepily, she smiled at him. It was a knowing smile. A smile that said *I'm just as eager as you.*

It was well past four o'clock, when they both, finally succumbed to sleep.

At eight thirty, the ships horn woke them, followed swiftly, by the Captain announcing that the ship was in Port. He advised that the gangplank was situated on deck four and reminded everyone who was disembarking, to take their stateroom cards and passports with them.

Gabriel was barely awake, he pulled a pillow over his head and groaned. Playfully, Willow grabbed the pillow and ran off towards the bathroom. Within minutes, he heard the sound of the shower and Willow humming a rather bad tune. He would have been quite happy to enjoy a nice lay in. It was a rarity for such a luxury these days. His work was so demanding and exhausting. Tentatively, he raised himself up the bed, resting his head against the luxuriously padded headboard. It was rather glitzy, he thought to himself. In fact, the whole room was a bit too glitzy for his taste. He noticed a programme was placed on his bedside cabinet. Picking it up, he began to read of the day's events. Interestingly, it was very informative; it even had the times of the sunset and sunrise, along with the day's forecast.

There was a comprehensive list of shore excursions and port information, in addition to port shopping advice. He guessed, that most people would have already arranged their excursions, perhaps they would be too late to get a place. Still, it was worth a try. He checked out the list of phone numbers in the directory next to the phone. Sure enough, the Port information contact number was listed. Worth a try, he thought.

A lady named Pippa answered the phone. She was very helpful and informed Gabriel that a couple had in fact cancelled, just prior to his call. She offered to fit him in on the full-day excursion to the medieval city of Bruges. He was to collect the tickets from the excursion desk on the promenade deck. However, he needed to be sharp, as the bus was due to leave from outside the ship, within the hour. Pippa took his stateroom number, which was linked to his credit card details. He promised to be up on deck to collect the tickets in twenty minutes. Pulling on a pair of jeans and an Oxford blue shirt, he opened the door to the en-suite. The room was steamy, to say the least. He called out to Willow and briefly explained the situation.

Racing out of the room, he couldn't decide whether to turn right or left along the main corridor. Either way, he hoped to find a lift to take him to the promenade deck. He noticed, there was a lot of activity. Not only was there lots of passengers, mulling around, but stateroom attendants were busy pushing trolleys of fresh linen and cleaning products. He called out to one of them.

'Which is the best way for mid-ship promenade deck, please?'

A young Chinese girl, dressed like a chambermaid, pointed to her right and smiled.

'Thanks,' called Gabriel, as he dashed off in the direction that she was pointing.

When he arrived at the excursion desk, there was quite a queue. 'Bugger,' cursed Gabriel under his breath. He had neither showered nor shaved and his mouth felt unclean. Still, he had no choice other than to wait his turn.

By the time he'd returned to his stateroom, Willow was ready to leave. She was dressed casually in a pair of white Capri pants and a royal blue cotton top.

'Do you have the time for a quick shower and shave, Gabriel?' asked Willow, as she opened the safe to collect their passports and euros.

He looked at his watch and smirked. 'Just you watch me,' he answered.

They made it on the coach with seconds to spare. Both breathless, excited and very hungry. Willow rummaged in her very large handbag. She passed a bottle of water to Gabriel and another one for herself.

'I could murder a coffee and some toast,' groaned Gabriel.

'Me too,' said Willow. 'Let's make it our priority when we arrive at the city. Coffee and croissants. Mm, I can almost taste them.'

As the bus pulled away from the cruise terminal, they took note of the size of the ship. It was magnificent, to say the least. Willow wondered at the engineering skills of keeping such a huge vessel afloat.

As they travelled through the Port Town of Zeebrugge, making their way to the medieval city of Bruges, they marvelled at the wide-open motorways of Belgium and how they contrasted with the busy motorways back home. Content, they sat relaxed, holding hands enjoying the journey together.

When they entered the city, it took away their breath; such was the splendour of the city, with its tree-lined squares, medieval churches, and buildings. They found a restaurant, close to the town centre and chose a table outside. While waiting for their order, they watched in wonder as the horse-drawn carriages rolled by on the cobbled roads. The drivers in traditional livery and the horses with red plumes and shining horse brass. The air around them was charged with the emotions of their feelings. For Willow, it was nothing short of magic. She felt as though in the middle of a fairy tale, with her own prince sat beside her.

Over breakfast, they made plans for the rest of the day, which was to include a boat ride down the beautiful canal. Arm in arm, they wandered the streets, drinking in the sights and smells of Bruges. Every hour listening to the clock in the square chime; standing still in wonder, at the magic of the city.

Making their way, back to the bus at five o'clock, they vowed to return again perhaps for the whole weekend or even longer. This day would always be engraved into their memory.

It had been a whirlwind of a day and there were still so many activities to enjoy. Tonight, was formal night on the ship. This involved extra special preparation for the ladies. Dinner was scheduled for seven o'clock, not allowing much time to make ready. Gabriel suggested that Willow have the first shower and him the second. That way, she can be getting dressed up in her formal clothes and take her time with her hair and makeup. Although he knew that she wore very little makeup, he guessed that she'd appreciate the extra time more than himself.

While Willow was in the shower, Gabriel went for a quick stroll around the ship. As he expected, the casino was closed, as they were in port. Without the bright lights and the hum of the machines, it looked like a graveyard to him. A stale smell of alcohol hung in the air. Gabrielle questioned himself as to why he felt compelled to gamble. What was the joy of losing so much money, he hoped that one day, he'd come away winning? He just needed to be patient. It was a nuisance, to him that the casino was shut. But there was still the online gaming as a good second best. He had begun his relationship with online gaming when he was working night shifts. The unsociable hours made it difficult for him to go to the bookmakers. Although not as exciting, it was easy to place a bet.

With the casino closed, the regular visitors to this part of the ship were either in the Yacht Club or the Bingo Hall. He knew the afternoon quiz was on in the Yacht Club, so he decided to head there. On arrival, he noticed how busy the club was. The quiz was very popular among the guests. He saw groups of people with their heads close together, discussing the answer to the last question. Gabriel knew the answer, for it was a medical question. Over at the far end of the bar, Seamus was sitting with his wife, Colleen. They waved him over, loudly proclaiming, for all to hear, that he was a doctor and sure to know the answer to the last question.

Gabriel waved back and made his way over towards the table where Seamus and Colleen were sat. He whispered the answer to them both. Gabriel noted that neither of them was dressed in their formal attire.

'Will we be seeing you in the restaurant tonight, for the formal dinner?' he inquired.

Colleen shaking her head told Gabriel that it wasn't for the likes of them. They planned to eat in a more relaxed manner in the Buffet restaurant.

'Might we be seeing you both in the casino later,' inquired Seamus, with a wicked glint in his eyes. Gabriel picked up the subliminal message loud and clear. He felt somewhat relieved that they wouldn't be joining himself and Willow at the formal dinner that evening.

Gabriel knew that once they set sail, later in the evening, the casino would once again be open for business. Smiling politely, he told Colleen and Seamus, that they hoped to catch the late show and would probably not get to the casino.

Secretly, he was already planning a way around this dilemma. The very idea of not getting to the casino filled him with apprehension. Somehow, he'd find a way. The more Gabriel tried to resist the temptation, the more demanding the obsessive thoughts became. From experience, he recognised that he should remove himself away from the location and distract himself by alternate means.

Right now, he needed to get back to the stateroom and prepare for the evening ahead.

Willow was putting the final touches to her hair when he let himself into the stateroom. She was sitting at the dressing table, clipping a diamante hair clip, into her up-swept hair. Her neck, he noticed, had a tiny fine line of dark hair at the nape. Her neck and shoulders looked smooth and tempting. Gabriel, walked up behind her, massaging her neck and shoulders with his warm masculine hands. He looked at her in the mirror, catching her smile at her own reflection. She was wearing a long, black satin evening dress that was covered in silver beads and pearl drops. The shoestring straps skimmed her bare shoulders. As Gabriel hovered above her, looking down, he saw that she was not wearing a bra. Her breasts were high upon her chest, shapely and firm. If only he'd returned sooner, then perhaps he could have reached his hands down into the bodice of her dress and caressed her sweet curvaceous breasts. He felt the familiar ache of desire, he was tempted to abandon all plans of the formal evening and the show. Something even stronger than his desire for Willow held him back.

He cursed himself for his own weakness.

'Are you nearly ready, Willow, is it okay for me to use the bathroom now, or do you need me to wait a little longer?' he inquired.

She stood up, moving away from the dressing table giving him the opportunity to see how truly sensational she looked. Willow moved over to the bed, she lifted her dress above her ankles and slipped on a pair of gold evening sandals.

'That's me ready, do I look all right?' she asked.

'You look sensational,' he replied. 'I hope that I can match up to your own expectations,' he answered, making his way to the shower.

While in the shower, Willow reached into the wardrobe and retrieved his dinner suit. She removed the cellophane wrapping and laid it out on the bed. Without wanting to be too presumptuous, she went into his bedside drawer, hoping to find the bow tie. While rummaging through the drawer, she picked up a pile of Euro lottery tickets. Thinking this rather odd, Willow checked the dates, assuming that perhaps they were old stubs that he'd emptied from his pocket. Willow was about to check the dates when she heard movement from the shower. She quickly closed the drawer, as Gabriel sauntered into the room, naked and obviously pleased to see her. Thankfully, he mistook her blushes, for something altogether different, as he proceeded to tease her as he dressed.

Willow helped him with his bowtie. The smell of his aftershave was quite intoxicating. Was this gorgeous man, genuinely in love with her? So, what, if he enjoyed a little flutter on the lottery. What man didn't like to gamble now and again? She put all thoughts of the lottery tickets behind her. Tonight, they both looked a million dollars, they were dining in style and going to see the equivalent of a "West End Show".

When they were shown to their dining table, Willow was surprised to discover, that they were the first to arrive for dinner. Gabriel did not appear to be surprised, when the Irish contingency, failed to put in an appearance. In some ways, for Willow at least. It was more romantic, with just the two of them at the huge, round table. The table was set to perfection, with crystal white table linen, heavy silver cutlery and white porcelain crockery. The crystal flutes, wine glasses and water tumbles, glistened under the huge sparkling chandeliers. Dressed in her evening dress of black satin and wearing her single row of pearls around her neck. Willow felt like a princess in a dream. She didn't want the dream to end. But end it must. She knew that very soon she'd be back in her green dungarees, soil under her perfectly manicured nails, and her steel toe capped garden boots. For the present, she was living the dream. A dream that she'd created when she booked the cruise.

Gabriel was unable to take his eyes away from Willow. In his opinion, she outshone every woman in the room, although she was so humble; he doubted that Willow realised this. Despite their relationship being in its infancy. He knew without a single doubt, that he wanted to make Willow, his wife. Currently, it was impossible to offer her marriage. He had another year to complete his studies and even then, his salary wouldn't be great. His only hope was to win enough money, to pay a deposit on a house and to afford to give Willow the wedding she deserved. He knew that his parents would be unwilling to help. He suspected that they would most likely disapprove of the match. Even try to dissuade him. He knew full well that they were expecting him to do missionary work for the church. Despite making it quite clear that this was not going to happen, he was concerned they might place undue pressure on him, to accomplish their dreams. His student loan was mounting, not to mention his overdraft. Somehow, he had to find a way of earning some money. Gabriel was so consumed with his thoughts, the wine waiter who was hovering around the table was getting impatient, awaiting an answer to the offer of wine.

'Sorry,' said Gabriel. 'Please bring a bottle of wine to the table.' He looked over to Willow. 'Do you prefer, red or white, darling?'

Not used to being called darling, Willow was taken back.

'White please, as I'm thinking of ordering fish for mains,' she answered.

Willow could see that Gabriel was distracted. She smiled and reached over to his hand.

'Are you worrying about work or your exams, Gabriel?' inquired Willow.

'Actually, neither,' he replied. Not wanting to saddle her with his financial worries, he made light of the situation, resolving rather to utilise the opportunity to talk about his sister, Victoria.

He explained that his sister, Victoria, had dropped a bombshell on the family. Not so much for me, although it will impact on my own life to some extent, he told Willow. He went on to explain that she was getting married to a fellow student from Scotland.

'His name is Duncan; that's as much as my parents know. They're not very happy about the whole situation, to be honest. It is so out of character for Victoria. You would have thought that she might at least have introduced him to us before announcing the proposed marriage.'

Willow thought otherwise. Remembering the cool reception that she received from his parents, she guessed that Victoria had likely anticipated a similar response. Secretly, Willow admired Victoria and was looking forwards to meeting her.

'Are you close to your sister, Gabriel? Do you think that she might want to discuss the matter in private with you before the meeting? After all, with your parents around and probably Duncan's too, I guess she will keep pretty tight-lipped.'

Gabriel considered this suggestion and decided to take Willow's advice.

'Yes, that's what I will do. Now, you and I are going to enjoy this meal and hopefully, if we finish pretty quickly, we should get good seats in the theatre.'

They did manage to secure exceptionally good seats which was just as well, for the theatre began to fill up pretty quickly. The show, as promised in the reviews, was outstanding. The audience gave a standing ovation. Willow was enthralled with the music and dance production. Gabriel enjoyed being with Willow, and appreciated the quality of the production but throughout the performance, his mind was somewhere else. He felt lucky tonight.

After the show, Willow needed to stretch her legs and suggested that they take a walk on deck. It was breezy on the outside deck and a little chilly. Gabriel slipped his dinner jacket around Willow's shoulders. Walking hand in hand around the entire length of the ship, both port-side and starboard looking at the ink-coloured sky was nothing short of perfection for Willow. Gabriel rather hoped that she was feeling tired and ready to return to their stateroom; so that he could slip off to the casino. It was midnight already and he guessed that the seats around the gambling tables would be all taken.

'Are you ready to turn in? It's been quite a day.'

Thinking that he was eager to return to the stateroom to make love, she feigned a yawn. They entered inside the ship, making their way towards the glass lift situated in the atrium. On the way down, Willow noticed a lot of activity around the champagne bar area and thought that it might be fun to have glass of champagne to complete the magic of the evening. It looked very trendy. Willow hoped that Gabriel was up for the fun of it too. When she suggested they do just that, Gabriel hesitated for a moment, before answering. She thought that he'd be happy to join in the fun and was disappointed when he declined, adding that he was tired too.

Maybe he was right, she pondered. Perhaps he was still tired from the night rota and needed to rest. There was always tomorrow. The last night on board. There was still lots to do. They would be spending the entire day at sea. Willow was hoping to go to the solarium and maybe have lunch in the huge winter garden. The champagne bar could wait until the last night.

Gabriel was glad to be taking off his bow tie and cumber band. The high collar of his shirt was irritating his neck adding to the rising tension relating to his urgent need to get to the casino. He helped Willow out of her dress, revealing the new lacy underwear that she'd purchased for the cruise. He gently kissed her and told her that he'd enjoyed the evening and the best was still to come. Lifting her up in his strong arms, Gabriel carried her to the bed, all the time kissing her softly until she ached for more.

After they'd made love, she snuggled close to him and quickly fell into a happy and peaceful sleep.

Gabriel had no intention of sleeping. He listened until satisfied Willow was soundly asleep, he disentangled himself from her and climbed quietly out of bed. He slipped on his trousers and shirt, leaving the neck open for comfort. After putting on his shoes, he quietly left the room.

Chapter Eleven

The casino was buzzing with activity and excitement, as he made his way towards the Black Jack table which was the least busy. He hoped to get a game or two while he waited for space at the roulette table. Gabriel felt lucky. He purchased five hundred pounds worth of chips using his stateroom card. He knew by the end of the night, his winnings would more than cover his losses over the past two days.

His first hand was good. He had an ace and a king. Perfect. This was encouraging for Gabriel; it was a good sign. He beat the banker in the first deal. His excitement mounting, despite losing the next four hands.

Out of the corner of his eye, he saw a gap at the roulette table, so he excused himself and made his way towards the possibility of winning big. Sitting high up on the cream leather stool, with its slick chrome trim, he felt his anticipation rise.

'Drink, sir?' The waitress was standing so close to him, he could see the line where her make-up began and ended. Her perfume was heavy and sickly.

'Vodka and tonic please,' he replied. The words sticking in his throat.

For a moment, a vision of Willow passed through his mind, he could almost smell the floral notes of her perfume.

'Place your bets,' called the croupier and the vision of Willow was gone.

He placed his bet, starting with a low stake, to get a feel for the game. Tonight, he planned to stick with red numbers only, perhaps if he kept to his plan then success would be assured. The croupier spun the wheel.

Gabriel took the opportunity to check out the other punters around the table. There was a mixed bunch of characters around him. Sitting directly opposite him was an elderly couple. Probably, man and wife, he guessed. The man in question looked very portly in stature. His abdomen was huge, his belly overhung the red satin cumber-band that looked about ready to pop. As he swung around in the chair, Gabriel chuckled. The man reminded him of Desperate Dan a cartoon character, broad-shouldered and obese around the abdomen, slim hips and thin legs. Totally out of proportion.

Sat next to him, the woman who was probably his wife looked to be a good ten years younger than the man. She appeared to be quite fit for her age. Her slim figure in proportion, hair swept up in a chic, French plat.

'Black wins,' called the croupier and once again, Gabriel moved his gaze from the couple to the roulette wheel.

The waitress came with his drink. Gabriel passed her his card so that she could add the cost to his mounting debt. Five vodka and tonics later and only four chips remaining, Gabriel looked forlorn to the point of his feelings being obvious.

'Don't be an eedjit and spend any more, you silly sod,' said Seamus, as he placed his hand on Gabriel's shoulder.

Gabriel swung around and realised that not only was Seamus there to witness his shame. So was Eugene.

'Let's be moving on now,' said Eugene. 'I expect Willow will be missing you.'

Gabriel picked up his four remaining chips, the ones he'd be winning back all of his losses with. Common sense prevailed. Head hung low and a huge knot of tension in his gut, he left the table with Seamus and Eugene.

'One for the road?' asked Eugene.

In for a penny, thought Gabriel, as he followed them to the bar. Seamus got the first round of drinks in.

'Where are your lovely women tonight?' Gabriel asked.

'The same place as Willow,' answered Seamus. 'Although, Willow is not in as much need of beauty sleep as our two,' he laughed.

Gabriel knew that he was just teasing and trying to create a lighter mood.

Just to be friendly, Gabriel got the next round in, then, of course, Eugene had to buy another round, just to be polite. And so, by the time Gabriel arrived back at the stateroom, having lost his way several times, he was well and truly stumbling around like a man on rubber legs. Trying, and failing miserably to be quiet, Gabriel practically fell into the room.

Startled, Willow sat bolt upright in bed, put on the bed side light, and found Gabriel on the floor. Knowing that he had to make up a half decent excuse, Gabriel scrambled to his feet. Trying his best, not to slur his words, he concentrated on his response.

'I couldn't sleep, Willow, so I decided to take a walk on the deck. I bumped into Eugene and Seamus on their way to the casino. Not wanting to be unfriendly, I joined them for one or two drinks. I'm really sorry if I frightened you.'

The lies were sticking in his throat, but the truth would have choked him. He was trying to rationalise his own behaviour as he weaved his lies to the woman he loved. As he looked towards Willow, her face looking dreamy from sleep, he once again vowed to himself that this would never happen again. He reasoned with himself that surely his life was exciting enough without needing the adrenaline rush of a potential win. Yes, that was the last of his gambling, it didn't feel like fun anymore.

Willow lay back down on the bed; she wasn't sure what to think. For some reason, he looked guilty. Perhaps he was embarrassed about being drunk, she pondered. Yes, that was likely the reason. In any case. With working the night shifts, there was no wonder his sleep pattern was disrupted. Satisfied that she'd reached a convincing conclusion, Willow snuggled up to Gabriel when he climbed in beside her. Within minutes, they were both sound asleep.

Their last day at sea was for leisure. Willow spent a few hours in the Solarium, enjoying a swim in the warm indoor pool. Gabriel who was feeling delicate, from the over indulgence of alcohol the previous evening, laid on a sun lounger admiring Willow. Although their relationship was fairly new in some respects, he felt a sense of responsibility towards her. Fundamentally, he knew that he had no need to explain himself to her or anyone else for that matter. His money was his own concern, and if he chose to gamble his money, then it was his decision. Except, it wasn't, his money, and he knew that. However, he felt confident that one of these days he'd have a big win enabling him to pay off his huge student debt and the overdraft that was mounting in the bank account his parents had set up for him.

After lunch, they went for a game of ten-pin bowling, followed by a visit to the cinema. It was a strange sensation, sat in a cinema that gently rocked and rolled with the movement of the sea. The film was in 3D, it was fascinating to both of them. Sci-Fi wasn't Gabriel's usual preference, but the film *Avatar*, he thought, was brilliant.

At Willow's suggestion, they had afternoon tea in the conservatory, giving Gabriel a good opportunity to suggest that they skip dinner in the restaurant that evening and just have a light snack in the buffet later. Willow, appeared to be happy with the plan, although, not as happy as Gabriel. He had just succeeded in preventing a meeting with Seamus and Eugene, with the potential for the truth being exposed. The holiday had been so perfect, he didn't want to risk anything spoiling the magic of the last few days.

Much to his relief, they disembarked from the ship, without setting eyes on any of their cruise friends. Although under other circumstances, Gabriel would have sort out his acquaintances, to wish them farewell; on this occasion, he declined to do so.

Willow and Gabriel firmly held hands as they stepped off the ship onto terra firma. They certainly looked to be a happy, loved up couple. Willow was glowing with happiness. Even the prospect of the long drive home did not displace the joy that she was feeling. The whole experience aboard a cruise ship was quite something. She had so much to tell her parents and her friends; who no doubt, will be asking her for every little detail. Some of which was too personal to discuss. After all, her love life was just that. Hers alone and not for sharing.

The thought of sleeping alone, without Gabriel by her side, was a little unsettling. After being together, day and night, she knew that she wanted to spend the rest of her life with Gabriel and couldn't imagine a life without him.

'Thank you, Willow, for being with me these past few days, I can't even begin to tell you how special it has been. I feel like the luckiest guy in the world. Please say that you will stand by me, no matter what,' pleaded Gabriel when she dropped him off outside of his home.

Willow was touched by his words and yet, extremely confused. What did he mean by 'stand by me'? After all, Gabriel was training to be a doctor, with a huge future in front of him. She considered herself to be the lucky one.

'It's been great for me too,' she replied. 'Can we make plans to meet this weekend, Gabriel?'

He wasn't sure how to answer. His mother had made it quite clear that Gabriel was to meet Duncan's family alone. Perhaps, he will speak with his sister after all and just maybe, she'd like to meet Willow, he thought.

'Can I get back to you about the weekend plans, Willow? I need to check my rota at work. I think that I'm off on Sunday, but there is always the possibility that my shifts have been swapped. I will call you tomorrow evening, we can make definite arrangements then.'

Willow was disappointed but understood. After all, he didn't work regular hours, like herself. She felt his loss, the moment she drove away. Willow couldn't understand why she felt so empty without him. *Is this how love feels*, she pondered. She knew that she'd fallen deeply in love with Gabriel. He was her first thought on awakening and her last thought as she drifted off to sleep. Her love for him was the sweetest of feelings and yet it frightened her. As she drove home, she spoke with Molly, her twin sister. Molly had not invaded her mind while she was with Gabriel. Now Molly knew that her sister needed someone to confide in, she was there in spirit. A presence that Willow relied upon, at times of contemplation.

Chapter Twelve

On his return, Gabriel decided, that he had to prioritise his life. He knew what he wanted for his future. His future was with Willow. He wanted to make her his wife. He tried to rationalise, the steps that he could take, so this was possible. The first priority, he needed to concentrate on was his studies; his whole future and Willow's, if she agreed to be his wife; depended on him, passing his Degree.

Although he considered his gambling to be no more than a lad's zealous hobby. He knew, that he needed to curb his spending. His current debts, amounted to £40,000, an amount he'd hoped to reduce by winning at the roulette table. He considered the possibility of approaching his parents for a loan, to pay off his debts. However, he knew, that at this moment in time, with Victoria's wedding hanging over them like the Sword of Damocles, it was highly unlikely that they would agree.

Thinking of Victoria, reminded him of Willow's advice, to ring her. *No time like the present*, he decided.

When he rang, she didn't answer, so he left her a message to ring him back. Within the hour, she returned his call.

'Hi, Gabriel, to what do I owe this very rare phone call. I feel quite honoured,' she teased.

Gabriel had just got out of the shower when she rang. With a small towel around his middle and his hair dripping onto his shoulders, he was speaking to Victoria, at the top of the stairs, when Leo accompanied by his latest girlfriend came in. Somewhat embarrassed, Gabriel pulled the skimpy towel closer to his body as Leo and his lady friend rushed past on their way to Leo's room.

'Just a second, Victoria, I need to make myself scarce. Leo is now upstairs with his latest girlfriend and I guess it's going to get a little noisy up here. Give me a minute while I pull on some jeans and go downstairs.'

'Okay, sis, now I'm decent, I guess that I should explain why I called.'

'I think that I can guess the reason, Gabriel. I know it's been a bit of a shock for our parents, but you know what they are like. I couldn't risk introducing Duncan any sooner. They would have frightened him off, and I love him so much, I didn't want to take the risk.'

Gabriel knew exactly what she meant. He told her about Willow and how their parents had been most unwelcoming. He told Victoria about how they'd met and how wonderful she is.

Victoria listened to her elder brother. She knew from the tone of his voice and the loving way he spoke of Willow that her brother was totally in love with this woman. Willow sounded intriguing, and probably not the kind of wife, their parents had in mind for Gabriel. It appeared that they were both in the same position. She knew that her parents wouldn't be happy with her choice of husband. Although a scholar, he was not the genteel god-fearing type of man who they would approve of. A typical broad Scotsman, with a strong body and an even stronger will of iron. Duncan could be very polite and well-mannered when called for. He and his family were from an exceptionally good blood-line. His ancestors were of high standing within their own community. However, she planned to keep this information to herself for now. The fact that he was a laird was to remain her secret and her trump card, should her parents become at all difficult.

'Tell you what, Gabriel, bring Willow along when we all meet up next weekend. It will be fun.'

'I'm not so sure, Victoria. Our parents aren't too happy about you and Duncan, never mind me and Willow. They will be fuming. Surely we need to avoid any confrontation when meeting your future in-laws?' answered Gabriel.

'Don't worry about Duncan's parents, I've forewarned them,' she giggled. 'Besides, safety in numbers and all that. What do you say?'

'When you put it like that, Victoria, how can I resist. Send me an e-mail with the venue details and the final plans. I will be there. Hopefully with Willow.'

Without wasting a second, he rang Willow, hoping that she'd be home by now. The phone was answered by her mum, Emma.

'Hello, Gabriel, Willow is getting her case from the car, she has just arrived home. Did you have a nice time dear? Oh, here she is now. I will pass the phone over to her.'

'Missing me already,' teased Willow.

Gabriel smiled; he felt a warm glow pass through his body. He was missing her indeed, but tonight he'd miss her even more so.

'I've just spoken with Victoria and she has invited you along next Sunday, are you up for a meeting with my parents again? I understand they can be difficult, but you will need to get used to them, for when you are a part of the family.'

Willow wondered if she'd heard right or if it was a slip of the tongue. Part of the family? Either way, she didn't mention it, just in case, it was a Freudian slip or something.

'That sounds great, thanks Gabriel. It will be nice to meet your sister and her future husband.'

Neither of them wanted to say goodbye, it was going to feel like an eternity until they could be together.

Gabriel had a busy week ahead of him on the Paediatric ward. Although he was covering the early morning rota, he was also to be on-call three evenings. The on-call duty meant that he had to stay at the hospital, to be available any time. He hoped Sister Clay was the night sister on duty. He knew that she had a soft spot for him because she had a son the same age as Gabriel. She confided in him once about her constant worry. Her son was on active duty in the army and each tour of duty put another grey hair on her head, she once told him.

The main advantage of the on-call was that it gave him the opportunity to spend time in the medical library and get on with some dedicated study. He carried his bleep with him and was able to get back to the ward quickly in case of an emergency.

Every morning on his way into work, Gabriel called in at the local newsagent to purchase a few scratch cards which he managed to check while parked up in the staff car park. In addition, he felt compelled to have a go on the Euro lottery. This had become, yet another ritual for him to manage. On his return home, he called in at either Coral or Bet Fred Bookmakers, to place a few bets on the horses. He reasoned with himself that it helped to wind down at the end of a stressful day. The adrenaline rush, as he watched the horses race around the tracks, gave him a few moments of peace inside. The excitement seemed to override his other emotions and cares, no other thoughts managed an alternative route into his mind, while with great anticipation he hoped that this time he'd been clever enough to back a winner. He did occasionally, back a winner, but somehow winning did not give him the same shot of electricity that he felt when he first placed his bet. The anticipation and excitement of a win almost always gave him the bigger buzz. There was also something about the atmosphere in the company of other gamblers that made him feel as though he was in an alternate existence. It was mostly men who frequented such places. That was not to say that the place lacked any feminine charms. Behind the very high, secure counter, there were usually two or three glamorous young women, taking the bets. Sure, he'd noticed them, even making occasional small talk. They were of no interest to Gabriel. There was only one woman for him. When the vision of Willow entered his mind, it always had a profound effect, encouraging him to walk away, from one more bet.

Gabriel now had a long-term plan taking root in his already overactive mind. In just over a year, he should have completed his studies. Since meeting Willow, he'd decided to apply for a position at one of the local surgeries to train as a GP Registrar. In time, he hoped to apply for a partnership with a practice. Gabriel visualised a future with Willow; a nice home with a garden she could lovingly attend. Just thinking about Willow, and the plans that he had for their future, should she agree to be his wife, gave him a feeling of euphoria.

Chapter Thirteen

Willow was glowing with happiness when she arrived at work on Monday morning. Dorothy recognised the signs. She was definitely in love; it was a certainty. Willow, already a beautiful young woman, was radiant and full of joy. As usual, they sat together enjoying a nice cup of tea and planning the daily tasks. Willow in her garden dungarees and painted nails looked like a model ready for a photo shoot. Dorothy smiled, knowing that by the end of the day, the varnish would be cracked and chipped which Willow wouldn't be troubled by at all.

Naturally, they chatted about the cruise ship and the visit to Bruges, the food, and the entertainment. Willow painted the most amazing picture to Dorothy. It all sounded too perfect, thought Dorothy. She'd noticed a hint of hesitation in Willow's voice when she was talking about the casino. Never having been in one before, she could only imagine what it was like, from the description that Willow gave her. However, Dorothy suspected that it sounded like Gabriel, might have enjoyed the casino a lot more than Willow. Still, they were both young, with so much adventure in front of them. For now, though, Willow needed to concentrate on the tasks at hand and not have her head in the clouds, no matter how bright the horizon looked.

The week dragged by for both, Willow and Gabriel. Each of them feeling more apart as every day they longed to be together. Willow rang Gabriel most nights. At first, she was worried that he might be concerned about this, and even consider her as being needy. But Gabriel was just as excited as herself when he heard her voice on the end of the line. They never ran out of conversation. Willow hung on to every word he spoke. Although he didn't give too much information because of confidentiality, Gabriel did manage to convey to her some of the interesting aspects of his job. He appeared to be enjoying working with the children and spoke with such compassion. During one such conversation, he enquired if Willow had considered a future with children. She was surprised by this question, explaining that she very much hoped to one day have a family of her own.

Willow told Gabriel that there was a possibility of twins as she herself was a twin. This was the first opportunity she'd had to talk to Gabriel about her twin sister, Molly. A subject she found extremely painful to discuss. Talking about her twin sister felt strangely disloyal as though she was exposing her sister to the world once more. A world that gave her life then quickly took it away.

He was most surprised to hear that she'd been an identical twin. She was the one to survive. He guessed that this may have had some kind of impact upon her, from a psychological aspect. Willow denied having any issues with survivor guilt. She explained that it was her parents who suffered the most pain, and that she felt a huge responsibility to be a good daughter to them.

Willow had no intention of telling Gabriel about the conversations she still had with her dead sister. She thought no one would understand that she felt as though Molly was still attached to her; close by her side at all times. She'd never discussed it with her parents either, although when she was a little girl, they knew about her pretend friend. Her parents heard Willow talking to her little friend, setting out a picnic place for her and sharing her toys. They suspected Molly had been her best friend throughout her childhood and just as they'd predicted, as Willow left childhood behind her. Molly was left in her childhood, along with the toys.

They decided to meet early on Sunday morning at her house. Gabriel's parents were making their own way to the venue. For this, she was grateful. The thought of being trapped in a car with them was the stuff of nightmares for her. As it was, Willow was tense, to say the least. The saving grace for her, was the idea of meeting Victoria and Duncan, whom she was looking forward to being introduced to.

Gabriel didn't give too much away when Willow enquired if his parents were okay about her joining the family on such an important occasion. The truth was. They were furious that Victoria had even considered the fact. It was bad enough that they were to be meeting their daughter's future husband for the first time, and on foreign soil, as far as they were concerned. The truth was, they were both upset because they felt as though they were losing control of their children. Neither of them even considered the reasons why Victoria didn't want to bring Duncan to her own home for the first introductions. Meeting in some strange neutral place they considered odd, not to mention the fact that it was a public space. They would have much preferred to have met them in their own home and maybe call into the church for evening mass.

Apparently, Duncan's parents lived in Edinburgh, so Victoria and Duncan who were travelling up from Warwick had arranged to meet them in Richmond, although not halfway; it was close enough.

Willow enjoyed the drive up, through the North Yorkshire countryside. The passing scenery was breath-taking. They arrived with a good half hour to spare. After parking up, close to the town centre, they strolled hand in hand, around the cobbled streets, enjoying a spot of window shopping in the quaint shops around the market square; finally making their way to the tea rooms, they'd agreed to meet in.

Duncan and Victoria had already arrived. Gabriel spotted his sister, the moment they entered the traditional and spacious tea rooms. Willow could see the resemblance to Gabriel, almost immediately. She was striking, with similar auburn hair, only hers was a mass of curls. She almost looked Celtic and could easily be considered as a Scot herself. She will fit right in with her new family, thought Willow. With open arms and a radiant smile, Victoria embraced Willow first and then her brother. Quietly, in her shadow stood Duncan. He looked to be at least six feet three, with broad shoulders and strong looking legs. His sandy hair was receding a little at the front, which he made up for, with a tiny ponytail in the nape of his neck. He looked like the kind of man who could toss a caber with no problem at all. He gave a huge grin when introduced to Gabriel. They did the usual man thing of shaking hands and thumping each other on the back. With Willow, he was as gentle as a lamb, giving her the sweetest of hugs and a warm smile.

Both couples sat down together at a huge, round table, set near a Georgian style window, overlooking the marketplace. Having had only a brief conversation with each other. Duncan announced that he'd just spotted his parents walk by the window. Victoria and Duncan made their way towards the entrance, greeted his parents and walked over towards Gabriel and Victoria. Further introductions were being addressed when a waitress approached the party. Duncan ordered a full afternoon tea for eight people.

Duncan's parents were an absolute joy. It appeared that they'd been to the Norman Castle, located in the town centre. They were very impressed with the whole town and planned to take a walk by the River Swale later in the day. Apparently, they'd booked into a quaint Bed and Breakfast for the night. Both retired, they had no commitments the next day and planned to enjoy the visit.

Engrossed in conversation while awaiting the tea, no one noticed the serious, drab looking couple who entered the tea rooms. Gabriel and Victoria's parents wandered around the premises for a good five minutes, before finally locating the very jolly party, sat close to the window.

'Well, thank you for meeting us so nicely, children and good afternoon to you,' said their father, as he approached the table, tipping his hat to the group.

Gabriel and Willow abruptly stood up, one of them caught the table leg which set the table into a tipping position and was immediately rescued by Duncan's father who was laughing loudly as he rescued the table from falling into the new guests.

'I'm very pleased to meet you both,' said Duncan's father, as he held out his hand in readiness for a polite handshake.

The gesture was not replicated. Feeling uncomfortable about the situation, Victoria approached her parents and directed them towards the two seats that had been left vacant for her parents.

'Mother, Father, I want to introduce you both to my fiancé, Duncan, and his parents, Gordon and Moira,' said Victoria. They both nodded their heads in acknowledgement and swiftly sat down at the table.

'It is good to meet you both, I've heard such a lot about you,' said Duncan to the parents of Victoria. 'I guess that today will just be a brief introduction to one another, and we can get to know each other much more at our wedding. Today is a good day, a time to celebrate. We are strangers at the moment. Victoria, my parents and I have just had the privilege of meeting Gabriel and his delightful girlfriend, Willow, and now you have joined us, perhaps we can start our afternoon tea. Ah! Look, I think that tray of food coming our way must be ours. I hope tea is all right, if not we can order fresh coffee?'

The uncomfortable atmosphere was dispelled for a moment, while the waitresses set the table and placed the tea, sandwiches and cakes.

Moira was the first to break the silence that ensued. 'Yes! I'm Moira and my husband is Gordon, and your names are…'

'Joan and Sam,' answered Gabriel's mother, without elaborating any further. Joan looked in the direction of Willow, giving her a steely look.

'I see that you have managed to get yourself an invitation to a family meeting,' she said.

Willow was not quite sure how to respond. The atmosphere was clearly getting more Icey, by the minute. She felt so hurt for Victoria, this was her and Duncan's special day. Willow flashed her a look of deep sympathy. Gabriel came to Willow's rescue.

Addressing his parents, he said, 'Willow, he hoped, will one day also be part of the family, and as such, when Victoria invited her along, he felt that it was a great opportunity to meet his sister and her future husband.'

A huge gasp went around the table. Willow pretended not to notice, despite her racing heart and flushed face. Victoria put her hands on her heart in a gesture of love. She smiled at Willow and then at her brother.

'Well, we do have a lot to celebrate. I'm sure my parents are quite overwhelmed by everything. It's not every day you see both of your children happy and in love. Duncan and I feel so lucky to have met each other and now I hear that I may soon have a sister as well. Perhaps after we've finished our tea, we could go across the road to the hotel and celebrate with something stronger?'

Duncan made his way over to Victoria, standing behind her resting his arms on her shoulders, he told them of his love for Victoria and how he would always take care of her. Victoria knew exactly what he was going to say next. She couldn't wait to see the expression on her parent's faces, who so far had not managed to crack the smallest of smiles.

'When we get married, your daughter will become Lady Victoria, just as my mother became a lady when she married my father. I'm sorry that this will mean we will be living in an old and draughty castle in Scotland, as that's what is expected of a Laird, even nowadays,' he laughed.

Willow looked around the table, everyone was smiling except Joan and Sam, who were both open-mouthed.

'What about your studies, Victoria? We have made many sacrifices for you and Gabriel to have a good education, surely you're not going to throw away all that knowledge, to become no more than a housekeeper in a draughty old castle?' said Joan.

An audible gasp could be heard by all at the table. Duncan was not amused; this was quite obvious from his expression. However, he remained polite and matter of fact.

'Both Victoria and I are grateful for the opportunities we've been given, our education will not go to waste, we've already looked into the possibility of research posts available locally. We have been reassured that should our degree results be satisfactory, then there will be employment for both of us. Don't worry, Victoria will be living a life of great comfort and dare I say it, she will never have to worry about money ever again.'

Gabriel stood up and to the amusement of Duncan's parents, he began to clap.

'Well said, Duncan, you have a great spirit, I admire that in a man. Welcome to the family. I'm looking forwards to visiting you and my sister in Scotland. Congratulations to the both of you.'

Willow felt so proud of Gabriel for the way that he handled a situation that could quite easily have got out of control. His parents sat stiff-lipped and quiet throughout the meal, while Moira and Gordon laughed, joked and made plans for their son's marriage. They appeared happy about the match that their son had made. Victoria was charming, well spoken, polite, and very amusing. Willow considered how Gabriel and Victoria had managed to grow up into such well-rounded adults, despite their parent's pious, ill-mannered behaviour. So, his mother's name was Joan, well, she was no Joan of Arc, thought Willow, in fact despite this being the second meeting with his parents, they were as cold towards her as on the first occasion. She didn't take it personally, for Willow observed that they treated Duncan and his parents with what appeared to be the same contempt as she was being given. Gabriel not only made her proud but also astounded her, with his announcement of her potential place in the family. She knew he loved her, for he had told her many times. But, to announce his intentions, before asking her was most surprising and something she planned to talk about on the way home.

They never did toast the couple with champagne or prosecco. Sam and Joan excused themselves within two hours of the meeting, leaving just the six of them in an awkward situation. Both Willow and Gabriel were at work the following morning and despite the pleadings from Victoria, they declined a trip over to the hotel for a drink for fear that one may turn into two and they couldn't risk that, with a drive ahead of them. Having shaken everyone's hand, with a promise to meet up again, before the wedding, possibly at the castle, Willow and Gabriel reluctantly left Victoria with her fiancé and parents-in-law to be.

'Phew! Thank goodness that's over,' said Gabriel, as they made their way towards the car. 'I must admit, I do like Duncan. Did you see the look on my parents' face when he dropped the bombshell about him being a Laird? Anyone else would be overjoyed, but no, not my parents. Do you know, Willow, I'm beginning to think that the only thing that would make them happy, would be for Victoria to be a nun and me a priest? In fact, I think they would even prefer for me to be a missionary, over and above being a doctor. For the life of me, I cannot fathom them out.'

Willow reached for Gabriel's hand. She found it hard to believe that his parents were so cold and humourless. What had happened to make them so?

'Have they ever been different, Gabriel? I mean, do you remember your childhood and times of comfort with your mother? Surely there must have been many moments of family laughter and joy?'

Gabriel squeezed her hand.

'Time enough to psychoanalyse my parents another day, for now, we have our own lives ahead of us. You and I are going to have such a great time, Willow. We have a long drive ahead of us. How about we stop somewhere halfway and have a meal in one of the country pubs on the route?'

'Sounds good, to be honest, although the sandwiches and cakes were delicious, I didn't enjoy the meal, because the atmosphere was so tense,' replied Willow.

It was after eleven o'clock by the time Gabriel dropped Willow off home and he still had a good forty-minute drive ahead of him. He walked Willow to the door, hugged her tightly and kissed her as though she was a movie star. Willow giggled.

'Gabriel, you have literally taken my breath away, where did you learn to kiss like that?'

'I've been paying close attention to the old films, so I thought I might steal a few tips from the likes of Dirk Bogart and that other heartthrob Sean Connery,' he laughed.

'Well, you have certainly left me with a kiss to remember,' she replied.

Neither of them wanted to part, it was getting more difficult by the day to spend lonely nights in bed, without each other. They had experienced the joy of sleeping together all night and now, for Willow at least. She wanted Gabriel by her side, every night.

Gabriel drove home with so many mixed feelings, turning around in his head. Victoria had taken the plunge; she'd made a commitment to Duncan. Perhaps he should take her lead. He didn't want to steal away the excitement from his sister, but neither did he wish to wait years before asking Willow to be his wife. He decided that he'd formally propose to Willow after his sister's wedding. With this thought still in his mind, he drove home, half euphoric and half concerned about the financial implications. He would find a way, somehow, he'd pay off his mounting debt. He remembered hearing that some of the student doctors had volunteered for medical trials. Apparently, they paid very well, sometimes a few thousand pounds. Maybe he'd start looking into it tomorrow. Yes, that's what he'd do.

Chapter Fourteen

The following day, Gabriel wasted no time in searching out an application for a clinical trial. He found a company who were currently seeking, healthy males between the age of eighteen and forty years of age to trial a new treatment. He felt that this was a low-risk study and if he was successful in his application, he could quite easily fit it into his schedule. The study was over two days, with an overnight stay under controlled conditions. No one needed to know. Not even Leo or Adnan. The fee, although not huge, would at least chip a little off his mounting debt.

Gabriel was successful in his application. Despite his primary goal to earn the much-needed fee, to help towards his gambling debts. He felt a sense of worth within himself. He felt proud to be helping towards the improvement in medical science. From what he understood of the trial, it was aimed at improving the understanding and treatment of viruses that affect billions of people every year during the flu season.

He was pleasantly surprised how well managed the trial was. Although over the past few years, Gabriel had studied many research articles and understood about the process involved to achieve accurate data; he never really considered much about the volunteers who willingly participated in the advancement of medicine.

He stayed overnight in a residential unit, had his own private room with en suite facilities, and even a flat screen TV and play station. Although there were other volunteers who each had their own room, they were kept isolated until the trials were complete. He understood the reasoning behind this and had come prepared. Gabriel used his time wisely, dedicating most of his time to study. He was interested in the study design and asked many questions throughout the trial. Overall, it was a unique experience. He suffered no side effects, for which he was grateful, and he left with more knowledge about medical research than he went with.

Spurred on by this, Gabriel applied for a further drug trial three months later. The trial with the previous drug was without complication and the payment was made directly into his bank account; making a small dent in the mounting debt. Meanwhile, he had a few modest wins on the horses, further raising his spirits and providing him with a little breathing space in terms of his anxiety that had started to creep up on him, when he thought about the responsibility that lay ahead of him.

Following the second drug trial which involved a double-blind study on a new statin drug. Gabriel was feeling generally tired and a little achy. He guessed that it was likely that he'd been given the active drug, as opposed to the placebo, but he felt that these temporary problems were worth it in the long run.

One evening after a difficult shift, he received an excited phone call from his sister, Victoria. The wedding was all arranged and was to take place in the castle grounds in

Edinburgh. Duncan's family were providing the wedding feast and everything. Victoria was sorting out her wedding dress and the bridesmaids, of which there were to be four of Duncan's nieces.

'Just one other important thing, Gabriel. The men will be wearing either kilts or a tartan sash. Do you think you might oblige?'

'Are you kidding me, Victoria?' he replied.

Victoria laughed. 'Just testing the water, Gabriel. Can you imagine Father wearing a kilt or sash? No, it will just be Duncan's clan.'

The wedding was set for mid-July the following year. His final exams were scheduled, for May twenty-first, but there was always the possibility of a potential resit in mid-August. He hoped that this wouldn't be necessary; still, he needed to factor this into his plans. Now was a crucial time in terms of studying for his final exams, the effort he put in now was essential for the outcome. He understood deferred gratification in terms of putting his life on hold temporarily in order to achieve later success. He hoped that Willow understood this too.

His plan to propose to Willow after his sister's wedding was now something that he should consider. The engagement ring he'd already decided was to be a solitaire diamond set in a traditional gold band. He had already started looking in the jewellery shop windows while in the city centre. Although Gabriel was still purchasing his regular lottery tickets and calling into the bookmakers a couple of times a week, his gambling habits had declined in recent weeks. Partly because of the many screening appointments he was attending for the trials reducing his opportunity and partly because he was so tired after work, he didn't have the energy to hang around at the bookies. The little energy that he was left with was spent on study.

Willow noticed that Gabriel was more tired than usual over the past few months since meeting Victoria. However, she didn't raise any concerns to Gabriel. He was working and studying hard, leaving very little time recently for them to be together. He seemed to be having less and less time off work. They spoke every day on the telephone and managed to meet a couple of times a week. Usually going to the cinema or out for a meal. The time they spent together on the cruise, seemed a lifetime away. She longed to recapture the magic again.

Still, in close contact with her friends Janet and Sharon, they arranged to meet up one lunchtime in the city centre for a spot of retail therapy and a nice lunch together. Willow caught a tram into the city centre. No driving for the girls today, they intended to share a nice bottle of wine and catch up on each other's lives. Both Janet and Sharon were now in serious relationships, so the girls all had exciting stories to share. Willow was eager to learn about their boyfriends and hoped they had lots of photos to show each other. She had lots of digital photos on her mobile phone, most were of the cruise but there were a few nice selfies of their time spent at the races. Early in their relationship, the races appeared to be Gabriel's favourite day out. Willow, now that she understood the racing scene, was more relaxed, allowing her to enjoy the days out much more.

Staring out of the tram window as the bendy tram coiled around the track, she thought that she saw Gabriel looking into a shop window. Willow convinced herself that she must be mistaken. Besides, it was a jewellery shop. Why would he be looking in a jewellery shop? A small smile crossed her face and her cheeks began to burn. No! It was just wishful thinking on her part. Her mind was playing tricks on her because she was thinking about the last time, they went to the races together.

During the journey, Willow reflected on how her own life was evolving. Although she felt totally secure in her relationship with Gabriel and knew without question that he loved her just as much as she loved him. She had a niggling worry at the back of her mind that she couldn't work out. His parents were hard work that she was certain of. However, his sister Victoria more than compensated for their behaviour. She was nothing like her mother, come to think of it, she was nothing like their father either. Willow thought it odd that Gabriel never mentioned any relatives. She wondered how many guests there would be at the wedding from Victoria's side of the family. She herself had a huge extended family. Gabriel had already been introduced to most of them. Her grandparents sadly were no longer alive, but she had fond memories of them from her childhood. In total, Willow had twelve cousins. Nowadays, they only managed to meet up at births, deaths, and marriages. *A sad fact of life,* thought Willow.

The tram creaked to a halt. The girls had arranged to meet in Yates Wine Lodge on Long Row in the city centre. This was one place that she felt comfortable in, even on her own, should she be the first to arrive. But she wasn't. Janet's loud, squeaky voice could be heard from above the noise of the crowd. In the distance, she saw a hand waving frantically, beckoning her to climb up the stairs to the next level. Pushing her way through the crowd, Willow eventually reached the foot of the stairs and proceeded to make her way to the top. At the very far end of the room, overlooking a balcony, sat Susan and Janet. They looked as though they had a head start on her, for they each held a wine glass in their perfectly manicured hands. Willow glanced at her own hands. Her nails devoid of colour looked insipid and plain by contrast. Undeterred, she waved her insipid hand towards them, indicating that she was going to the bar. She gestured to them a sign indicating if they would like a drink. As predicted, they nodded their heads almost simultaneously in a resounding yes.

Willow made her way to the bar and ordered a bottle of Chardonnay. The waiter passed her a tray with the wine and three glasses. He winked at her, then grinned and told her that he'd be over with the wine bucket and ice within a few minutes.

Over to the girls, she carefully walked in her high heel shoes, all the time balancing the heavy tray. It was a relief for her, to lower it down onto the table. As promised, the waiter was right behind her with the ice bucket. He seductively took the bottle from the tray and placed it into the bucket, looking at Willow the entire time.

'Thank you,' said Willow politely.

'My pleasure, gorgeous. Has anyone ever told you that you have the most amazing eyes, not to mention your thick, shiny hair? I swear I was in heaven when you walked in.'

Willow blushed scarlet. For some reason, she was speechless, struck dumb and feeling shy to boot.

'Has the cat, got your tongue?' he continued.

Collecting herself, in order to be kind and not frighten the young man off, ever giving a girl a compliment again, she said, 'Thank you for the compliment, you're quite a charmer. I see that you have a lot to offer the right girl, whoever the lucky girl is. Sadly, it's not me, for I'm already spoken for.'

Happy with her reply, he grinned and swaggered off, back to the bar.

'You look radiant,' said Susan. 'Love suits you, Willow, you're glowing. Right, pour the wine and let's check out the menu. Enough flattery, we have a lot of catching up to do. I'm starving, don't know about you girls.'

Willow looked across the table towards her two best friends. They had shared so many wonderful experiences together as school friends and teenagers. Now, here they were, all in their twenties, about to embark on the next stage of their lives. The three friends never came up for air. The conversation was almost non-stop, between sips of chardonnay, until their meals were delivered to the table. This time by a young female waitress.

'I see you've met Fabrizio,' she said to the girls. 'He is so handsome, don't you think?' They all answered a resounding yes, which seemed to please her very much.

'I thought he looked Italian,' said Janet. 'Although, he doesn't have much of an accent. Probably the second generation, I would guess.'

'I do hope that she is the one for him,' said Willow. 'Just look at her, she's besotted.'

'Are you besotted, Willow? Are you and Gabriel making any plans?' enquired Janet.

She told them of Gabriel's proposal of sorts and about his sister's forthcoming marriage. Her friends listened intently, without interruption, when she described Victoria and

Duncan's wedding arrangements. The girls were fascinated to hear of Duncan, being a Laird and having a castle.

'It's like a fairy story,' said Susan.

Willow grinned. In her imagination, she visualised Victoria as a Scottish Princess and Gabriel's mother as the wicked witch. Her imagination once again went into overdrive, which she was prone to do, especially after a couple of glasses of wine. Over the years, Willow had imagined all kinds of scenario's related to her own life. Sometimes at night, just before sleep eased its way in, she let her mind wander through the different paths of life she may one day take. No matter which path her mind explored, there was always one constant. A constant that had been present since her early teens. She saw her life in front of her, with children. Always in her dream-like state, she saw her sister, Molly, as being her own child. Molly would come back to her; she'd live the life that had been so cruelly taken away.

'Willow, Willow,' called Janet. 'You are in one of your daydreams again I see, no doubt thinking of your own wedding.'

'I think that's some years away,' she answered. 'Gabriel appears to be set on training to be a general practitioner; he has a further two years of study to undertake as a foundation doctor in a teaching practice first. Then he needs to apply for a partnership or work as a salaried GP. Either way, a wedding is unlikely to be his main priority. He is currently studying for his final exams in May that's why we've spent so little time together recently. I miss him so much; I can't even begin to explain how empty I feel without him. It is as though I'm incomplete without him. Crazy, I know. I've always considered women who talk like that as being weak and needy, so I need to work on my inner warrior woman.'

'You! A warrior woman?' laughed Susan. 'This I've got to see.'

The three friend's swapped stories, complimented each other on recent achievements and enjoyed the atmosphere of their meeting. Neither of them wished to leave, however, both of her friends had arranged to meet their partners in the evening and reluctantly waved Willow farewell.

After they left, Willow sat alone staring out of the balcony window. She looked over towards the Market Square where the city council had erected a roller-skating rink. It was very busy, she noted. There were many families and young people enjoying themselves. For a few moments, she watched a young couple who stood out from the crowd. The young woman was striking. She had ebony black hair cut into a Cleopatra hairstyle and was wearing Goth type fashion. Her young man was tall with dark hair and brooding looks. He wore similar style clothes with high leather boots. They were not conventional and dared to be different she thought. Even from the distance that she looked, Willow could see by the way that they were holding each other and the body language as they tumbled towards each other laughing that they were happy.

Walking towards the square was a group of three women, probably in their forties, she thought. One of the women was a little underweight she looked as though she'd recently been unwell. The other two ladies looked to be hale and hearty, both of them slightly bohemian in their dress. They appeared to be on a mission, the way they marched across the road.

Enough people watching, thought Willow. *Time to go home.*

She called into Marks and Spencer food hall, before catching the tram, purchasing a rich fruit cake for her parents to enjoy with a nice cup of tea. On leaving the food hall, she entered the women's fashion department and noticed some pretty blouses on a rail. It was her mum's birthday in a few weeks' time and they looked just the style she'd wear. Willow chose a cream coloured, short-sleeved blouse for her mum, hoping that size fourteen was correct.

When she arrived home, they had visitors. Her mum's sister Aunty Violet and her cousin Rebecca. They looked rather despondent as they greeted Willow. She guessed that this was a formal kind of visit and was very upset to hear that her Uncle Levi had died of an acute heart attack the previous day. He was a few years younger than her father, which made her feel even more distressed. Remembering the cake that she'd purchased, Willow passed it to her mum.

'I'll put the kettle on mum, while you get the cake plates and forks,' she said.

Putting her arms around Aunty Violet and then Rebecca, she passed on her feelings of sadness for their loss. While busy in the kitchen, Willow reflected on the fact that her uncle Levi had been a fit and active man, just like her father; his brother. It occurred to her, that maybe there was the possibility of a genetic tendency, something she planned to discuss with Gabriel when she rang him later. Her day had started with the joy of meeting her friends and ended with the sadness of losing her uncle Levi. Life is hard at times, thought Willow.

Around nine in the evening her mobile phone began its familiar ringtone. It was Gabriel. She was pleased that he'd rung her, for she was feeling a bit low in spirit, and was contemplating whether to ring him.

'Hey, sweetheart, how has your day been so far?' said Gabriel sounding chirpy.

She was pleased that he sounded in better spirits and less tired. After catching up on each other's brighter aspect of the day, she told him about Uncle Levi. Gabriel confirmed her suspicions that, heart disease can indeed be hereditary. He offered to check her father over, on his next visit and bring his blood-pressure monitor with him.

'I would advise him to make an appointment with his own doctor to arrange a few routine blood tests, for example, his cholesterol level,' he informed Willow.

Gabriel spoke of his sister's forthcoming wedding and how he was looking forwards to spending some time with his sister and getting to know Duncan a little better. Willow felt the same although the thoughts of spending time with Gabriel's parents rather took the shine off the event. He told her of Victoria teasing him about wearing a kilt which momentarily put a smile on her face. Gabriel asked if Willow might take a few days off work so that they could stay over in Edinburgh and explore the area after the wedding.

She did not hesitate; it was the best offer that she had in days. Immediately, her mood was lighter, just the thoughts of spending quality time with Gabriel gave her a warm glow, pushing away any unhealthy doubts that were beginning to take root in her mind. He was due to finish his hospital placement at the end of the week. He told her that he had mixed feelings about leaving the paediatric ward and returning full-time to university, in readiness for his final exams.

He explained that he had made up his mind to work in the primary care sector as a GP. Working as a family doctor means that I will still be treating babies, children and people of all ages. It will be a privilege getting to know the patients as I help them through their medical journey. I cannot imagine specialising in one body system for the rest of my career. He spoke enthusiastically and with such passion telling her that the role of a traditional doctor has changed a great deal over the years and he wished to be a part of that change. Do you think that I will be suitable as a family doctor, Willow? The hours of the surgery will mean no more night shifts.'

Willow liked the sound of that very much. She knew how important it was to enjoy one's work. She felt truly lucky, to be working in a job that she enjoyed so much. Job satisfaction contributed to her own well-being and happiness, so she understood Gabriel's perspective.

'You will make a fine family doctor, Gabriel. Can I be your first patient?'

'Mm… I don't think that would be ethical. It would be considered a conflict of interest. However, I'm happy to examine your beautiful body on a daily basis, if only…' he laughed.

They made arrangements to go for a walk, followed by a pub meal on Sunday, that week. Willow knew exactly where they would go. She'd been planning to visit Newstead Abbey for a while since one of the customers had told her what a wonderful wedding ceremony, she'd been to in the Orangery, situated close to the cloisters of the old Abbey. In Willow's mind, this location would be her own dream wedding. What could be more perfect? Surrounded by history and beautiful grounds. Thinking such sweet thoughts lifted her spirit after the upsetting news of Uncle Levi.

There was a funeral to attend and later, a wedding. Life is full of ups and downs, she told her sister Molly that night, as she lay in bed thinking through the day's events.

Chapter Fifteen

The days dragged by for Willow made all the worse by the sadness that enveloped her home. Both of her parents were in a low mood especially her father, who was beginning to think about his own mortality. He spoke to Willow about making arrangements to see a solicitor to draw up a will While her mum became unusually clingy and appeared to be losing interest in the garden. Despite being weary after working in the nursery she tried her best to help with the household chores.

It was a busy time at the moment, in preparation for the summer planting. She usually enjoyed this time of the year, but somehow the shine had been taken away. Dorothy was beginning to see a change in Willow and inquired if things were fine between her and Gabriel. On hearing of the family bereavement, she insisted that Willow took a few days off in order to support her family. For this, Willow was grateful and not for the first time acknowledged what an amazing boss Dorothy was.

On her first day off work, Willow set to work with her parent's smallholding. There was digging and planting to do and still plenty of harvesting. Her father was watching her from the window. He smiled for the first time in days; pulled on his Wellington boots and donkey jacket and joined Willow on the land. They worked compatibly together, her father whistling and her humming along. Together, they achieved a great deal of work. Feeling exhilarated from the fresh air and exercise, they entered the house, bringing with them, a renewed feeling of life, into their previously sombre home.

Their improved mood must have been contagious, for within a short time her mum had joined them both in the cosy kitchen nook, bringing with her, a tray of tea and toasted crumpets. Instead of being sad, they began to reminisce about their lives, only bringing up the most positive aspects and steering clear of any subjects that could reduce the mood. Her mum rummaged in the Monks Bench that was situated close to the back door. Inside was where they stored the family photo albums. Emma said that these were her most prized possessions. She kept them close to the door, in case of fire, so they could drag the monk's bench through the door as they left.

Looking through the albums, was bittersweet for all of them. When Emma turned the page and saw the image of herself in full pregnancy, she swiftly moved on to the next page. Willow noticed a tear, rolling down her mum's cheek. Her pain evident for all to see. Tom moved over to his wife and hugged her tightly.

'One day, Emma, we will be bouncing a grandchild on our knee, now won't that be grand?'

He looked towards his daughter, willing her to respond.

'That's right, Mum, in fact, if and when I get married, be sure to expect a brood of grandchildren running around your feet,' she said.

Her words seemed to have a calming effect on both of her parents, for Emma continued to turn the pages of the album. Willow enjoyed looking at the many happy, family pictures. Each special event had been recorded on film. Some of her early teenage school shots, made her cringe. Sporting a spotty chin and a greasy fringe on one such photo was so embarrassing, that Willow considered surreptitiously creeping back and removing it from the album. For fear that it might one day come to the attention of Gabriel.

After their evening meal while sitting comfortably in the lounge, Willow gently told her father of Gabriel's advice for him to have a health check. Her mum thought that this was a sensible idea and encouraged her husband to take Gabriel's advice. However, he appeared reluctant, until Emma suggested that perhaps they could go together, as it would be sensible for them both to be screened. Satisfied that both of her parents were in agreement, Willow said that she'd ring up the surgery the following day and get them an appointment. When Gabriel rang her that evening, she thanked him for his suggestion and informed him that they'd both agreed to a health screen.

'Do your parents keep good health,' she inquired. 'What about the rest of your family, your grandparents, aunts and uncles?'

Willow was surprised to discover that Gabriel knew next to nothing about his family. He said that he'd never met any of his grandparents, who, it appears, had died before he was born. Apparently, neither of his parents had siblings. When she enquired about his childhood and lack of relatives, he said that he and Victoria had each other and lots of friends from school and the church. Gabriel, swiftly moved the conversation on, telling her that he was looking forwards to seeing her on Sunday.

'Oh, yes! About that, Gabriel. Do you fancy a visit to Newstead Abbey, we can call at The Hut, for a meal afterwards? Please say yes, I can book a table, shall we say two o'clock for lunch?'

Her enthusiasm touched him. He knew how much she was missing him. He was also struggling with the lack of intimacy. He craved for the time that he could spend a whole night with Willow, to fall asleep in her arms and wake up to her soft, sweet-smelling body. July seemed a long time to wait until they could spend a few days together in Scotland. But wait they must. His whole future depended on the outcome of his exam results, Willow's future too if she agreed to be his wife.

'Okay, that sounds good,' he replied. 'I will pick you up around eleven o'clock.'

Gabriel was aware that Willow found it strange that he had no true knowledge of his family. It was something that himself and Victoria had never concerned themselves about. They accepted it as fact and just got on with their lives. He began to think back to the conversations he had with his parents as a child. He vaguely remembered how quickly his parents closed the conversation down, without giving away any answers. Their family home was so different from their friends, even the friends they met at Sunday school, whose homes they occasionally went to for tea; when his parents were invited along. He recalled his friend Mathew who lived quite close by. His house was always filled with family, including his grandma and aunt, who seemed to call most days. Their house had photographs set in fancy frames of the entire family. Mathew once joked with Gabriel about his

139

home having more framed pictures than a stately home. Now he came to think about it. Gabriel does not remember, ever seeing a family photograph, other than his and Victoria's formal school photos.

The following day, he made it his mission to visit his parents. He knew that they would be surprised at his impromptu visit, but nonetheless, it needed to be done. His curiosity was getting the better of him.

To say that his parents were surprised to see him was an understatement, which was made obvious by their greeting.

'So, what do we owe the pleasure, Gabriel, is it money that you're after or have you got that gardener girl of yours pregnant?' asked his father, within two minutes of Gabriel crossing the threshold.

'Neither, as it happens,' he replied. 'I'm hurt that you would even say such a thing.'

'Nonsense,' joined in his mother. 'You know perfectly well what our feelings are. There are plenty of lovely Catholic girls around here, all good girls who go regularly to church. Why do you go out of your way to annoy us so, Gabriel?'

Gabriel felt that he'd walked into a den of wolves and doubted very much if he should bring up the real reason for his visit. His parents had always been stern but the older they got, the worse their un-endearing habits became.

'Do you feel the same about Duncan, Mother?'

'Yes, we both do,' she answered. 'But Victoria's mind is set, she has started the ball rolling and no doubt she will follow it through. But you, Gabriel, have time to change your ways. Find a nice, young Catholic girl and go into the priesthood once you have completed your final exams.'

'I know that you don't like Willow, but I happen to love her very much and plan to make her my wife,' said Gabriel in a much more controlled voice, than he actually felt. 'And another thing, you can forget any plans for the priesthood. I've made up my mind, to work in general practice as a family doctor and I will not be persuaded otherwise.'

'Marry her,' growled his father.

'Yes, you heard right, Father. It is my intention to spend the rest of my life with Willow, she makes me a better person. I came here today to ask you about our family. My grandparents, aunties and uncles, any relative alive or dead, come to think about it. But right now, I don't think that I could stand listening to your opinions of how your ancestors were so very righteous and how they went into a monastery or nunnery or over to Africa to free the slaves. No, that can wait. In fact, I don't think I wish to know how grand they all were.'

Without waiting for a reply, Gabriel marched towards the door and let himself out. Once he was inside of his car, he breathed out long and slow, to compose himself. He hadn't achieved what he'd set out to do. In fact, the situation was a whole lot worse.

Anger, frustration and a deep-rooted loathing for his parent's attitude were emotions that surged through his body as he made his way home.

Unable to relax after the traumatic encounter with his parents, Gabriel decided to vent his anger and release the tension that was creeping into his shoulders. He did this the same way as always. He called at the betting shop on his way home. Entering the familiar room with the dull sound of the racing report in the background and the sound of the rollers as the fruit-machine wheels tumbled around, gave him a sense

141

of belonging. Gabriel approached the high counter of the bookie's desk and placed his first bet of the day.

Chapter Sixteen

Walking around Newstead Abbey grounds holding hands with Gabriel gave Willow the peace of mind that she'd been craving since the sad news of Uncle Levi's death. Although both of her parents were still coming to terms with the loss, they'd started to connect once more with the daily routine of life, so long established. Willow felt a little guilty that she was abandoning them for Sunday lunch as this had become a traditional family gathering. A time to relax and unwind, a time to reflect on the events of the week.

When Willow suggested that she might cancel the arrangements with Gabriel, her parents told her she was to do no such thing.

Despite a chill in the air and the likelihood of rain; if the gun-metal grey sky was anything to go by. Gabriel also began to feel more relaxed than he'd been since the encounter with his parents. Having time to reflect on the events of that day had given him some clarity on the situation. Realising that there was an alternate way to find out about his ancestors, Gabriel enrolled on the *Genes Reunited* website. Although he hadn't yet begun his research, he felt confident that the information he was seeking would soon be found.

Over lunch at The Hut, a quaint fifteenth-century country pub on a turnpike road opposite the Abbey. Gabriel told Willow of his plans to research his ancestors. Without giving too much away about the visit to his parents, he told Willow that he'd decided to do a bit of digging into his family history.

'Sounds fascinating, Gabriel, but do you have the available time, you already work so hard and study long hours. Can I help in any way?' said Willow.

Although tempted to take her up on such a fine offer, Gabriel declined; citing that there was no real hurry to discover his roots. He was considering speaking with Victoria about their extended family and if she had any plans to contact any of them about her forthcoming wedding.

The pub was quite busy with customers, the low roof and ceiling beams making for a noisy but lively atmosphere. Having checked out the menu, they both decided on something from the carvery. A young attractive waitress wearing the traditional uniform of a crisp white blouse and a black pencil skirt came to their table to take the order.

'Hi Gabriel,' she quietly said, as if not to draw attention to herself.

'Fancy seeing you here. You are a long way from the High Street of West Bridgeford.'

Gabriel introduced Willow to the waitress, explaining that they'd been to visit the Abbey before lunch and that Willow lived quite close by.

She smiled sweetly at Willow and proceeded to take their meal order. After the waitress left, Willow asked Gabriel how he knew her, for he hadn't returned the introduction.

Gabriel had been put into a difficult situation. The waitress knew him as a regular punter at the betting shop on his local high street. She must be working part-time at the Hut on her weekends off he concluded.

'She works in the Coral betting shop, where I sometimes purchase a Euro lottery ticket,' he told Willow, with tongue in cheek.

Willow could see that Gabriel was feeling uncomfortable about something. She didn't want anything to spoil their day together, especially as she was hoping that they may extend the day into night. Although she'd not discussed it yet with Gabriel, she was rather hoping that they would go back to his place for the night. In anticipation of this happening, Willow had packed a few overnight essentials in her oversized handbag. Having researched the tram and train times, she planned to make her way to work and back, on public transport. There was always a spare set of dungarees and wellington boots at work.

Thankfully, they didn't have to wait long before a different waitress arrived at their table with two steaming plates of food. Both hungry following their brisk walk around the Abbey grounds, they enjoyed the delicious meal. Unable to drink anything containing alcohol because of driving; Gabriel was drinking Becks Blue, an alcohol-free lager, while Willow enjoyed a small glass of Merlot wine.

Willow got the impression that Gabriel was in a hurry to leave after the meal. He seemed unsettled and not his usual self. She began to wonder if the waitress who had taken their order was more than just an assistant in the bookmakers. Perhaps she was an ex-girlfriend, and he was feeling uncomfortable and embarrassed. Either way, she wasn't about to allow anything to spoil this precious time with Gabriel.

Each day, she fell deeper and deeper in love with him. So intense was her feelings that she savoured every single moment of time spent in his company. Whenever Willow was with Gabriel, her body felt alive and highly responsive to his every movement. The curl of his lip as he smiled and the way his eyes looked like the windows to his soul, mesmerised her. She felt totally under his spell whenever they were together. She felt as though they were the positive and negative ends of a magnet, being pulled towards each other. Willow wanted to believe that nothing would ever block the powerful magnetism that they shared.

As if reading her thoughts, Gabriel stood up from the table and beckoned her to join him, as he walked towards the bar to pay the bill.

At the other side of the bar, Becky the waitress who knew Gabriel and his mounting debts at the bookmakers stood in silence and wondered if Gabriel's girlfriend knew just what she was letting herself in for.

Holding hands, they ran to the car as little spots of rain quickly turned into a sudden downpour.

'That was close,' Gabriel said. 'I hope you haven't got too wet?'

'Don't worry, I can dry off at yours,' replied Willow.

Gabriel turned towards her with a huge grin on his face.

'I was hoping you'd say that.'

She turned her face towards him, as he stroked her damp hair and kissed her with the exact deep longing that she herself was feeling.

'I can stay the night, Gabriel, and leave for work in the morning. I've missed you so much. Every night, I feel the same. Ever since we went on the cruise, my bed feels the loneliest place in the world without you.'

'Ditto,' he replied, as he put the car in gear and drove in the direction of West Bridgeford.

On the way, Gabriel pulled in to a service station and returned carrying a bottle of Merlot.

'I know that you prefer to stick to the same drink, Willow, so how about we share this and watch a good movie this evening,' he said, looking very pleased with himself.

'Sounds perfect,' Willow replied.

They did not get to see much of their chosen movie, which incidentally they'd both seen a number of times previously, for *Love Actually* was one of their favourite movies. However, they did manage to finish off the wine, before falling into a post-coital sleep that was interrupted only by the sound of Gabriel's alarm the next morning.

Bleary-eyed and fatigued from the hours of love-making, both Gabriel and Willow managed to call on their reserves for one more display of their love, before frantically rushing off to work.

Although in theory, catching the tram and train seemed a good idea. On a wet Monday morning, joining the other commuters in the rush to work was less exciting than the rose-coloured vision that Willow had conjured up in her mind.

Arriving at the Garden centre with her long, dark hair wet and lank, Willow looked more like a drowned Labradoodle dog than the glamorous assistant to Dorothy as she was known by some of the male members of the team.

'Well, good morning, Willow,' said a cheery looking Dorothy. 'I won't mention the fact that you look like a drowned dog. Whoops! Sorry, I just did,' she laughed.

'Here you are.' Dorothy passed Willow a steaming mug of tea. She reached over to the sink and offered Willow a towel.

'Go and dry your hair, I can't have my best member of staff coming down with a head cold,' she chuckled.

Willow did as she was told and was grateful that Dorothy, as usual, tried to mother her and this morning she was extremely grateful for the attention.

While changing into a pair of overalls that were stored in the female cloakroom, Willow caught sight of her reflection in the mirror. She looked tired, yes. But there was a radiant glow that was unmistakable, and she knew that Dorothy had noticed it too.

Chapter Seventeen

Gabriel felt troubled by the chance meeting with Becky while dining with Willow at the Hut. He realised that she'd know about his mounting debt and his frequent visits to the bookmakers to try to recoup back some of his losses. What she wouldn't be aware of, was his debts to a rival bookmaker. He managed to regain some trust with that manager after paying back most of his debt using the money, he earned from the last drug trial that he volunteered for.

Gabriel knew that he was just having a run of bad luck and it was only a matter of time before he could pay it back. For now, he must concentrate on his studies. Once he was in a full-time post as a GP registrar, his life will be turned around.

Victoria rang him later the same week to speak with her brother about the wedding arrangements. It appeared that Duncan was having a stag weekend two weeks before the wedding and wanted Gabriel along to join in the fun. It was to be held at the family residence. The castle no less. Apparently, the castle had some kind of great hall that the men used for such occasions. Duncan planned to make a weekend of fishing, shooting and hunting as well as the drinking of copious amounts of ale and spirits.

'Sounds a blast,' said Gabriel. 'Count me in.'

'Just out of interest, Victoria, how many guests will you be inviting from our side of the family?'

'Good question, Gabriel, and the answer is just you, Mum and Dad, and Willow, of course. I hadn't really thought about it before the wedding, but don't you think that it's rather odd that our parents had nothing to do with their respective families?'

'I do,' answered Gabriel. 'I'm going to do a bit of digging around on an ancestry website, I'll let you know what I come up with. It's pointless asking Mum and Dad, they refused to talk to us about our family when we were children and I can't imagine them changing their minds now.'

The stag weekend was definitely something for him to look forwards to and such a great location. Having Duncan for a brother-in-law sure was going to be an advantage. He couldn't wait to share his news with Willow.

Willow struggled to keep her emotions under control at the best of times, but over the following few weeks after the incident at The Hut, she felt a little insecure in her relationship. The little voice of Molly persistently whispered in her ear. Some days, she felt an irrational jealousy over some imaginable female who had somehow manifested in her mind. Molly was Willow's conscience; she was the other half of her brain. Sometimes, Willow thought that the fanciful side of her mind belonged to Molly. The serious side of herself. It was the serious side that she tended to display to the world. Her fanciful side, the side that was Molly. She kept private and never divulged the existence of.

Gabriel told her about the stag weekend, she was happy for him and excited about the wedding that was fast coming around. The weekend of the stag party, Willow made arrangements to meet up with her friend Janet in the city centre. She arrived at the train station with minutes to spare. Four teenagers were gathered around the ticket machine and appeared to be struggling with it. Willow assessed the situation. There was probably not enough time to wait while the young people fathomed out how to use the ticket machine. Willow climbed aboard and sat on the first available seat which happened to be the first table seat on the left of the carriage.

A few moments later, the four young people, two male and two females, sat opposite her. They made themselves comfortable and continued chatting away. As the train began to pull away from the station, the female train manager approached Willow. Tall and imposing, with a short back and sides masculine style haircut she scowled meanly at Willow.

'May I have a day return ticket to Nottingham please?' requested Willow.

'Why didn't you buy a ticket from the machine at the station?' said the manager with an edge of bitterness to her voice.

Pointing to the group of teenagers opposite. Willow explained her reason, pointing out that she'd assessed the situation and reasoned that there was a possibility that she might miss the train. The manager gave her a filthy look and proceeded to tap away at her ticket machine.

Willow had shown her discount rail card and her credit card before the train manager had started the process.

'Twelve pounds fifty pence,' she growled.

Willow knew that this price was not correct as she'd done the same journey on many previous occasions.

'I'm afraid that's not correct,' said Willow. 'Have you taken off the discount? I showed you the rail card?'

The manager looked ready to do another battle of words. She tutted and tapped away at the ticket machine.

'Eight pounds thirty-eight pence,' she answered, as she hovered meanly over Willow.

Willow nodded her head and proceeded to give her credit card.

'Well,' she growled. 'Being as you're so clever, I guess you know what to do next?'

She passed a different type of chip and pin machine that was used on previous trains. This was small and compact as opposed to the large machines that resembled old Motorola mobile phones. Having slipped her card into the slot. Willow politely enquired if she needed to press the enter button first as no message had appeared on the screen.

'Not so clever now, are you?' she sneered.

Willow felt the colour rising in her cheeks. She was not in the mood for conflict. Her life was complicated enough. She wondered what was making this woman so bitter and angry. Perhaps she had her own demons and was taking her anger out on others. Willow took in a slow deep breath, pressed the enter button and proceeded to follow the instructions. When the paper copy of the tickets was printed off, the train manager slammed them on the table and stormed off.

Willow leant forwards on the table, supporting her head with the flat of her hand resting on her left cheek. She could feel a tightness creeping up her neck and knew that before the day was out. She would have a full-blown migraine.

Looking out of the train window, passing over the historic viaduct in the town of Mansfield, she watched as the local people went about their day. Willow tried to force a smile as she saw a young mother pushing an old-fashioned yet stylish Silver Cross pram across the road. Her head held high with pride. Willow thought about her parents and how terribly upset they must have felt, when they swapped their twin pram for a mono-style, after losing Molly. As the transient thought of Molly sent messages to the rest of her brain, her auditory senses became triggered; resulting in her sister once again speaking to her.

These messages from Molly had become a little more frequent of late. And while Willow enjoyed the closeness of her twin sister, she rationalised with herself that it was not conducive to her own mental health. Hopefully, meeting with her friend, Janet, would be a good distraction, one that she so desperately needed.

Janet was already on the platform waiting for Willow. Dressed in the latest fashion and looking a million dollars as always; she waved and called out to Willow as she disembarked the train.

'You look a bit peaky, Willow, are you feeling okay?' said Janet, looking all concerned.

'Phew!' gasped Willow, while touching her temple. 'I seem to be developing a migraine, do you mind if we call into the Pumpkin Café on the platform so I can get a drink of water and take a couple of Migraleve tablets?'

Janet linked her arm through Willow's and led her away from the platform towards the café. She purchased a bottle of water for her friend and a latte for herself.

'I guess we should put the wine on hold,' smiled Janet. 'Not to worry, there are plenty more times that we can drink wine. Now, please tell all, I'm in need of a good love story.'

Willow smiled and proceeded to tell Janet all of her news.

'Any sign of a ring yet,' Janet teased.

Willow smiled at the very thought that one day soon she'd be wearing an engagement ring. Although Gabriel had not disclosed his plans, she had a fairly good idea that it was imminent. She knew that he loved her, for he made his feelings known in so many ways. There was no doubt in her mind that it would happen.

'He is under a lot of pressure to pass his medical degree at present,' Willow replied. 'Did I mention that he is planning to do further training as a General Practitioner?'

'A doctor's wife, Willow. How fantastic. Will you continue working at Ollie's after you're married? Just think, you will be attending all of those fancy dinner parties and corporate events put on by the big drug companies,' replied Janet, getting quite carried away on her friend's behalf.

'Let's eat,' said Willow. 'Maybe my blood sugar is low. It won't be helping me with this headache.'

They made their way towards the canal-side where there was a number of good eating places. Sitting outside in the fresh air eating lunch and chatting with Janet, helped to block out the occasional murmur from Molly. It wasn't that Willow wanted to dismiss her sister; it was more of a distraction method.

There was certainly a lot of catching up to be done. Janet was eager to talk about her promotion at work and all that it entailed. She was also in a new relationship.

'This is the one, Willow, I'm sure of it. He is definitely the man for me. He ticks all of my boxes. He is kind and loving. Not only to me, you should see him with animals, he is a proper softy. Did I mention that he is a vet and works with the RSPCA?'

'No, you didn't, but I know now,' Willow replied. 'What other qualities does he have that ticks your boxes, Jan? And by the way, what is his name?'

Janet spent the remainder of the afternoon describing every detail of her new boyfriend, Matt, his family and friends. By the time Willow waved goodbye to her friend, she knew everything there was to know about Mat and his family. The truth was, she knew more about Mat's family than she did Gabriel's.

Chapter Eighteen

Willow was excited. Not only was she spending the weekend with Gabriel, but of all places, they were staying at Duncan's parent's castle. This was the stuff of dreams for most people. Willow included.

They travelled the day before to settle in and to meet the extended family in advance of the wedding. Unsure of the protocol on such occasions, Willow couldn't stop worring if she'd chosen the right outfits to wear. There were so many questions that she'd have liked to ask Victoria. For example, did she need some sturdy walking boots and trousers in case they went for a walk in the Glen? Maybe there was to be a formal evening the night before the wedding and she needed a cocktail dress. There were so many unanswered questions in her mind.

For Gabriel, there was only one burning question he needed answering. Would they be allowed to share a room, or would they be separated by the thick castle walls?

The drive to Edinburgh though long was very pleasant; made all the more so by the soundtrack to their journey. To get them in the mood for things to come, Gabriel played a variety of Celtic tunes on the car CD player. By the time the imposing gates to the castle were in view, both Willow and

Gabriel were well and truly in the mood for a Scottish welcome. Which is exactly what they received.

They were met on arrival by Duncan's parents who immediately made them both welcome, putting them much at ease. Within minutes of their arrival, Victoria came bounding down the grand stairs and flung herself at Willow, as though she'd known her all of her life. Victoria looked radiant, exuding happiness from every pore of her body. Duncan was not far behind her. With a huge grin on his face, he shook Gabriel's hand, slapped him on the back and offered them both a drink of Scotch. The atmosphere throughout the castle was of excitement and joy, the happiness was almost tangible. They followed the happy couple through to a garden room at the back of the castle where they all sat comfortably drinking large measures of single malt whisky. This was the scene that greeted Victoria and Gabriel's parents as they were shown into the garden room by Duncan's father.

'It's a bit early in the day to be drinking whisky, children,' said their father, in a tone that suggested utter disgust.

'Nay, let the young people enjoy themselves, it's a special day tomorrow, let them be,' said Duncan's father in a loud and jovial voice that suggested he'd already partaken of a few drams himself. He winked at Victoria and Gabriel, then proceeded to direct their parents to a large plush sofa, some distance from the others.

'Can I be getting you both a drink now,' he said mischievously.

'Perhaps a pot of tea for us please,' answered their mum with an air of attitude about her.

'Then tea it is,' he replied courteously.

Following a delicious evening meal, they all retired to their rooms early, in order to be well rested for the celebrations the following day. Gabriel need not have worried about the room situation. Duncan and Victoria had that well organised. Although they had separate rooms, there was an adjoining door discretely inside. Gabriel and Victoria's parents wouldn't have the slightest idea, and neither would anyone else. Other than Duncan's parents, who had no objections at all?

On the morning of the wedding, Victoria invited Willow and Duncan's mum into her room, to help prepare for her special day. It was an absolute joy for Willow although, she couldn't help but wonder, why Victoria chose to omit her own mum from the honour. Whatever the reason, it did not deter the bride from looking radiant. Victoria had chosen a simple and elegant gown of ivory satin, trimmed with the finest Nottingham lace.

Before she slipped on her stockings and shoes, Victoria sat on a small stool while Duncan's mum washed Victoria's feet. Apparently, a traditional custom for an older, married woman to perform before the wedding.

When Victoria was satisfied her hair and make-up were as perfect as she'd hoped, her mother-in-law to be placed a tartan sash over her shoulder and draped it across her waist then passed a small gift box to her.

'It is a love token from Duncan,' she softly said.

Victoria opened the blue velvet gift box. Inside was a silver brooch. It was two hearts combined, with Victoria and Duncan's names engraved upon them.

'It is *a luckenbooth,*' said Duncan's mum as she pinned it to the sash.

'Something new and something blue, I have something for you to borrow,' said Willow, as she passed her best pearl necklace to Victoria.

'It's perfect,' said Victoria. 'Thank you, Willow.'

Without knocking, Victoria's mum entered the room. She was dressed in a brown tweed two-piece suit, with a feather brooch attached to the lapel. Ignoring everyone except Victoria, she strode over and passed her a large silver cross.

'Have you said your prayers this morning, Victoria?'

Without waiting for a reply, she handed the cross to her daughter.

'I expect you to carry this with you to the ceremony, Victoria. Don't let me and your father down.'

'Thank you, Mother, I was in need of something old,' she replied.

Without a word of compliments to her beautiful daughter, she strode out of the room.

'Phew!' said Willow. 'What are you going to do now?'

Victoria went over to the table where the bouquets were arranged and standing in water.

She placed the cross in the centre of the large bouquet of white roses and carnations. Duncan's mum handed Victoria a sprig of white heather to put next to the cross. Another traditional good-luck token. Although the flowers were somewhat displaced by the cross, she managed to confer with her parents' wishes. By arranging the flowers closely around the cross, Victoria managed to salvage the appearance of the bouquet.

A sudden knock on the door, followed by loud giggles, signalled the arrival of the four young bridesmaids.

Willow excused herself to get ready and left Victoria surrounded by four little girls and their mothers.

Willow very quickly changed into her own wedding outfit, a sleeveless sheath column, scoop neck, navy dress; made of satin with a white lace trim on the bodice. Her friend Janet helped Willow to choose the dress and gave her a white satin bolero style jacket to compliment the outfit.

While looking in the mirror and pinning in place a navy and white fascinator, Gabriel entered the room.

'Swit swoo, Willow, you look amazing, come here and allow me to ruin your lipstick,' he laughed.

'You don't look so bad yourself, Gabriel. What happened to the kilt?' replied Willow.

'Never mind that now, come on, you gorgeous creature, I'm the luckiest man in the world to have you on my arm. Let's go down and join the wedding walk to the chapel.'

They joined the rest of the party who were waiting for the bride and groom. As the piper began the first notes of "Highland Cathedral", Duncan and the bridesmaids made their way to the front of the party. A huge gasp from Duncan heralded the arrival of Victoria in all of her splendour. She held on to the arm of his best man. They stood immediately behind Duncan and the bridesmaids. When the piper raised the notes an octave, he signalled to the party and lead them on their way to the chapel.

The wedding ceremony was the most touching ceremony that Willow had ever attended. When the traditional English wedding march was played on the bagpipes, it gave a whole new perspective to the music. Her father walked Victoria down the small isle with barely a smile on his face. By contrast, the bride looked radiant and proud.

Victoria and Duncan chose the traditional wedding vows out of respect to their parents and chose a variety of traditional English and Scottish prayers as part of their service. The occasion was tastefully organised and as the piper played them out of the church as man and wife; the tune of Mair's wedding rang out above the joyful shouts from the congregation.

Gabriel squeezed Willow's hand affectionately, 'Our wedding will be just as perfect as this one, Willow.'

Willow turned towards Gabriel. 'Is that a proposal, Gabriel, if so, I think we'd best keep it to ourselves. This is Victoria and Duncan's special day and we should allow all the focus on them.'

'And if it is, then what is your reply, Willow?' enquired Gabriel.

'My reply would be a resounding yes, Gabriel, I would be honoured to be your wife.'

He lifted her up in his arms and kissed her, much to the surprise of the guests who were walking behind them. One of the younger bridesmaids, who was with her parents, giggled and skipped on ahead to the bride, holding her hand as they walked towards the castle.

With the piper still playing merrily away, the bride and groom and the guests all entered the great hall where the wedding party was to proceed. Following a huge banquet, Duncan and Victoria took to the dance floor for the traditional Grand March, followed by the best man and Duncan's parents.

Traditionally, the in-laws joined the grand march, but his parents were having none of it. Seeing the disappointment on his sister's face, Gabriel grabbed Willow's hand and joined the family. His parents watching from the side-lines as though the whole event was beneath them.

Later, Willow joined Gabriel's parents at the top table to try to get to know them a little better. Unknown to them, they were to be her in-laws in the not-too-distant future, so she felt duty bound to make an effort with them.

'Didn't Victoria look amazing, she looked so happy as did Duncan. I'm pleased for them that the whole day has been just perfect. Even the weather has held for them,' said Willow, as she made herself comfortable next to them.

'Oomph... Too much Scottish tradition and not enough of the true Catholic ceremony for my liking,' grunted Gabriel's father.

Not for the first time, Willow took note that Gabriel was nothing like his father. Not in looks or temperament. Apart from his auburn hair that was greyer than anything else, there was not one family trait on display.

'Thank goodness we made her carry the Catholic cross,' interjected his wife.

'It is a wonderful setting though, isn't it?' said Willow, who was searching her brain to think of something they might find positive to say.

'There is nothing wrong with our local Catholic church and the school hall if you ask me. Why she has had to drag us all the way up here when our friends of the church could have attended, had it been more local, is beyond reason,' said Gabriel's mother.

Grasping the opportunity, Willow enquired about their own family and what was the reason there were no blood relatives from their own side.

At the mention of relatives, Gabriel's father swiftly stood up and said to his wife.

'I do believe that it's time we left the party, shall we go back to our room and pray that God blesses this marriage? Perhaps he will listen to us in the quiet of our room, with no loud pipes and drums in the background.'

Dutifully, his wife stood up and left Willow feeling as though she'd driven them both away from their own daughter's wedding.

'Cheer up, it may never happen,' said a smiling Victoria, as she approached Willow.

'I'm sorry,' said Willow. 'I think I may have put my foot in it with your parents.'

'What's this I hear about putting one's foot in it?' said Duncan as he came up behind his new wife and hugged her.

'Just the usual miserable behaviour from my parents,' Victoria replied. 'But there is nothing they can do that will spoil our day, come on husband, it's time to pass the *Scottish Quaich* around.'

Victoria and Duncan made their way to the table where a two handled silver bowl stood and beside it was more than a dozen bottles of whisky. Victoria filled the bowl with whisky and with each of them holding the bowl, they drank together from the bowl; having wiped the rim with a white linen cloth, they passed the bowl to his parents who proceeded to pass the *loving cup,* around the room.

The Ceilidh band played until the early hours of the morning, long after the bride and groom left the celebrations, for their honeymoon. A destination to be undisclosed until their return.

Chapter Nineteen

Willow's parents wanted to know every detail of their daughters visit to the castle and her first Scottish wedding. In many ways, they lived their lives vicariously through their daughter. Happy to spend their time together, tending the smallholding and raising their daughter; neither of them had the desire for travel. That's not to say that they wished the same for Willow. Indeed, they hoped for a much more exciting life of travel and enlightenment for her. But whatever path she decided to take, they would always support her decision.

She did not disappoint them. Willow relayed the whole proceedings to them with a glint in her eye that told them all they wanted to know. Her mother was excited to hear about the order of the ceremony and the bride's dress. By contrast, her father was fascinated to hear about the pipers and the traditional music played. He wanted to talk about the men going out into the glen to do the clay pigeon shooting and the hunting.

It was no different when she arrived for her first shift at the garden centre. No sooner had Dorothy put the kettle on, she was requesting every minor detail of the wedding.

'Has it given you any ideas for your own wedding?' laughed Dorothy. 'I see an extra special glint in your eyes, Willow. You know you can't keep anything from me.'

'You will have to wait and see, Dorothy, but don't worry, I will give you advance warning so you can buy a hat. Besides. The next big event is Gabriel's graduation ceremony. I hope… I'm keeping my fingers well and truly crossed. He gets his results in a few weeks' time and I plan to be with him to celebrate. To be honest, from what I've seen of his parents, they lack any kind of passion. I can just imagine his dad saying I should hope that you have passed, rather than a well done, son, I'm proud of you.'

'Are they so bad?' said Dorothy.

'Oh yes, and his mum is the worst,' she replied.

'Life is treating you well, Willow. I'm happy for you, don't allow their spite to spoil anything for you and Gabriel,' said Dorothy.

But Willow wasn't so sure. She still had a few niggly doubts and wasn't at all happy with the way her meeting had gone with Gabriel's parents at Victoria's wedding. Still, it was out of her hands and she had no need to see them, until the graduation ceremony.

Gabriel was getting anxious about his exam results and so was Leo and Adnan. They decided to go to the student union bar on campus to join all the other nervous students. Gabriel missed the company of Willow, but it was good to be with the lads. All three of them were now in serious relationships and although they lived together their shift patterns and social lives, left very little time to have a lad's night out.

'Had any good wins at the races lately?' Enquired one of the students waiting to be served at the bar.

'Do I know you?' asked Gabriel.

Holding his hand out to Gabriel, he introduced himself as Mike, a third-year math student.

'I do a bit of part-time work at the bookies and sometimes see you in there. Not that I'm one for wasting my money gambling… No offence.'

'None taken,' replied Gabriel, as he walked away.

Although he suspected that Mike had a good idea of the mounting debt that he owed. Still, he wouldn't have to worry about that soon. The moment his results were through, he intended to apply for a registrar post in general practice. He knew that it would take some time before a suitable position was available. Meanwhile, he needed to complete his competency-based foundation programme before he was entitled to the full GMC registration.

The debt could wait a little longer. The first thing he intended to do was to buy an engagement ring for Willow from his first wage packet. If things went to plan, they would be married within a year, by which time he hoped to be in general practice.

For Gabriel and his fellow students, the hard work and study paid off. When the results were announced, a huge roar of triumph rang around the hall. After the hand-shakes and shoulder slapping were over, Gabriel rang Willow.

'Well done,' she cried down the phone. 'I'm so proud of you, what did your parents say? They must be overjoyed.'

'I haven't told them yet, I wanted my future wife to be the first to know,' replied Gabriel.

'Wife, I love the sound of that, Gabriel.'

Willow knew that Gabriel was saving for her engagement ring. Truth be known, she didn't want a huge diamond. Just a simple ring declaring to the world his love, was enough for her. But she was willing to wait if it was Gabriel's wish. She hadn't mentioned the engagement to anyone and was waiting until Gabriel slipped the ring onto her finger.

'You must phone them now, and Victoria too. Next year, it will be her turn to celebrate,' replied Willow.

'I'm on to it,' laughed a jubilant Gabriel.

Victoria and Duncan were ecstatic about his news.

Brilliant news Gabriel. With any luck, me and Duncan will be celebrating our own success next year.

'Three doctors in the family, what more could our parents want, Victoria? I'm about to tell them my good news. Wish me luck?' answered Gabriel.

On the very last ring, his father answered the phone.

'I hope you're ringing us with good news, Gabriel, after all the years we've financially supported you?' Were the first words that he was greeted with.

He didn't expect any other and knew that he'd now be on his own in terms of finance. The good news was that Leo and Adnan also planned to complete their competency-based foundation programme; allowing them to share living costs for another year at least.

His ecstatic mood from earlier when he received his results, went from one-hundred to zero, such was the tone of his father's voice.

'Yes, Father, it's good news. Will you put Mother on the phone, please?'

'No need for that, I will tell her,' he replied, and swiftly put the phone down.

Oh well, thought Gabriel. It was as expected.

The university organised a ball to celebrate the success with their students. It was a black-tie event and was to be the finest event that Gabriel had taken Willow to, so far.

He already had his dinner suit, but Willow needed a ball gown. Her friends, were once again up for the quest to help Willow choose a gown that made her stand out in the crowd. They loved anything to do with fashion and knew exactly were to take Willow. Having already done their research, they took her to John Lewis in the centre of Nottingham.

'Take a look at this gown,' said an excited Janet, as she held up a beautiful floor-length chiffon dress of the palest blue.

'Wow,' said Willow. 'It is perfect and the right size too. Come on girls. I will need some help to get into this.'

They all trooped into the small changing cubicle and helped Willow with the dress.

'It is a perfect fit, just look at the bateau beaded bodice, and the price, Willow. It is less than one-hundred pounds. Just think,' said Susan, 'you can wear this when you go on your next cruise. A honeymoon perhaps?'

Willow smiled, but she wasn't about to give anything away.

'Thank you both, it's perfect. Come on, you two, when I've paid for this, the drinks are on me,' said Willow.

Just as Gabriel promised. It was the most splendid event that Willow had the privilege to attend. The event was held at Colwick Hall, a Georgian country mansion house, nestling in sixty-acres of parkland. The views were stunning as were the magnificent flower borders along the paths.

Following the speeches and the main meal, Gabriel took Willow's hand and suggested that they take a walk in the garden. It was a soft warm summers evening as they walked hand in hand along the path leading away from the hall. The fragrance of the magnolia filled the air and a hint of recently mowed grass added a crisp clean freshness to the mix. Walking hand in hand with Gabriel through the gardens felt so liberating and romantic for Willow. She wished that the night would never end. Everything about the evening felt surreal, almost magical. As the distant hum of the music faded into the background, she could pick out the sounds of the crickets and the evening bird-song. The swish of her skirt as they slowly walked along the path added to the romance of the evening. In the distance was a rose harbour with a beautifully carved seat in the centre. They made their way to the seat and rested for a few moments. The scent of the white roses climbing around the harbour frame was delicate and sweet, adding to the romance of the evening.

Gabriel turned to face Willow. He slipped his hand inside of his jacket and produced a red velvet box. Expertly, he flipped open the lid, revealing a solitaire diamond set in gold.

'Willow, will you be my wife? I promise to love and care for you until the end of my days. Please say yes,' said Gabriel, as he removed the ring from the box.

Willow held out her hand in response and as Gabriel slipped the ring onto her third finger left hand, she replied.

'Yes. My answer is a resounding yes. I promise to be your wife and I too will love you until the end of my days.'

They sat together on the rose harbour for a long time, both marvelling at the occasion. Willow repeatedly looked at the ring.

'Do you like it?' asked Gabriel.

'It is perfect and so well cut. Just look how it sparkles. It is brighter than the star that's above us,' answered Willow.

Gabriel looked up and sure enough, one star was twinkling brightly in the sky. Catching her hand, he beckoned to Willow for them to make their way back to the ball.

No sooner had they entered the main hall when Leo and Adnan came running towards them.

'Is it now official then?' enquired Leo, as he held out his hand towards Gabriel.

'It certainly is,' replied Gabriel with a huge, smug grin on his handsome face.

Adnan put his arms out towards Willow. She went into his arms. He hugged her gently, then moving away slightly, he said, 'Gabriel is a lucky guy. Good luck, mate, and you too Willow.'

Leo followed suit, then together they joined the throng of activity, all the more exhilarated by the occasion of the engagement of their friend.

There were two stages, providing entertainment to suit everyone. The music continued until two o'clock in the morning, by which time exhilarated and exhausted the happy students and their plus ones were ready to leave, having celebrated their own personal achievements.

They didn't go back to Gabriel's house. After using the transport into town that had been organised for the students, they managed to get a room at a decent hotel in the centre of town. A perfect end to the night.

It was a little awkward for Willow the following morning as she left the hotel in a ball gown. Gabriel didn't look quite so out of place, having removed his jacket and bow tie.

Fortunately, the hotel receptionist very kindly ordered a taxi to transport them home.

The sight that greeted Willow's mum, as she opened the lounge curtains that morning would remain etched into her memory for eternity. Her daughter practically floated up the garden path in her chiffon ball gown, holding on to Gabriel. There was an aura of happiness around them that was almost tangible.

'Tom. Tom, come quickly and greet Willow and Gabriel. I think they may have some good news for us,' called Emma.

Sure enough, when the young couple entered the house, Willow held out her hand, proudly showing the sparkling diamond ring in pride of place on her wedding finger.

'May I please have permission to marry your daughter, Tom?' asked Gabriel.

Tom held out his hand to Gabriel. 'Welcome to the family, son,' he replied.

Although too early for a celebration drink. Emma insisted they have breakfast together. Well prepared for such an occasion, she had some bottles of sparkling wine mixed with fresh orange juice that would suffice for the time being. Following a traditional English breakfast, the four of them raised a glass to a happy and wonderful life together. During the toast, Willow quietly whispered to Molly, 'Absent friends.' Molly was still very much a part of her. Day and night, she was beside her and inside her. Her twin and she were one.

Chapter Twenty

Dorothy couldn't have been happier when Willow showed her the engagement ring.

'That sure is a beauty, Willow. Much too precious to wear at work. Perhaps you might wear it on a chain around your neck. We don't want to dig around in the compost bin if it should get misplaced or even worse, chase up one of the customers on the off chance it had been planted along with their prize marrow,' laughed Dorothy.

'Mm… Good point,' replied Willow. 'I will do it now.'

'So, have you thought about the wedding plans?' enquired Dorothy.

'To be honest, I've been thinking about nothing else. I'm not a follower of religion and feel that it would be hypocritical to be married in a church. My problem is that Gabriel and his family are serious about their religious beliefs and I respect that,' she replied.

'Mm, I hear your dilemma, Willow. It is very hard to keep everyone happy and be true to yourself. I think it sounds as though Gabriel will need to decide. Most men want the day to be perfect for their wife and therefore, I suspect that Gabriel will let you have the final say,' said Dorothy.

'What about your parents, do you think they might want a church wedding for their daughter?' she continued.

Willow shook her head. 'No, I don't think so. They wouldn't want to be hypocritical either.'

'Then what is the ideal location for you, Willow? Just supposing that you could choose any place? Do you fancy going abroad to get married? I hear it's popular to scoot off abroad and tie the knot,' Dorothy replied.

'I would prefer to be married in the countryside, close to nature, surrounded by trees and wildlife. I know it sounds a little bohemian, but a stuffy stone-cold church, with high ceilings and wooden pews, just doesn't feel remotely romantic. In fact, the more I compare it to my ideal, the more I dream of it happening,' said Willow.

'Well! In that case, I believe that I know the perfect location,' said an excited Dorothy.

'It is in the middle of Ransom Woods and I know for a fact the place has a licence for civil ceremonies. I don't want to raise your hopes, Willow, so wait to find out Gabriel's thoughts on the matter. I do know that it's very popular and you will need to book it well in advance, so the sooner you decide, the better.'

Willow couldn't contain her excitement. 'Please tell me the name of this exciting venue so that I can start my research, Dorothy.'

'It is called Forever Green,' replied Dorothy, with a huge grin on her face.

Meanwhile, Gabriel was deciding the best way to inform his parents. Should he just drop it out casually in conversation or should he make a formal announcement? The latter would involve taking Willow to visit his parents. He suspected that she'd prefer to give that a miss, but she was a woman who liked to do the right thing, regardless of any discomfort to herself. In the end, Gabriel and Willow went to visit Sam and Joan in their home to announce their engagement.

The news of their engagement was received just as they'd anticipated. With a cold and bitter response. Neither of Gabriel's parents appeared remotely happy for their son. Their body language told them everything they needed to know, even before a word was spoken.

'And how do you propose to pay for a huge Catholic wedding, Gabriel?' inquired his father. 'Your mother and I have supported you through medical school and to our knowledge, you have no savings. You had better get yourself a hospital porter's job at the weekend to supplement your income. Within a year, you should have enough to buy a wedding ring if nothing else,' he continued.

Gabriel's mother was nodding her head in agreement.

'Perhaps a few years working as a missionary in Africa before you commit to being a husband, might be a good idea and give you both the chance to save,' added his mother.

Gabriel looked embarrassed and ashamed.

Willow interjected for she couldn't take any more of their unkind behaviour.

'There will be no huge wedding; from what I have seen, you have no family and outside of the church, no friends. Therefore, to avoid further embarrassment to Gabriel, we prefer a small affair. In fact, the smaller the better. My love of nature draws me to a country location and I have the perfect place in mind.'

'Then you're on your own, young lady, and if Gabriel is not married in the eyes of God, then we consider him not married at all,' said Joan.

'Fine by me,' replied Gabriel.

'Perhaps I should mention that my parents are very happy about the news and hold Gabriel in high esteem. They have already agreed to pay for the wedding and other than Gabriel's suit and my wedding ring, there will be no expenses incurred. In fact, he doesn't need to worry about a thing. We don't need your money. However, it would be nice for Gabriel to have your blessing, but I guess that's too much to ask,' said Willow, as she held Gabriel's hand and made her way to the door.

'Well, I never.' Were the last words from his mother that she heard, as they swiftly closed the front door behind them?

Once inside the car, Gabriel let out a huge sigh of relief.

'Willow! I never knew that you had it in you to be so assertive. I feel so ashamed of the way my parents received our news. I'm both shocked and happy that you will not be pushed around by anyone. And what is this about your family paying for the wedding, it's news to me?'

'Sorry, Gabriel. I felt so angry when your father deliberately and cruelly mentioned money. I've been saving for years. I get it that you may feel awkward letting me pay a deposit for a house and my parents pay for the wedding, but please. Let us do this, who knows, in the future I may be busy raising our family, then you will be providing for us,' smiled Willow.

'I don't know what to say, Willow. On one hand it takes a lot of pressure off me, but on the other hand, I feel as though I'm letting you down,' replied Gabriel.

'The important question I need you to answer is, do you mind if we don't have a Church wedding? It is not who I am, and I wouldn't feel comfortable getting married with all of that religious ceremony and chanting in a foreign language that neither I nor my family and friends understand,' said Willow.

'Willow, I will marry you anywhere you want. I don't care, as long as you are happy.

Sam and Joan were looking through the window watching their son and his future wife chatting in the car.

'Sam, we will have to tell Victoria and Gabriel the truth. Willow has been asking questions about our family and it's only a matter of time before they find out,' said Joan with a tremble in her voice. 'I cannot keep this façade up any longer.'

I suppose now we have no choice,' replied Sam.

They watched as Gabriel pulled away in his old Ford car, his future wife sat beside him. Their whole future ahead of them. A future full of promise, a future that no one could predict.

Gabriel drove Willow home with mixed feelings. On one hand, he felt ashamed and embarrassed at his parent's behaviour and on the other hand, he felt somewhat relieved. Inadvertently, his parents had more or less forced out Willow's plans about the wedding arrangements. At least now the pressure was off in some respects. Hopefully, in time, his parents would come around to their wedding plans and soften a little. Besides, his graduation ceremony was the next thing to celebrate, it was only a few weeks away. Surely his parents could behave themselves for one day. He had already invited Victoria and Duncan to the graduation ceremony and planned to have a chat afterwards with his sister about his forthcoming marriage. Although there was always the possibility that his parents might break the news before then.

He felt some of the burdens of his gambling debts lighten a little. He realised that Willow inadvertently had provided him with much-needed breathing space. With luck, his debts would be wiped out before he was married and maybe, he might have some savings. Perhaps today would be the day it was his turn to win the Euro-millions. After taking Willow home, he called at the newsagent to purchase a dozen lottery tickets. Yes! He was feeling lucky.

When he arrived at his place, Adnan and Leo were in the kitchen surrounded by empty takeaway cartons and piles of leaflets and paperwork.

'Phew, smells like an Indian takeaway in here guys, is there any left, I'm feeling ravenous,' said Gabriel, as he made himself comfortable at the table.

'I think there is some rice and a portion of korma left,' said Leo, while shuffling through some paperwork.

Gabriel sorted through the cartons and salvaged a portion of food. It was still warm, so he transferred it to a dish and hungrily ate up.

'What's with the paperwork?' he enquired.

'It's mostly graduation information and how we apply for our first year on the foundation programme,' answered Adnan.

'Pass over the relevant stuff and I'll check it out. Anything that needs immediate attention, guys?' said Gabriel.

'Not really,' said Leo. 'Apparently, we will need another CRB check before we're given our contract.'

The colour drained from Gabriel's face. He wasn't altogether sure what it entailed. He knew that the disclosure and barring service was to enable safe recruitment. What he didn't know was if his gambling debts would show up. Surely not, he began to rationalise to himself.

'Are you all right, mate? You have gone a little pale,' said Leo, as he passed the documentation to Gabriel.

'Probably low blood sugar,' responded Gabriel. But his mind was doing over-time.

That night, he tossed and turned in bed. Unable to sleep. His mind was in turmoil. On one hand, he felt overjoyed that he was successful with his medical degree, but to move forward, he must sort out his finances. He guessed that most of the university students accumulated large student debts in order to pay for their studies and their accommodation. He had already loaned the maximum amount and depending on his salary while working as a foundation doctor he may have to start the repayments. He decided to consolidate all of his debts by getting a new credit card to pay off the existing credit in order to reduce the interest. Having settled this in his mind, he eventually managed a couple of hours sleep.

'You look rough this morning,' said Adnan, as he passed Gabriel a coffee. 'I'm going to spend a few weeks with my parents until the graduation ceremony and I think Leo is planning the same. What about you, Gabriel, will you be going home to spend some time with your parents?'

Gabriel had no intention of spending time with his parents after the reception they gave to Willow, but he didn't wish to discredit them to his friends.

'No, I think I'll chill out here and make a love nest for me and Willow while you guys are out of town,' chuckled Gabriel.

Later that evening, he rang Willow and suggested that they might spend the following two weeks together in his student digs. It would mean a long drive to work for Willow unless she could take some of her holiday entitlement. Gabriel almost persuaded Willow to stay with him for the whole two weeks when he teased her about it being a trial run for when they got married. In the end, she stayed with him for the one week which Dorothy agreed to take off her annual entitlement.

They enjoyed a wonderful week together playing house as though they were already a newly married couple. Every morning involved a lazy and enjoyable lay in bed, following their frantic love-making. The evenings they spent snuggled on the sofa watching old movies and box-sets. Willow practised her culinary skills and not only surprised Gabriel, but herself, with some of the dishes she cooked from Jamie Oliver's cookbook.

On the last evening before Adnan and Leo were due to return, Gabriel became quite serious as they lay in bed, which was unusual because normally he was playful and tormenting, something she rather enjoyed.

'Willow, I've been thinking.'

'Mm, that sounds ominous, and serious. Do you want to share your thoughts? I do hope so, as you have got me in suspense,' she joked.

'How do you feel about bringing the wedding forward, say by six months? Do you think that's possible? It has been great these past few days, just the two of us. When we have our own home, it could be like this all the time. When I'm working as a junior doctor, my earnings will be upwards of £26,000 in my foundation year then £30,000 in the second year. I know it isn't a great deal to start with and I will have to pay a small amount off my student loan, but if we're careful, we could just about manage.'

Willow threw her arms, her legs and then, the entire weight of her body onto Gabriel.

'Hey! Steady on,' said Gabriel. 'What do you say?'

'I do, I do and I do. A million times yes from me, Gabriel.'

'That's settled then. We will go and check out some venues this weekend and depending on the availability, we will book a registrar. With luck, we can announce our intentions after the graduation ceremony. Victoria and Duncan will want to celebrate with us. Do you think I should have a stag night, Willow?'

'Well! I'm certainly having a hen night, Janet and Susan would never forgive me. Not to mention Dorothy. I've heard nothing but hats and wedding outfits since I told her of the engagement. She is so excited I dare bet she's already decided on the colour scheme.

Chapter Twenty-One

On the morning of the graduation ceremony, the weather decided to change. For days, it had been settled, with nice blue skies and a balmy warmth. Based on this, Willow chose a deep royal blue, taffeta full skirted ballerina length skirt and a short-sleeved lace camisole top. However, as the wind changed, she regretted her decision. The ceremony was in one of the Great Halls on the campus. She was to meet Gabriel and his family, in the reception area. Gabriel had given Willow, all the directions and was now looking out for her arrival.

'Here she is,' called out Gabriel to Victoria and Duncan and he waved her over to join them.

As Willow walked across the forecourt to a waving Gabriel, a huge gust of wind blew her skirt high above her chest and it was billowing out like a sail in full wind. She struggled to keep her balance as she tripped along in her little ballerina pumps.

Gabriel came rushing out towards her and pulled down the wafting taffeta with a grin.

'Love the black lacy G-String, Willow. Duncan's eyes nearly popped out of his head,' he laughed.

'Oh no, I'm so embarrassed,' answered Willow.

'No worry, Willow, at least Mum and Dad didn't witness it. I can just imagine the look on their faces. Come to think about it. Maybe it could have been a good thing, for them to crack a smile. Come on, let's join the others,' said Gabriel, who thought that he'd be the envy of the faculty having such a beautiful fiancé.

An embarrassed Willow joined the rest of the group, trying her best not to let the unfortunate event spoil her day. While Gabriel made his way to the front of the auditorium to join the other students, of which there appeared to be many. Willow waited with Victoria and Duncan for the arrival of Sam and Joan. They were so busy catching up with each other that they almost missed their arrival.

Willow noted, with some disdain, that they greeted their daughter and son-in-law with a curt nod of their heads and gave her no acknowledgement at all. No hug for Victoria nor a handshake for Duncan. They hadn't visited for months; she'd have expected some show of emotion. Still, not everyone is as loving and affectionate as her own parents she thought.

Making their way towards their registered seats on the first tier, Willow peered out towards the crowds of students below.

As if Gabriel could sense Willow searching for him, he stood up and turned around to face the families who were all now taking their seats. There among the crowd, he saw Willow, frantically waving and blowing him kisses. Waving back, he blew her a kiss before taking his seat once more.

The auditorium was full to capacity. Excited students sat patiently waiting for their moment of glory. Years of hard work and sleepless nights had culminated into this momentous occasion. Willow surreptitiously peeped at Victoria. She looked relaxed and happy and probably thinking about the day that her and Duncan would be taking to the stage to collect their own Degree certificate. She felt a strong affection for Victoria and hoped that in time they would form a sisterly bond. Although it wasn't the right time to be discussing wedding plans, Willow desperately needed to chat with Victoria to see what her thoughts were about them bringing forward their wedding plans.

An orchestra announced the arrival of the Dean. Along with other members of the faculty, he spoke of the great success of the university and gave a brief outline of the university history.

One by one, the graduates were called to the stage to collect their certificates. Bound up as a scroll with a red ribbon attached.

Holding her breath, Willow watched Gabriel climb the steps up towards the stage. The Dean said a few words to him, shook his hand, and passed the all-important certificate. Having received it, Gabriel turned towards the crowd and waved to Willow and his family.

It was another hour before they finally left their seats. Willow was glad to stand up and stretch her legs. Closest to the aisle seat, she was the first to leave the row they were in. Victoria put her arm through Willow's and began to walk towards the stairs, leaving Duncan to escort her parents.

As they walked together, Victoria and Willow shared their news and reminisced about Victoria's wedding and how amazing the whole event had been.

'What plans do you and Gabriel have?' enquired Victoria.

Willow explained that she preferred a simple ceremony without too much fuss or splendour.

'I've found an amazing location,' she said excitedly.

Just then, she spotted Gabriel walking towards them with his gown flapping in the breeze behind him and an excited look on his face.

'In fact, Victoria, if you and Duncan have the time to spare, I would love you to come and look at the venue I have in mind. Gabriel and I are planning to visit tomorrow, and I would appreciate your opinion. Please say that you will come?'

Gabriel arrived in time to hear Victoria agreeing to visit their intended wedding venue.

'It has been quite a day, hasn't it?' he smiled.

Putting his arm through Willow's free arm, together they walked. With Victoria on one side and Gabriel on the other, Willow felt a great surge of pride that very soon she'd be married into their family. *If only their parents were as lovely as these two*, she thought.

The next day, all four of them followed the directions that Dorothy had kindly provided. The venue was called Forever Green. It was on the outskirts of Mansfield Town. Set among the woodland of Ransom Woods, stood a modern building with large glass windows and doors giving views of the surrounding pines and conifers. Outside on the large patio was pretty tables and chairs. Perfect for a summer wedding, thought Willow.

Inside the light and airy reception area were comfy sofas and chairs and a bar area that sold healthy food and drinks. A dance area with a variety of seating arrangements and tables completed the downstairs area. They made their way up a modern sweeping staircase which led into a huge banquet space with formal tables and chairs and another large bar area. The view from the windows was fantastic as it overlooked the tree canopy.

Willow knew without a doubt that this place was exactly what she'd hoped it would be. She hoped that Gabriel was as thrilled with it as she was.

Victoria was the first to speak. 'This is perfect for you, Willow. With your love of nature and all things natural it looks great.'

Duncan was nodding his head in agreement. Gabriel just grinned.

'Perfect, Willow, just like you. Let's go and check out the menus, the sooner the better as far as I'm concerned. I wonder what the earliest availability is.'

Excited, they all trooped down the stairs. Willow imagined herself walking gracefully down these stairs to the ground floor where the ceremony would take place. Luck was with them as the manager told them that they had availability the following June. Although nine months away, Willow felt that it would be worth the wait. The weather should be good enough for them to sit out late into the evening on the patio. The nights in June would be getting longer and the guests could enjoy the beauty of the surrounding woods. She began to formulate a plan in her mind of decorating the trees around the patio area with solar lights and butterflies to make the place magical. Looking around, her mind went into overdrive. She imagined tea lights on the tables outside, flowers on the inside tables. The possibilities were endless. She hugged Gabriel, as he formally agreed with the manager that they wanted to book their wedding.

Willow felt as though she was walking on air as they made their way back to the car. Unfortunately, Victoria and Duncan needed to be making their way back home and were unable to join them for lunch. After lots of hugs and farewells, Willow and Gabriel drove to see Emma and Tom to share their good news.

As usual, Gabriel was made most welcome by his in-laws to be. He felt blessed that he was joining this family who was full of love and kindness. Emma insisted that they stay for lunch and was putting two extra place settings on the table, as she asked.

'Looks like we can't refuse,' smiled Gabriel.

Over lunch, they told Willow's parents about the wedding venue and how it reflected Willow's personality and theirs too. Willow was unable to contain her excitement, as she went into great detail about her plans.

'What about Gabriel's wishes, Willow?' enquired her father, looking somewhat concerned.

'Don't worry about me, Tom. If Willow is happy, then I'm happy,' he replied.

'I see you're a man after my own heart, Gabriel, and already understand my daughter,' said Tom.

'We have been saving for this day, a long time and have a substantial amount put away, please allow us to pay for the reception and the cake and of course the refreshments. We will have a day to remember,' said Tom.

Gabriel shook Tom's hand and hugged Emma. 'Thank you both, I promise to love and care for your daughter all of my life, I'm one lucky guy.'

Willow couldn't wait to start making plans and was eager to arrange the registrar. Gabriel was free for the next few weeks until he started his new placement, so he told her to leave it up to him to sort out the registrar. He requested a copy of her birth certificate, as he felt sure that this would be a requirement.

Monday morning over coffee, Willow told Dorothy about the venue and how perfect it was. She described in great detail how the canopy of trees surrounded the building which itself appeared to blend into the forest. How the smell of earth and pine permeated the air making her feel alive and close to nature.

Dorothy was eager to hear all about the arrangements, she so much wanted to be a part of the planning but realised that she needed to take a step back. Although there was one aspect of the event that she felt perhaps she could help with. When Dorothy finally managed to get a word in, she put her idea forward.

'Willow, can I provide the flower decorations and bouquets? My gift to you and Gabriel.'

Hugging Dorothy and almost squealing with delight, they drew the attention of the other staff members who were now eager to have their own coffee break. Suddenly, they were all involved in the colour scheme and design of the bouquets and table decorations.

***

The next nine months flew by in a flurry of wedding plans and house searches. Willow had not realised the amount of planning involved for even a small wedding. She had no hesitation in who she wanted as her bridesmaids, so quite soon after the preparations began; she met with her friends, Janet and Susan Together, the three girls enjoyed a day in town searching for the perfect wedding dress and contrasting bridesmaid's dresses for her two friends. After trying on lots of different style wedding gowns, some of which were so uncomfortable, she wondered how any bride could move, never mind dance in some of the designs. True, they looked feminine and magical, some even glamorous. None of these styles appealed to Willow she was looking for a wedding dress that not only looked elegant but also comfortable. She'd been to weddings where the bride was constantly pulling up the bodice to prevent her breasts from falling out or having to un-lace the bodice for fear of fainting. Finally, she found the perfect dress. It was in Monsoon while looking for the bridesmaids' dresses that she spotted the dress.

The floor-length elegant tulle skirt draped romantically from the waist. It had a high-necked bodice embellished with crystal gem and pearl detail. The back of the dress was styled with a V-shaped detail, drawing attention to her slim silhouette.

Looking at her reflection in the dressing room mirror sealed her approval. It was a perfect fit and draped gently to the ground just skimming her ankles. No train to worry about while dancing close to Gabriel. No tight corset bones or laces to be fastened. She swirled around the cubicle admiring herself for a private moment before giving her friends a sneak preview.

'Perfect,' they cried in unison. 'Simply perfect!'

'Now girls, let's get you two sorted,' said a very happy Willow.

Janet and Susan chose a similar design in a pretty shade of peach with a diamante clasp on each strap. They all chose a pair of satin shoes with a diamante clasp to complete their outfits.

'We need to help you choose a veil,' said Susan.

Willow smiled. 'No need, I have one already. I will be wearing my mum's veil, it's so perfect. Do you know, it has been packed away in tissue for the past thirty years?'

'Wow, fantastic,' replied Janet.

'Come on let's get lunch…my treat.'

Chapter Twenty-Two

Gabriel meanwhile was enjoying his work as a junior doctor and although the hours were long and the work demanding, he was buoyed up by the fact that his life had a real purpose. Not only was he doing a worthwhile job, helping society as a whole, he was also living his life to the full. In the short term, everything was in place. The wedding plans were going well, and they had begun to research the property market.

Although his gambling debts still hung over him like the Sword of Damocles, he felt that his life was in a good place. His gambling of late was more under control. His visits to the bookies were less frequent and a couple of good wins had allowed him to keep the bookies sweet in terms of his debt. Each month he paid off the minimum amount from his credit card and although the total amount was reducing slowly, he felt confident that in time, he'd close the account.

On the odd weekend off, he took Willow to the races, where he enjoyed the thrill of watching the race in anticipation of that one big win! The huge adrenaline rush that he felt as he watched the horses run towards the winning post gave him a feeling of euphoria. He still purchased a substantial amount of lottery tickets in the hope of winning the Euro-millions. Yet despite this, Gabriel felt in control and was looking forward to his life with Willow.

One weekend, while visiting Southwell Races, they decided to check out a new development of properties that were being marketed for first-time buyers. They agreed that location was important when choosing a property apparently according to a well-known property programme it is better to buy the worst house in a good area, than the best house in a bad area. So said her parents. In any case, they both had a car, and the route was fairly straightforward. Willow rather liked the idea of living in Southwell. The schools were good and the village itself picturesque. The village boasted a wonderful cathedral; Southwell Minster. Historical connections with the civil war added a touch of mystique to the place. Yes, she could envisage settling here and raising their family.

Looking around the show home they both felt a huge wave of anticipation flood over them. Could this be it? Had they found their future home? Holding hands, they walked into each room with a feeling of elation. After they'd seen the final bedroom, their minds were made up. Gabriel hugged Willow.

'Well, I think it's great, what do you think?

'I love it, but can we afford it?' she replied.

'There is only one way to find out,' he answered. 'Let's go and speak to the manager of the development and see what she has to say.'

They were in luck. One, four-bedroom detached property was available. It was on a corner plot and boasted extra land, but also with an extra price tag attached. A quick assessment of their combined income revealed that they could afford to take on a mortgage although only if Willow continued to work.

'It's a bit risky, Gabriel, what happens if one of us is unable to work. How will we manage?'

'Let's not worry about that now,' he replied. 'Besides, within less than two years, I hope to be working in general practice and my wages should be enough to support us both.'

'In that case, let's sign the agreement now,' said an excited Willow.

Having agreed to probably the largest investment they would ever make, Willow felt a mix of emotions, but compared to Gabriel's concerns, hers were minuscule. Amid the excitement, he realised the enormity of the situation. This was a huge responsibility. On one hand, he was confident that his career as a doctor was safe from such things that might affect his earnings. After all, it was unheard of for doctors to be made redundant or their hours reduced. He wanted to provide a good life for himself and Willow. A life that would be befitting for a family doctor, which is the path that he was certain to follow.

'What days are you free next week?' enquired Willow. 'As we need to go to my bank and set up the mortgage. I have enough in my account for the deposit, but I'm afraid there will be very little left after the deposit and conveyancing fees are paid.'

Gabriel was feeling guilty about his future wife paying the deposit. It made him feel less of a man. No matter how often Willow reassured him that one day it was likely to be his wages that paid the mortgage and all the household bills. He still felt ashamed. His redemption came from the fact that Willow thought his debts were due to financing his years at university. There had never been the need to explain to her that he also had other huge debts, linked to his gambling. The time had never been right and now was too late.

Putting his fears aside, Gabriel held Willow's hand.

'Let's celebrate. I know just the place,' said Gabriel.

They went to The Saracens Head, a historic pub reportedly built in 1463. Willow was fascinated as she read about the royal connections with King Charles 1. While Gabriel was at the bar, she checked the menu and the information about the pub's historic connections.

Gabriel had been a number of times before on his return travels from the race track. Sometimes with a good win in his pocket, but more often than not nothing but loose change and enough to buy a half lager. He was pleased to see that the bar staff were changed since his last spree, enabling him to relax and chat with Willow.

'Do you know much about the history of the town, Gabriel? I'm finding the whole place fascinating. There are so many interesting places to visit. I've read somewhere that there is an old Victorian workhouse here that has been taken over by the National Trust.'

Gabriel smiled. 'Did you know that during the civil war the whole town suffered at the hands of Oliver Cromwell's troops? Apparently, they plundered the town.'

How about we check out the area around the Cathedral after we've eaten and get a feel for the area?'

They chatted constantly throughout the meal, full of anticipation of the wonderful life ahead.

She allowed her imagination to transport her thoughts to joining the local community and planned to do as much research on the area as Google allowed. Her thoughts drifted from one event to the other. The wedding, the honeymoon and moving into their very first home together.

It was like a fairy tale; one she wanted to tell Molly about. Her sister of late had not whispered in her ear, but that was not unusual. For some reason, Willow felt the need to feel a connection with her once more, a chance to share her feelings about the new life they were planning.

Having checked out their schedules, they made arrangements to see the bank manager the following week. Willow was keen to set up a joint account as soon as they were married, but Gabriel had reservations about this. Willow felt a little hurt that he hesitated when she first brought up the subject. Being sensitive to his needs, she suggested that there was no hurry, they could make alternative arrangements to pay the shared bills. Willow always assumed that they would manage their joint finances as her parents had. They trusted one another implicitly to be sensible and always discussed major purchases before going ahead. It occurred to her that Gabriel's parents may have managed their joint finances differently, therefore he needed time to reflect on the best way forward for themselves.

The mortgage adviser provided them with a number of options, explaining in detail the pros and cons of each type of mortgage. They settled on a fixed-rate mortgage of 3.69% over three years followed by a standard variable rate over the remaining twenty-five years. They both agreed that with a fixed rate for the first few years of their marriage, it would enable them to plan their finances.

Happy with their decision, the paperwork was signed with both of their names to be on the mortgage as it would be on the deeds of the house. Now all they needed to do was wait for the process to proceed. The time frame they'd been given, meant that if all went to plan, they could begin moving into their new home two weeks before the wedding. *Perfect*, thought Willow, as her mind went into overdrive thinking about colour schemes and furnishings.

'Let's go and tell your parents our good news, Willow,' Gabriel said, as he swung her around in the air, much to the surprise of the customers waiting patiently for their turn to see the bank teller.

Willow grinned, she felt as though they were living in a bubble of happiness. Everything was falling nicely into place; she could hardly believe her luck.

As anticipated, her parents were overjoyed to hear of their plans and insisted they stay for a light supper before leaving to visit Gabriel's parents. As a consequence, it was just past eight o'clock in the evening when they rang the doorbell of Gabriel's family home. It was some time before the door was answered by his father, who stood there in his checked dressing gown looking not too impressed.

'It's a little late for visiting, don't you think?' he said brusquely.

'Sorry, Father, can we come in, we have some good news to share with you both,' said Gabriel, who was looking extremely embarrassed.

Moving aside to let them pass, they walked towards the lounge.

'I'm here in the kitchen,' called his mum.

They found her sat at the breakfast bar in a fleecy robe, hands curled around a mug of what looked like warm milk. Willow detected a whiff of alcohol in the air, maybe brandy or possibly whisky.

'Are you all right, are you unwell only it's a little early for bed, isn't it?' said Gabriel sounding anxious.

'If you visited more often, Gabriel, you would be aware that we try to turn in before ten o'clock most evenings,' she sourly replied.

Turning towards both his parents and holding Willow's hand, just a little too tightly, he told them of the good news about their home in Southwell. *He would have been better saving his breath,* thought Willow, as she carefully observed their reactions. Not a smile of goodwill passed over their faces. No handshake as her father had done. No hugs and congratulations either. Willow wondered what had happened in their lives to make them so cold and unemotional.

'Are you going to be able to keep up the payments, you two, it's a huge commitment and when it goes wrong, don't come crawling back to us to dig you out,' said his father.

'No chance,' Gabriel replied. 'I would rather live in a caravan than come seeking your help. Why are you both being like this, what have we done to make you so angry?'

Neither of his parents responded. Taking it as their cue to leave, they turned towards the door. Before leaving Gabriel called out to them,

'See you at the wedding then and not a minute before.'

Somehow, the joy of their day became deflated. Gabriel's parents had a habit of lowering their mood, but Willow understood that Gabriel wanted to share his news with them, no matter what. Knowing that Gabriel had an early shift the following morning, Willow declined the offer of a visit to the pub on their return journey. Instead, she suggested that after he dropped her off at home, perhaps he should spend some time with his friends.

'After all, Gabriel, haven't you got a stag weekend to organise?' she teased him.

'Yes, I've been thinking about that,' he replied. 'I was going to ask your father and mine to join us, but now I'm not too certain. What do you honestly think?'

'Mm, I…think that it will be polite to ask them both and I will hazard a guess that they may equally politely refuse,' she playfully replied.

It was Duncan who came to the rescue in terms of the stag party arrangements. When Gabriel rang him the following day to ask him to be his best man, he immediately agreed and invited Gabriel and his friends up to the castle for a proper "stag do".

'I will make all the arrangements,' Duncan told him. 'Be prepared for a brilliant weekend of shooting, fencing, and archery, not to mention a few extra activities thrown in.'

Gabriel was relieved that Duncan agreed to be his best man. He couldn't possibly choose between Leo and Adnan. Instead, they were to be his grooms.

Willow was wrong with her prediction for much to her surprise, her father wholeheartedly accepted the offer of joining Gabriel on his stag weekend, explaining that he thought it was a great opportunity to get to know his new son. Gabriel's father declined with no explanation, which helped to make up Willow's mind. She decided not to even raise the subject of her own Hen party with her mother-in-law to be, for fear of having to justify her intentions.

Meanwhile, Willow was in a dilemma about her own hen weekend. If the truth be known, she didn't really want much fuss and certainly didn't want to make a weekend of it. Janet and Susan threw a few ideas forward, but none appealed to her until Dorothy suggested a weekend at a spa retreat. Now that did grab her interest, especially when Dorothy told her of a place in Huddersfield called the Titanic Spa where they could share an apartment overnight. Having checked out the details online, Willow was finally convinced that this was the ideal location; suitable for her friends, Dorothy and her mother.

Two weeks before the wedding. Dorothy kindly drove the five of them to Huddersfield having left Ollies in the capable hands of her under-manager. It was located in beautiful surroundings. The Titanic Spa was located in a renovated mill and looked huge.

'Wow! this looks amazing, Dorothy, thank you so much for suggesting this place, it's perfect,' said Willow when first setting eyes on the huge building.

'It's hard to believe that this was once a working mill,' replied Dorothy. 'Apparently, it's also eco-friendly, how about that? Just up our street, Willow.'

They made their way to the reception where they were greeted with a complimentary drink. The smell of aromatherapy oils drifted through into the reception, inviting a mood of tranquillity and calm.

'I feel relaxed already,' said Janet, as they were being given a guided tour of the Spa area and flat.

The check-in for their apartment was two o'clock, giving them plenty of time to enjoy a swim and a nice relaxing dip in the hot tub, before lunch. They were all provided with robes, towels and slippers, before making their way to the spa area.

'This is the life, Willow,' whispered Emma to her daughter, as she relaxed in a comfortable recliner, close to the salt pool.

'I'm so glad that you're enjoying it, Mum. Am I right in thinking this is your first spa experience? I don't imagine it was the kind of hen night you had in your day?'

'No,' Emma replied. 'But don't imagine for one minute that I didn't have fun. My hen night was quite exciting and believe it or not, it was the night before I married your dad.'

'No way, wasn't that a bit risky,' replied Willow.

'It certainly was, as I nearly didn't make it home.'

'Do tell more,' called out Susan, who was surreptitiously listening in on the conversation.

Emma laughed. 'Tell you what, girls, tonight when we're in the flat sharing the four bottles of prosecco I've hidden in my weekend bag, I will spill the beans. After all, it's a hen weekend, we're here to have fun, don't you agree?'

Willow hugged her amazing mum, although she'd heard the story before and many more besides, it meant the world to her, that she had a mother who was so honest and open.

'Time for lunch, I think,' called Dorothy. 'And it smells really good. Come on, you lot, let's go grab a table.'

After a delicious light lunch, they went in search of their apartment. They found it to be modern, light and airy. There was a full-screen DVD television and a huge selection of films. The television sported lots of different channels. Enough choice to keep everyone happy. They unpacked their travel bags. Willow noted a number of bottles going into the fridge and a selection of cheeses, pate, and antipasti.

Dorothy winked at Willow and placed a gift basket of fruits, crackers and olives, next to the continental breakfast hamper on the breakfast bar that divided the kitchen from the lounge.

'I think it will soon be time for our facial and manicure girls,' said Emma. 'Come on, let's go and find which treatment room we need to be in.'

The rest of the day, they all relished in the pure luxury of the surroundings. After a two-course evening meal, they all retired feeling as though they were walking on air.

It was agreed that Willow should choose which film they were to watch as they settled down comfortably in the lounge. Dorothy and Emma made their way to the kitchen and prepared a host of food for them to enjoy throughout the evening. They opened two bottles of prosecco, pouring generous amounts into the over-large wine glasses.

'Cheers, Willow, we all love you!' they cried in unison, as they toasted Willow on her forthcoming marriage.

Willow chose *"Notting Hill"* as the first film of the evening, followed by *Titanic* which they all agreed was a great choice.

Many drinks later and after much frivolity and laughter, they retired to their beds, having enjoyed a brilliant day together.

Meanwhile, in Scotland, Gabriel was enjoying his stag weekend. Duncan had certainly pulled off all that he'd promised. He had set up a mini camp-site in the grounds of the castle with a campfire and hog roast, an archery board and rifle range. It was pure genius. Duncan's father, joined in the activities but it came as no surprise to Gabriel that his own father declined to join the stag party.

At first, Gabriel was disappointed and embarrassed at his father's lack of support, but Gordon and Duncan more than made up for his no-show. The fact that Tom, his father-in-law to be, had made the effort to join in the celebrations, reinforced his feelings of acceptance into Willow's family, who were embracing him as one of their own already. Adnan and Leo were fascinated by the castle and the way that Duncan had arranged such a unique stag weekend. They all thoroughly enjoyed the weekend and although a little worse for wear, arrived home on Sunday evening feeling that it had been a successful bachelor party for Gabriel.

Tom enjoyed the camaraderie of being with a group of men. Although nothing much fazed him, he was a little concerned that Gabriel had a tendency to put a wager on a number of activities and appeared to be enjoying the game of poker they played late into the night; a bit too much. Although it niggled him somewhat, he put it down to high jinks and the atmosphere of the weekend. By the time he was sat with Emma on the sofa, as they both discussed their weekend away, it was almost forgotten.

Chapter Twenty-Three

Precisely as planned, they got the keys to their new home two weeks before their wedding. The kitchen was fitted with all the white goods being integral in the units. Wooden floors throughout the house meant that they could take their time choosing rugs and runners. The windows were fitted with white wooden shutters, omitting the need to rush out to buy blinds or curtains.

Holding hands, they visited every room in their first home. They had already decided which was to be their bedroom. It was light and spacious with an en-suite bathroom and fitted wardrobes.

'I guess that we'd best prioritise choosing a bed, Willow, do you have any preferences?' enquired Gabriel.

'Mm… Now let me think. How about a single bed so that we can lay close all night long,' teased Willow.

'I'm up for that,' he replied with a twinkle in his eyes.

That afternoon, they went shopping to IKEA in Kimberley, not only to choose a bed but also all the necessary items required for their first weeks in their new home.

The next two weeks were incredibly busy for them. Working full-time and making final arrangements for their wedding left little time to prepare their new home in readiness for moving in following their two weeks honeymoon. Willow had no idea what Gabriel had planned. The only clues he gave her was to bring her passport and sun cream.

Her mum and Aunty Violet came to her rescue in terms of the house. They cleaned the house, top to bottom. Her father assembled the bed and a few other pieces of furniture, enabling her mum to make up the bed with freshly washed, new bedding. They put towels and other essentials in the bathroom and kitchen. Her father transported the many storage boxes of Willow's personnel belongings, storing them in the smallest of the bedrooms. By the time the wedding was upon them, their home was ready except for a sofa and other large pieces of furniture. Both Gabriel and Willow agreed that they wanted to take their time in choosing the larger pieces of furniture. They wished to savour the experience together without feeling rushed.

On the eve of her wedding, Willow finished working on the table and tree decorations. She'd lovingly created an array of butterfly table settings. Each table was to be named after a species of butterfly, enabling the seating plan to be easily followed. For the outdoor tables, she made tea-light decorations of damselflies, dragonflies and birds; a theme that she extended with the tree decorations. Happy that everything was finally completed, Willow went to bed content.

Bright and early the next morning, she awoke to the sound of laughter tinkling in her ear. It sounded familiar although distant and as though it was an echo. Confused, Willow sat up in bed looking around her old familiar bedroom. Of course, there was no one there. Why would there be? For the briefest of moments, she thought of her sister, Molly. This bedroom was to be their shared room and now Willow was leaving it for good. She quickly dispelled the thought, after all, this was her wedding day. She was to be married to her soulmate, her one true love and nothing was going to spoil the occasion.

Willow went over to her bedroom window. Bright sunshine was creeping through the crack in the curtains. Even before she opened them, Willow knew that her wedding day was set to be bright and sunny. And so, it was.

All of their well-organised plans fell neatly into place. Quietly along with her father and bridesmaids, Willow went up the sweeping staircase of the wedding venue to prepare themselves for the first few notes of music to announce the wedding ceremony was about to begin. Holding gently onto his daughter's arm and with Janet and Susan in attendance behind her, they returned to the ground floor area, were the guests sat waiting for the ceremony to begin. Gabriel and Duncan who were facing the Registrar, gently turned their heads towards the bride as the music changed, announcing the beginning of the ceremony.

The entire event was perfect for everyone except Joan and Sam, who reluctantly attended and quickly departed immediately after the final speech. Willow saw the disappointment on her husband's handsome face and the horror on her own parents' face, for they didn't have the courtesy to even say goodbye.

'There's something not right there,' Tom said to Emma, as they saw Gabriel's parents discretely depart.

'I agree, its unusual behaviour,' said Emma. 'Do you think it's because Willow wouldn't agree to a Catholic ceremony?'

'I'm not convinced that's the whole reason,' replied Tom.

Gabriel and Willow were not about to let his parents' behaviour put a damper on their wedding day. Nothing was going to mar their absolute joy. The wedding celebrations went on well into the night until Gabriel and Willow waved off their final guests.

'Are you ready for your honeymoon surprise, Willow? I have your suitcase and hand baggage stowed away in the boot of my car which is parked at the hotel I've booked for this evening. Your carriage awaits, wife,' laughed Gabriel, as he pointed to a taxi driver waiting patiently by the exit.

Their wedding night was spent at the Hilton Hotel and the following morning after fetching their travel bags from his car, they changed into their travel attire.

'Gabriel, stop teasing me, you still haven't said where we're going,' said Willow, pretending to be cross.

Gabriel passed her an envelope marked "Celebrity Cruises".

'Is this what I think it is?' shrieked Willow.

'I'm afraid it is, Willow, I hope you're up for another cruise, only this time it's around the Med.'

Willow whooped with joy and threw herself at Gabriel.

'I'm tempted, Willow, to take you back to bed, but we have a flight to catch at East Midlands Airport and we need to be leaving ten minutes ago,' said Gabriel, as he ran his fingers through his hair in an attempt to tidy it.

Their honeymoon proved to be everything they'd hoped for. Cruising around the Eastern Mediterranean, calling into so many interesting destinations was the icing on the cake for Willow. Places such as Dubrovnik, Montenegro and Croatia among others opened up a whole new world for both of them. Making memories and taking many photographs to share with their friends and family became the focus of their days spent in harmony together.

Gabriel, who truly couldn't afford such a luxurious honeymoon, was hoping to win a good deal of money on the roulette tables. He had taken out another loan to pay for the cruise and had every intention to make full use of the onboard casino.

This did not go un-noticed by Willow, who at first was alarmed at her new husband's interest in the casino. However, she came to the conclusion, it was his holiday too, and therefore she let it ride. No point in spoiling such a special time.

Chapter Twenty-Four

On their return, they moved into their new home. Emma and Tom left a fridge full of essential foods and a few luxury items to welcome them home. In addition, they'd picked a huge bunch of fresh flowers from their own garden and arranged them in a vase which was a family heirloom. Now passed to Willow.

'You are lucky, Willow, to have parents like Tom and Emma. They are so removed from my own, it's hard to believe that they are of the same generation. One of these days when things have settled down and I'm working in general practice, I swear that I'm going to get to the bottom of this. I never did check the ancestry website, despite signing up for membership. Something always distracted me, maybe we can do the research together. There must be a reason why they are so cold and distant. And, another thing. This situation about my extended family, or lack of it. I really do need to know, for when we have a family of our own. What am I going to tell them when they ask about their ancestors?' said an exasperated Gabriel.

Truth be known, there was more to his mood than just his concerns about his family. Gabriel once again had lost a substantial amount on the gambling tables, making him anxious and ashamed. Try as he might, the urge to gamble rose up inside of him and he was unable to resist. A number of times, he tried setting himself boundaries, but he was weak. His shame meant that he felt unable to speak to someone who could help him. Rationalising his behaviour often left Gabriel feeling depressed, reinforcing his low self-esteem that he'd hidden for most of his life.

He was well aware of support groups such as Gamblers Anonymous, but that meant admitting he might have a problem. He wasn't convinced that it had reached the stage where he needed to address his gambling, by seeking professional help. He decided that it was time to take back control and vowed to himself that he would end this destructive activity before it impacted further on his life. There was so much to look forwards to and no way was his behaviour going to sabotage his happiness with Willow.

Life for the newly married couple fell nicely into place. Over the next year, they gradually furnished their home. Although they had no savings, Willow was confident that the increase in her husband's wages in a few months' time, would enable them to put a little aside each month.

She had lots of plans for the garden, to the rear and side of their home. When they moved in, there was just a plain lawn and empty borders. Within weeks, she'd drawn up extensive plans to create an exciting yet functional space for them to enjoy all year around. Unable to plant the spring bulbs and some of the perennials until later in the year, she decided to concentrate on the herbaceous borders and the small rockery which would eventually be the backdrop to a small pond. Dorothy had kindly given them a nice water feature and a number of plants. In her little cloud of happiness, Willow felt relaxed and content.

Sadly, bubbling under the surface was a mountain of debt that Gabriel amassed due to his gambling, which even he began to realise was now an addiction that he needed help with. Feeling terribly ashamed and not wishing to distress his wife, Gabriel kept his concerns bottled up inside. His gambling had gone from a fun, innocuous diversion to an unhealthy preoccupation with serious consequences. He knew that he needed to break the habit and find a method of distraction which wouldn't draw attention to himself. With this in mind, he suggested to Willow that they join the local gym, citing that exercise was a healthy pastime they might enjoy together.

Unaware of the real reason, Willow jumped at the chance to spend quality time together. Of late, Gabriel had been working long hours at the hospital to complete his foundation course, often returning home after she retired to bed. She understood of course. After all, he was not only working but also studying to pass that all-important exam, to enable him to get a training GP position.

At first, going to the gym helped to distract Gabriel away from the betting shops. However, it proved to be a temporary respite. Triggered by a reminder from his credit card provider that despite paying the minimum payment each month, the interest was slowly rising; he succumbed to his addiction in the false hope of winning on a sure bet. Even when he knew the odds were stacked against him, he continued to gamble, chasing losses that were impossible to win.

Willow totally understood when Gabriel's visits with her to the gym petered off; after all, he was now busy securing a placement at a training practice and knew how much this meant to him. Recently, she missed a few visits herself due to a spate of bladder infections; resulting in the necessity to take a course of antibiotics.

Gabriel, she noticed, was becoming very distracted and although he showed her empathy when she struggled with the pelvic pain associated with the infection, he didn't seem to take it on board. Willow made allowances for him and was relieved when finally, he was offered a position at a local training practice that had an excellent reputation. It was a large practice, boasting three senior partners and a number of salaried general practitioners. The practice population of over twelve thousand patients meant that Gabriel would get lots of hands-on experience.

Genuinely relieved that there was light at the end of the financial tunnel which was consuming his every thought, Gabriel's mood gradually improved. Willow noticed the old Gabriel return to her and for that at least, she was grateful. Over the next two months, despite feeling out of sorts, she joined her husband on a number of social activities, arranged by the partners in order to get to know their new team members. He was becoming a popular doctor at the practice; as reported by the partners to Willow on their last little soiree that was held at a local Indian restaurant.

Unfortunately for Willow, she must have eaten something that did not agree with her, for immediately following the first sip of breakfast tea the following morning; she had to make haste to the sink. Where she expelled the contents of her gut.

'Hey! Willow, are you okay?' called Gabriel from the bathroom.

'I'm not sure,' she replied, before starting another round of heaving.

'Must have been that curry you ate last night. Do you think Dorothy will mind if you take a day off?' said Gabriel, as he made his way towards his wife, who still had her head hung over the sink.

'To be honest, I've been feeling tired and nauseous for the past few weeks, but you have looked so tense of late, that I didn't want to worry you,' replied Willow trying to hold back the next round of vomit rising into her throat.

Alarmed at the implications of what his wife had just said, Gabriel sat down on the nearest chair.

'Willow, have you had a period recently?'

Realising what Gabriel was getting at, she headed for the nearest seat and despite feeling dreadful, she tried to recollect the date of her last period.

'It isn't unusual for me not to have a period, Gabriel, as you know. Most women don't have a period at all when taking the progesterone only pill. I take it at the same time every day as prescribed and I know for sure that I haven't missed any.' When I was on the depo contraception, it was the same.

'I trust you with that, Willow, but you were on antibiotics a couple of months back and it's common knowledge that they can affect contraception.'

'What?' said Willow, in alarm.

Gabriel sighed deeply before his response. 'It's partly my fault, I've been so distracted of late that it never occurred to me to take extra precautions, when you were taking them.'

Willow felt confused. If she was pregnant, then although it was too soon, perhaps it was meant to be. If so, she couldn't deny that a part of her was a little thrilled at the aspect of becoming a mother.

'Let's not jump to conclusions, Gabriel. After all, it might be the curry from last night,' she said nervously.

'You are right, but just to be certain, I will bring a pregnancy test kit home with me tonight,' said, Gabriel, as he made his way out of the front door.

Safely in the car, he breathed out a huge sigh. Just as things were becoming a little less tense in terms of managing his debt, he was now faced with the prospect of becoming the sole provider of income. He loved Willow with all his heart and the thought of having a family together filled him with joy. What should be a time of celebration and anticipation of the test being positive, was in fact ruined by his underlying dread.

Later that day, his fears turned into reality. As the faint blue lines on the test strip appeared, Willow's hand began to tremble. She hadn't planned for this so soon and didn't feel prepared. In the space of a few seconds, her life was turned upside down. Amid the initial thrill and excitement, came an overwhelming sense of responsibility and uncertainty. So many questions raced through her already overactive mind. Would the pregnancy go full term? Would the baby be strong and healthy? Already, her anxieties were mounting as she turned to her husband for his response.

Gabriel had practised exactly how he would handle the situation if the little blue line appeared. His medical knowledge and the probability of the result being positive was something he'd been thinking about all day. Now, for the sake of his wife, he said the exact words she'd want to hear.

Lovingly, he took her into his arms and told her, how happy he was, to become a father.

'But, Gabriel, can we afford to have a baby, will we be able to pay the mortgage and the household expenses, as well as paying off your student loan. There are still so many things we need for the house and I haven't completed my work on the garden,' said Willow, who was now becoming more anxious than ever.

'We will manage, sweetheart. My salary will be enough for the three of us, please don't worry. The important thing now is for us to celebrate, not worry about money. Yes, we're starting our family sooner than expected but think about it, Willow. We are so lucky that we're able to have a family. Only today, I saw a young couple who have been trying for a family for the last ten years. With no success. We are so lucky to have each other, and now… We have made a baby with our love.'

Over the next few weeks, Gabriel continued with his act. Willow was keen to tell her parents and friends, who all congratulated them both sincerely. She also insisted they tell his own parents together and arranged to visit the weekend after breaking the news to her own.

Gabriel was dreading this. Neither of his parents had visited them in their new home, despite the occasional phone call he made, inviting them over. He didn't know what to expect. After all, he was making them grandparents; a role that he doubted they would relish.

Upon hearing their news, Sam stepped forwards and made an unusual remark, to Gabriel; who thought he must have been mistaken in what he'd heard. Willow thought so too and dismissed it from her mind. Joan mumbled something about being a grandma and she hoped that it would be less trouble than being a mother. *Odd thing to say,* considered Willow, but then again, they never failed to surprise her. Although it was a short visit, it hadn't been quite as bad as Willow anticipated. For that, she was grateful.

Over the next few months, Willow gradually began to feel better. By the time she was in her second trimester, she was positively glowing with health and happiness. Unfortunately, Gabriel was looking more and more anxious. Many a night, he tossed and turned in his sleep and, in a bid, to sedate himself had taken to drinking whisky before bed.

The smell of whisky on her husband's breath did not impress Willow. Once again, she made allowances for him. Despite thoroughly enjoying his work at the practice, she guessed that it was taking its toll on him, especially since he'd become involved with some of the financial transactions.

Trying to ease his burden, Willow took control of all things related to the baby. Along with her mum, she chose the nursery fittings and the pram. Her parents insisted they buy the pram for their first grandchild. Her father decorated the nursery in primrose yellow and assembled the white furniture. Willow and her mum, made a matching blind and curtains to complete the nursery. Everything was coming together nicely. It wasn't until after her second scan, which provided the news that she was having a boy that Gabriel finally began to take an interest in the preparations.

'A son, eh? How wonderful,' was the first response to the scan results. Kissing his wife tenderly on the lips, he quietly whispered, 'Thank you.'

He stroked her swollen belly, then kissed her once more.

'I don't deserve you, Willow, you're so pure and good,' he continued to say in a low voice.

In an attempt to lighten the situation, Willow suggested a few boys' names. Most of them of which she had no intentions of calling her son. That evening, they looked through a book of baby names and finally agreed to call their son Jacob. From that day on, Gabriel spoke of Jacob every day, as though he was already a part of their family.

Chapter Twenty-Five

It was two o'clock in the morning when the first labour pains started. Gabriel once more had been restless in his sleep and calling out to someone. When Willow gently nudged his shoulder to rouse him from his tormented sleep, he muttered something about being sorry. Giving him a further nudge, Gabriel finally woke and realised that his wife needed him. As he helped her out of bed, her waters broke, signalling that their son was well and truly on his journey into the world. Gabriel never left her side throughout every stage of her labour. For him, it was the most amazing of all births, it was nature at its sweetest.

Later that day, Jacob came screaming into the world, pink and perfect, a world full of hope and promise, a world full of love.

Gabriel held her hand tenderly and told her how happy and proud he was. He wasn't the only family member in the delivery room that day. Her twin sister, Molly, was also there to whisper congratulations. At first, she thought that it must be the drugs playing tricks with her mind, as she hadn't heard from her sister in such a long time.

The link with her twin sister seemed to be once more growing inside of her, the connection reignited following the safe delivery of Jacob.

The following day, as her family and friends buzzed around, oozing goodwill and congratulations, she began to feel strangely detached from reality. Watching her parents lean over the clear bassinet where Jacob lay sleeping, Willow felt an overwhelming sense of dread or was it fear? The emotion clearly etched into her face. This did not go unnoticed by her mum.

'Are you all right, luv?' said her mum, looking most concerned. 'You have gone very pale, Willow, do you want me to fetch Gabriel?'

'Just tired, that's all. Please don't worry Gabriel, I will feel better after a good night's sleep. Besides, he is busy at the surgery tying a few loose ends up.'

In truth, he was doing no such thing. He was with his new mistress, for gambling had become his muse. His companions were the electronic machines, the flashing lights and the sound of his coins, dropping into the mouths of the hungry bandits – sucking every coin from his pockets until they were bare.

He knew that he was becoming de-sensitised to the world of gambling, much like addicts of illicit substances who moved in circles where such behaviour was accepted. When he finally returned to his wife and baby, he felt full of remorse and shame.

As he held Jacob in his arms, Gabriel vowed once more to himself that he would not return to his mistress, there was to be no more chasing back his debts, no more lies. He realised that it was time to share the truth of his situation with Willow.

He planned to wait until she was stronger and emotionally stable enough to cope with the truth.

Ideally, rest should have helped Willow, but in fact, it seemed to be having the opposite effect. Too much time to think just gave her the opportunity to fill the void where negativity was taking hold. She began to worry that she was not good enough to be a mother, not nice enough or perfect enough for her precious son and husband.

As one by one her visitors left, her brain began to throw around ideas and worries that had no place in the mind of a new mother. She felt as though she was screaming inside, her misery intense and consuming. How she longed for plain vanilla thoughts instead of the crazy mind-blowing thoughts that were playing games and torturing her mind.

Following discharge from the maternity ward, Willow became adept at acting as though everything in her life was perfect. The reality was very different.

Gabriel was allowed two weeks paternity leave to provide support for his wife. Although in effect this was a good opportunity to bond with Jacob and help his wife, Gabriel was anxious that his little misdemeanour might be discovered in his absence. What should have been a joyous time for them turned into a daily routine of spiralling anxiety and tension. Jacob appeared to be picking up on the atmosphere and wouldn't settle. Most nights, Willow was pacing the floor with him, reinforcing her own stress levels and adding to her already sleep deprived exhaustion.

Unable to establish a routine with Jacob was adding to Willow's insecurities about her being a good mother. Despite the Health visitor, reassuring Willow that it was normal to feel this way, she was not convinced. Added to her concerns about

Jacob, was Gabriel's behaviour. He appeared to be distracted, frequently calling the practice to discuss administrative issues. The most romantic gesture that Gabriel offered Willow, was to have the baby monitor on his side of the bed. A gesture that in many ways was an empty one; for Gabriel was unable to settle Jacob after he'd fed him and still needed to wake Willow.

By the second week of Gabriel's leave from work, he was looking worse than Willow. The phone calls from the surgery began during this time, leaving Gabriel looking ill and behaving in an agitated and irritable manner. He appeared to be constantly pre-occupied and distressed.

It was during this second week that Gabriel's parents came to see their grandchild for the first time. Knowing that her in-laws were to visit, Willow gathered her remaining strength to clean and tidy the house. The pile of washing was getting higher, the bins over-flowing and the whole place looked dusty. Somehow, she managed to make a token effort to clean the house, but the washing had to wait, so this was pushed inside of the washing machine, whites and colours mixed together until she had the energy to separate.

Sam and Joan arrived bearing flowers for Willow and a soft pram toy for Jacob. Willow was surprised and quite touched, as they'd never brought gifts before.

'You look terrible,' were the first words that came out of Sam's mouth when Gabriel put in an appearance.

He did look shocking, thought Willow. In fact, she'd never seen him looking so scruffy. He hadn't bothered to shave in two days and she remembered him wearing the same clothes for the past few days.

'Dad, surely you remember what it was like when me and Victoria were born. All of those sleepless nights?'

Sam gave Joan an odd look, then proceeded into the lounge where Jacob was screaming his head off and kicking his little legs wildly about. Joan immediately went to lift him from the crib, she rocked him in her arms, speaking softly to Jacob, soothing him until he calmed down.

'Looks like, neither of you has been getting much sleep,' said Joan.

'Does he suffer from colic, Willow? Victoria had terrible colic and I swear, if she'd been my first baby, there would have been no more. Fortunately, Gabriel was a good baby. I can see some of Gabriel in Jacob. Just look at that mop of auburn hair. I do believe I can see a little curl.'

Willow had never seen this side of her mother-in-law and was pleasantly surprised.

'Thank you, Joan, do you mind holding him while I go and make a pot of tea?' said Willow, who went off to the kitchen in a trance.

While in the kitchen, she heard muffled voices coming from the living room. They all appeared to be in conversation with one another. She overheard Joan reprimanding Gabriel for his scruffy appearance and quite clearly told him to buck his ideas up.

Knowing that Jacob was in relatively good hands for the moment at least, she practised the deep breathing technique that the Health visitor had encouraged her to do during times of stress. Closing her eyes tightly shut, Willow paid attention to the area at the bottom of her rib cage and followed the sensations of her breath going in and out. It was in those few moments of relaxation, that she suddenly heard a commotion coming from the lounge, followed by the doorbell ringing.

Who could that be, thought Willow? They weren't expecting anyone as far as she was aware. By the time Willow was in the hallway, the door had been opened by Gabriel and there stood two police officers.

'Please come in,' called Willow, as she approached the door where Gabriel was stood like a mute statue.

The taller of the two police officers removed his hat but did not enter the hall. Looking directly at Gabriel, he told him that they were there to take him in for questioning.

'There must be some mistake,' cried Willow.

'Gabriel, tell them this is a mistake. What is it they want to talk to you about?'

Gabriel, head down and shoulders slumped felt unable to answer.

'Tell your wife what this is all about,' demanded Sam, who was now visibly annoyed and making his way towards the door.

'Well!' shouted Sam. 'Speak up, I can't hear you.'

'Please leave this to us, sir, you are not helping the situation,' replied one of the officers.

Willow made her way towards her husband who made no attempt to comfort her or give any explanation.

'Please, Gabriel, please, what is going on, what have you done?'

Emotionally drained, Gabriel did not reply. Instead, he followed the officers out to the police car without looking back. He held his head down in shame for fear of looking up and facing the prying eyes of the neighbours, some of who had gathered on the street when the police car arrived.

'Just like his father,' muttered Sam, as he went to collect his coat. 'Come on, Joan, I don't intend to go through this scenario again. Once is enough in my lifetime. All of those years wasted on his education. For what? He has turned out just like that waste of space no good brother of mine.'

'I'm not leaving Willow,' she replied to her shocked husband.

'I know exactly what she is going through and I wouldn't wish that on anyone. You go home, Sam. I'm staying here with Willow until we know the truth of this matter.'

Confused and in a dream-like state, Willow returned to the lounge and slumped down onto the sofa. Jacob was asleep in his crib and finally looked as though whatever was distressing him had settled. Joan went into the kitchen and returned with the tea that Willow had begun to prepare only minutes earlier. Setting it down on the coffee table, she began to pour the tea.

Willow broke the silence.

'There must be an explanation for this, it has to be a mistake. Do you think that it might be linked to the surgery?'

Joan couldn't look Willow in the eyes, but she knew for certain, that now was the time to deliver the truth. A truth that even Gabriel and Victoria were not aware of.

'Do you remember when you asked about our relatives, Willow?'

Looking up, Willow nodded her head.

'The truth is, Willow. Sam is not Gabriel and Victoria's father. He is, in fact, their uncle.'

Willow looked up and saw tears in Joan's eyes.

'Their father was Sam's youngest brother. He was a gambler who got into debt and committed suicide rather than face a jail sentence. He left me distraught and destitute with two young children. Sam and I fell in love. The whole family were against our relationship, saying that it was wrong, they disowned us leaving us with no choice other than to do a moonlight flit.

'We upped sticks and moved here to Nottinghamshire, where Sam was able to find work. We both worked incredibly long hours to save enough money to put down a small deposit on a business. You have no idea, Willow. We went without for years. The church gave us some grounding and restored our self-esteem. Gabriel and Victoria were too young to remember. They had the same surname as Sam. In fact, Sam was their real father's middle name. So, you see, it was easy to hide. We got married in a register office with two witnesses off the street. Not ideal, and in many ways, it broke our hearts. We have never been in touch with our respective families and have no wish to do so.'

Willow was shocked. Joan had no need to share this with her before telling either Gabriel or Victoria and she wondered what had prompted her to do so.

'Why are you telling me this, Joan? Has it something to do with Gabriel going with the police?'

'I'm telling you so you can prepare yourself, Willow. I've always worried that Gabriel inherited his father's tendencies. For that reason, we've not indulged him. We knew what he was like as a child. Always spending his money in the arcades while Victoria buried her head in books. Why do you think we wanted him to become a missionary? He needed to be removed from temptation.'

Willow knew that Joan was right. Worries that she'd long buried, began to surface. From the early days of their

223

courtship, she knew that he enjoyed going to the races and buying lottery tickets and that was only the tip of the iceberg. The amount of time he spent in the casino while cruising on their honeymoon was something that had greatly concerned her.

'Let me take care of Jacob, while you go to the police station and find out what this is all about,' said Joan.

Willow felt the walls closing in around her. She felt unable to breathe.

'I need my parents,' cried Willow and proceeded to collect her mobile phone and car keys. Before driving to the police station, she rang her parents, giving them a brief explanation.

They arrived within twenty minutes, during which time Willow had been left to wait in the family room. On arrival at the station, her parents were directed to the family room where they immediately opened their arms out to their daughter. They were still hugging when the duty officer came into the room.

'Please take a seat. We have charged Gabriel with corporate fraud and it's my duty to inform you that he is to be sentenced according to a process set out in the UK Sentencing Council's Definitive Guidelines,' said the officer in an animated voice that lacked any kind of emotion.

On hearing his words, Willow slumped in the chair, causing it to rock back where she landed on the floor, catching her face on the edge of the chair arm. Blood began pouring from a gash on her cheek. Emma raced over to her daughter, cradling her in her arms.

The police officer shouted for the duty medic to come immediately. Meanwhile, Tom began to assist his daughter into a more comfortable position, before transferring her to a chair, with the help of the officer.

After attending to her wound, the duty doctor enquired if Willow would like some counselling to help her to deal with the emotional side of the situation.

Willow was not feeling in her right mind. It was the wrong time to be making such a decision. Her baby was just over a week old, and she'd been dealt a blow that no new mother should have to face.

'No, thank you, I just want to go home,' she pleaded.

'Can I see Gabriel now?'

'I'm afraid not today, perhaps you should go home with your family and rest. You have had quite a shock,' replied the doctor.

'Don't worry about your car, it will be safely parked here until someone can collect it,' he gently told her.

Tom drove Willow home, where after thanking Joan for her help, she collected a few belongings for herself and Jacob in preparation for spending the night at her parents' home. They insisted she was to stay for one night at least until they knew the full situation.

Chapter Twenty-Six

Gabriel was sentenced to three years imprisonment for corporate fraud. His future as a practising doctor was very much in doubt and Willow by all accounts was left to raise Jacob alone while facing an uncertain future.

Every week, she went to visit her husband in prison where he was getting professional help to deal with his gambling addiction. He had commenced a course of cognitive behavioural therapy to help him focus on changing his unhealthy behaviours and thoughts. Gabriel was getting the help he so badly needed, but Willow was left high and dry. Unable to move on with her grief, her own mental health beginning to decline.

As each day went by, she struggled more and more to hide her depressive feelings. The negative thoughts plaguing her mind were reinforced by the decline in her physical health as her weight began to drop. Her parents couldn't fail to notice the changes their daughter was displaying. They became increasingly worried about her health and wellbeing.

Dorothy made several attempts to contact Willow, without success, eventually going directly to visit Willow without giving any warning.

One evening after the garden centre was closed, Dorothy arrived at Willow's unannounced holding a Japanese Azealia that was well established and planted in a large terracotta pot. Dorothy in her kindness had wanted to contribute towards Willow's recent attempts at landscaping their moderate sized back garden. She knew how much her friend admired the species of Azealia. Hurt and confused, Dorothy was surprised when Willow did not answer the door. She knew that her friend was home for she'd noticed Willow move the lounge blind up a fraction to peer underneath. Jacob was quite clearly playing up and being very vocal. Even so, this was unusual behaviour from Willow, causing Dorothy a great deal of concern.

Leaving the plant outside of the front door, in the shelter of the porch, Dorothy made her way home, feeling extremely hurt. She understood how embarrassed her friend must be feeling in view of Gabriel being sent to prison. Logically, one would hope that at times like this, Willow needed her friends more than ever. Not one to give up, Dorothy planned to call again later in the week, in the hope that Willow would at least let her cross over the threshold.

Hearing the garden gate close, Willow surreptitiously peeped under the blind once more. She saw Dorothy walking towards her parked car. From the corner of her eye, she saw the edges of the foliage from the plant, as the leaves rustled slightly in the breeze. Staring at the plant in a Trans like state, she wondered for a split second if she was dreaming. What was she to do?

Counting loudly to ten, she made her way to the front door. Opening the letter box, she peered through the crack. Directly in front of her vision, the Azealia stood proud and firm. The leaves splayed out in glorious colours of greens and burnt orange. Willow felt the corners of her mouth begin to form a smile. It did not quite reach the fullness of her mouth, but was enough to give her the courage to open the front door. She stroked the leaves of the plant and marvelled at its beauty. She didn't have the energy to lift the heavy pot and was surprised at her weakness. Where was Gabriel? *Perhaps he will help me later*, she thought. With a mighty shove, she pushed the plant into the far corner of the porch to protect it for the time being.

Jacob's crying had reached fever pitch by the time she returned to him. An overwhelming feeling of guilt washed over her. She should not have left him in his crib while she went to the door. She convinced herself that she was a bad mother and really must try harder.

At times, Willow felt in a very dark place full of despair and futility. Jacob was the one person who kept her going. She became obsessive about hygiene and safety and lived-in constant fear of something happening to him. Her love for Jacob became all-consuming. Of late, she'd taken her obsession with her son's safety to the extreme, by removing all sharp objects from the home. She buried them in the garden for fear that he'd hurt himself. Even as she was burying the scissors and knives, she knew that it wasn't rational behaviour, but couldn't help herself. She felt confused about her own behaviour and yet felt a prisoner to the irrational thoughts that plagued her.

Not knowing the full history of events, her health visitor reported to Willow's doctor that she was displaying evidence of postnatal-depression and at times possible psychosis. Based on this, he paid her a home visit. Mornings, for Willow, were never good, each morning for a few seconds after waking, she could almost believe that Gabriel was with her in bed. Those few delightful seconds before reality hit home, were the only time of relative normality she encountered.

When Dr Smith arrived, she was back inside of herself, down that long bleak tunnel full of heartache. He was very thoughtful and kind in his manner; encouraging Willow to talk about her feelings. She was unable to share her innermost feelings with a stranger, she hadn't found the courage to tell her parents exactly what she was going through so no way was she about to unload her innermost fears to someone else. Although in fact, she did have someone very close to her, that she felt totally connected to and whom she regularly shared her innermost fears. Her sister, Molly, was the one person she spoke to on a regular basis, unloading herself of all the self-loathing that was poisoning her beautiful mind.

Willow blamed herself for her husband's desperate attempt to pay off his gambling debts in order to hide his shame. In retrospect, the signs were there. She chose to ignore them for fear of confronting Gabriel and putting their relationship at risk. It was her weakness that drove him on to commit fraud. All of those days out at the races when she ignored his excessive gambling, thinking that he was just having fun. Blowing off steam to relieve the pressure of his anxiety about exams.

Having made his assessment, Dr Smith suggested that it might help if she was to see someone who specialised in her kind of problem. Thinking that it was pregnancy related, he referred her to the postnatal psychosis unit advising Willow that she'd receive an appointment within the week.

The following day was her day to visit Gabriel. She never took Jacob, for fear of him catching some unknown prison germ. Gabriel had pleaded with her to bring him along, but she was firm and she didn't tell him the real reason, as he wouldn't understand her rationale. She told her husband that she couldn't bring Jacob to such an establishment, it didn't feel right. Gabriel was not convinced of her reasoning. Every week, he saw his beautiful wife disappear before his very eyes. The sparkle was no longer in her eyes, she was thin and pale. Her thick, shiny hair looked dull and lifeless. Gabriel knew that he'd done this to Willow and for that he was ashamed.

Since her last visit, his mother had been. It was the first time she'd graced him with her presence. He was confused as to why his father had not come with her until she revealed the purpose of her visit.

'Has Willow mentioned anything to you about a little heart to heart I had with her when you were first arrested, Gabriel?' enquired his mother.

'No!' answered Gabriel. 'What is that all about?'

Joan told Gabriel word for word, what she'd told Willow. He let her continue without interruption, and when she finished, he simply stood up, turned his back on her and left the room.

Now Willow was sat in front of him, looking more unwell than ever. He had done this to her, but his parents must take some of the blame. Knowing his family history, they should have protected him by warning him of the possibility of such a fate happening to him. His whole life had been a sham. He wondered how Victoria was going to feel when she found out the truth. Surely, his mother was going to tell her. If not, the whole messy business would be left to him. She was planning to visit him the following week, something he was very much looking forwards to. Now he wasn't so sure. He hoped that he wasn't going to be the one to shatter her world.

'Willow, I know!' Those were the first words that greeted Willow. Not, Willow, how are you? Willow, I love you.

Desperate to let her know that his mother had been, he failed to acknowledge these wouldn't be the words she wanted to hear. He was rewarded with silence and an odd expression on his wife's face.

'Sorry, Willow… Please forgive me. I'm going through hell in here and now I've been informed by mother that my life has been a sham. How could they have lied to me and Victoria for our entire life? I doubt if the truth would have come out at all, if not for my own stupidity. Perhaps if I had known the truth, I would have felt able to discuss how my addiction was getting control of me. I have made so many mistakes. The biggest being unable to admit to you that I had a problem. The truth is, Willow… I felt ashamed and embarrassed. Say something please.'

Still no response from Willow. She sat there with her eyes wide open though they may have well been wide shut. It was as though her brain had gone to sleep. The light had gone out inside of her.

'Please say something, Willow,' he pleaded.

She hesitated before finally giving her reply.

'I must go back to Jacob, he needs me. I'm worried that he might be ill,' spoke Willow in an animated, monotone voice.

Recognising that his wife was not well and likely having some kind of emotional breakdown, he spoke gently, hoping to coax more from her.

'What do you mean? Who is taking care of him, Willow?'

'My parents of course,' she replied.

'And what makes you think that he might get hurt?' he said.

Willow didn't reply. She knew that Gabriel wouldn't understand her phobia about sharp objects. Only Molly understood her fears. Only Molly understand her obsession with checking things over and over again.

'I must go now. He needs me…you do understand, don't you, Gabriel? I'm responsible for his safety. He needs me… He needs me, Gabriel… He needs me.'

As Willow walked away from Gabriel, he felt that his heart would surely break into a million tiny fragments of tissue. The pain in his chest was restricting his breathing, so he clutched his chest tightly. The guard called over to him to make sure he was all right. He didn't want any prisoners having a heart attack on his watch and this guy had turned a strange colour of grey.

'I expect I will survive, but I'm worried about my wife and feel so helpless,' answered Gabriel, as he walked back towards his cell.

Willow had no idea how she arrived home. One minute, she was walking out of that dreadful prison and the next, here she was, walking into her home. A home that she thought would bring such happiness. Instead, it was now her prison. Gabriel was in prison and so was she. A prison of her own making; filled with repetitive behaviours, anxiety and fear.

Emma noticed the change in her daughter and she was concerned. Now, seeing her so pale and thin was the least of her problems, she feared for her daughter's mental health.

'Willow, I think you should pay the doctor a visit and soon,' said her mum. 'For the sake of Jacob, please.'

Willow turned to face her mum, with tears in her eyes, she hugged her mum tightly.

'Please, Mum, I don't want to cause you and Dad any worries. I've already seen the doctor. He has referred me to the hospital. I'm waiting for the appointment coming through the post.'

The look of relief was evident on her mum's face. Emma was never able to hide her emotions and today was no exception.

'That is a weight off my mind, Willow. Make sure you attend the appointment.'

The following morning, she received an official-looking letter. The appointment was in a few days' time. One more worry to add to her ever-growing mountain of stress.

The same day that the letter arrived, Susan and Janet paid her a visit. Although they'd both sent her text messages to let her know they were coming, Willow appeared surprised to see them.

With huge grins on their faces and their arms open wide, her friends embraced Willow until she felt as though the life was being squeezed out of her.

Standing back and surveying Willow properly, Janet enquired if she'd been losing weight deliberately.

'You look to be about a size six I would guess,' she said in a voice full of concern. 'Are you eating all right, Willow?'

Susan interjected. 'From where I'm standing, I would hazard a guess that you're putting so much effort and love into your motherly role, that you're neglecting yourself. How about you sit down and put your feet up while I make us all some tea and sandwiches?'

Willow did not have the strength to argue. And so, like a dutiful friend, she made her way to the sofa, picking Jacob up out of his crib before flopping among the many cushions that were piled up for comfort. She saw the glances pass between Janet and Susan, followed by a look of sympathy in her direction.

Not quite knowing where to begin a conversation with her two best friends, Willow began to feel a strange sensation, creep up inside her. It seemed to be rendering her speechless. The words were in her head, but she couldn't get the message to her lips. Janet and Susan tried their best to engage Willow in conversation, but she sat there mute and expressionless.

'Let me hold Jacob while you enjoy a nice cup of tea, Willow, and how about having one of these tuna sandwiches that Jan has made us,' said Susan in a gentle and kind manner.

Reaching out for Jacob who was nestled in his mother's arms, Susan began to realise that Willow was most definitely ill and needed help. Whatever help she needed was way out of hers and Janet's scope. Holding Jacob in her arms, she began to pace up and down the room; now and then, jiggling him in her arms and was awarded with a gummy smile.

'He is so gorgeous, Willow, you must be very proud of him,' said Janet, who may well have spoken in a foreign language for all the response she got from Willow. The tea and sandwiches, she did not touch. The smell of tuna fish filled the room and the tea formed a skin on the surface making it undrinkable.

Trying to make light conversation was proving most difficult and eventually they conceded. Placing Jacob in the crib, Susan moved in close to Willow on the sofa. She put her arms around her friend and kissed her lightly on the cheek.

'Say something please, Willow, you're freaking us out and we cannot leave you like this,' pleaded Susan.

As though snapping out of a trance, Willow stood up and gave her a hug. Making her way over to Janet, she heaved a huge sigh.

'I'm going to the hospital tomorrow to see someone who can help me feel normal again.'

As Willow spoke, she stared off into the distance as though searching out for someone.

'I feel that I'm living a half-life at the moment. The world seems to have slowed down around me and I feel as though I'm screaming inside. I'm screaming at Gabriel. I'm screaming at myself for not realising what was happening. How could I have failed to notice.

Looking towards her friends with a manic expression on her tired stressed face, Willow began to cry. Softly at first, like a small breach in the river bank allowing the trickle of tears to escape, then building and building into a crescendo of sobbing. Her hands began to tremble followed by the tip tapping of her feet on the floor.

'Can I call for your parents to come over?' enquired Janet.

Willow shook her head in response.

'Please don't bother them. I'd rather they didn't see me like this. I feel as though I've been building up to this moment since I heard of the charges against Gabriel. I've been unable to cry until now. This moment was destined to happen, I'm so glad you're both here with me. The pressure has been building and building and now I have let off steam…literally.'

'Funny saying, don't you think?' said Janet to Willow 'You make yourself sound like a pressure cooker?'

Susan giggled and looked to Willow to see the funny side.

Willow gave them a weak smile. 'Thank you both for coming, I'm really exhausted now and need to sleep. Please don't bother my parents. Everything is already arranged. I'm off to see someone in a couple of days. I know that I need help and for that I feel ashamed. Who would have thought my future would turn out like this?'

'Are you sure that you can manage?' said Susan, who was already making her way to the door.

Chapter Twenty-Seven

Willow knew that she desperately needed to attend the appointment at the postnatal psychosis unit on Friday. Her sister, Molly, had even told her so last night when she whispered in her ear. She'd only spoken a few words of encouragement, but it was enough to convince her. Just listening to her sister's sweet voice for a fraction of a moment, gave Willow a little respite from her own tormented mind.

Only two days away, but such was her anxiety that just thinking about the appointment and all that it entailed, was driving her deeper, and deeper inside of herself. Psychosis seemed such a frightening word, making the word depression pale into insignificance.

She ran every scenario through her troubled mind. Envisaged every question that they may ask. How deep would they go into her mind? How would they untangle the labyrinth of thoughts that had wound themselves around her brain; growing and tangling themselves around her cortex?

Yet amid all of her crazy thoughts and ideas, she'd somehow managed to seek help from Dr Google. She could always rely on him, to answer any of her questions. No psychobabble, using words that she was unlikely to understand. Of course, it was a one-way process. With no one to argue with her or question the validity of the written words on her PC.

She knew a little about her brain and how it was supposed to work. She'd read about the chemical imbalance that can occur following pregnancy. Apparently, childbirth can trigger hormonal shockwaves. Another possibility was her thyroid, and she knew that was easily treatable.

She wondered if they would decide that ECT therapy was the only way forward for her. Oh yes! She'd also read about the electroconvulsive therapy; an old-fashioned treatment that was still being used in some of the psychiatric units. Willow wondered if she might save them the trouble and expense, of putting her through the endless hours of counselling and cognitive behavioural therapy. Perhaps she should just stick a fork into an electric socket and be done with it. But what if it went horribly wrong and instead of killing her outright, she might suffer terrible burns and shock?

No, she'd have to think of an alternate method.

The following day, Willow went to visit her parents. She needed to put plans in place for them to take care of Jacob while she attended the clinic appointment. Jacob slept soundly for most of the journey. Willow continuously checked on him in the mirror which she'd attached to the rear seat where the baby seat faced. Willow repeatedly counted to ten, then looked into the mirror, to check on Jacob. Although distracting and exhausting, she continued with this ritual, the entire journey until she parked outside of her parents' home.

When the noise of the car engine had died down, she sat for a moment, enjoying the familiar view. Memories of her childhood, came flooding back. She wound down the window and breathed in the heady scent of the lavender and the sweet smell of the Roses. Closing her eyes momentarily, she was once again a carefree, young girl. No tension in her neck and shoulders; no constant anxiety, guilt or self-doubt. Feeling the way, she did, was exhausting. Her depression was like having a full-time job that sapped away her energy.

Willow, heard the creak of the garden swing, as it gently rocked back and forth. As a child, she spent hours swinging to and fro, talking to Molly about her day.

She lifted Jacob out from his car seat and carried him over to the swing. Holding him securely in her arms, she sat on the old familiar smooth wooden seat. Kicking back with her legs, she set the swing in motion.

'Molly, Molly, come and play with me, I need you,' she called. But Molly did not come.

Jacob was becoming restless in her arms. She was kissing his soft warm cheek when Sandy came rushing towards them, barking and jumping in the air with excitement.

Hot on the heels of Sandy, were her parents. 'Love, what are you doing out here, come on in, I will put the kettle on,' called her mum, walking towards the swing.

Like a dutiful child, Willow followed her parents into the house. The house was welcoming. All the familiarity was like a huge comfort blanket, wrapping itself around her. She pressed her cheek against the softness of Jacob's neck, breathing in his scent and feeling the warmth of his young body against her own.

'Can I hold my grandson for a moment?' asked her father, as he held his arms out towards Jacob, who smiled with delight as Willow passed him over.

'Willow, you must be so proud of little Jacob, he is such a gorgeous boy and so much like you at the same age.'

The joy in her father's eyes was quickly replaced with sadness as the memories of his twin girls flashed before his eyes.

'Come along, you two, there is tea and scones on the table waiting to be eaten,' called her mum in an over cheerful voice in the hope of lifting the dark mood that had descended over the house.

Dutifully, Willow followed her father into the kitchen. He placed Jacob into the little crib that belonged to Willow when she was a baby. It had been given a coat of paint and her mum had made a new lining of crisp, white cotton broderie Anglaise fabric. Jacob kicked his little legs, as a soft fleecy blanket was placed over him.

'I've agreed to go to the hospital tomorrow to see a psychiatrist,' whispered Willow to her parents, as they sipped their tea wondering how they might help their beloved daughter.

Her mum heaved a great sigh of relief. Her dad reached over to touch Willow's hand.

'That's good news, lass, and a great relief to your mum and me. Have you let Gabriel know that you have decided to seek help?'

'He doesn't need to know,' replied Willow. 'I don't want to worry him any more than necessary. It must be terrible for him as it is, in prison like a common criminal, when his only crime was to try to provide a nice home for me and Jacob.'

'I think there was a bit more to it than that, Willow,' her mother gently said. 'Gabriel needs help. A different kind of help to you but help all the same. Is he getting any treatment for his addiction do you know?'

'I'd rather not talk about it, Mum, I'm sorry but the thought of Gabriel locked up in prison, makes me feel all confused, it brings so many thoughts to my mind. Some are so irrational that I feel like I'm going insane. Sometimes, I imagine that it's all a dream, a very sick dream.'

Her parents looked at each other, their pain apparent on their faces. Both of them unsure what to say in order to help their daughter return to them. She seemed so distant and nothing like the happy girl she once was. Although it was only four months since Gabriel was sentenced to prison, it felt like a lifetime since they saw the light go out of their daughter's eyes. Her soft features no longer shone out beneath her sweet personality. Her hair once dark and shiny, hung limp and dull, falling onto her thin shoulders. Her weight loss she could no longer hide despite the elegant skirt she was wearing that looked as though it had been pressed at least a dozen times in order to get such a sharp crease in the back pleat.

As usual, the family sat together around the kitchen table enjoying the ritual of tea and scones. Her parents chatted about the garden and how much planting still needed to be done while trying their utmost to avoid any subjects that might distress their daughter. Jacob lay in the crib making little cooing sounds as now and then Tom reached over and gently rocked the crib.

'Would you mind taking care of Jacob for me, Mum, while I attend the hospital appointment tomorrow?' whispered Willow, without making any eye contact.

'Of course, Willow that goes without saying now don't you go worrying about a thing,' replied her mum.

Emma looked towards Tom. 'Tom, will you drive Willow to the hospital tomorrow, I'd rather that she didn't go alone. It will be such an ordeal for her?'

Before he had the opportunity to answer, Willow interjected.

'I prefer Dad to be here and help take care of Jacob. Please don't worry,' pleaded Willow.

She did not want anyone to go with her to the appointment. It was humiliating enough without having her father witness her suffer the indignation of attending the psychiatric outpatient department. She made scenes up in her mind as images of crazed women holding pretend babies in their empty arms paraded up and down the imagined corridor of the unit. She could almost smell the disinfectant and hear the sounds of wailing women. The more Willow thought about the appointment, the more she reinforced the pain and torment that was surging through her delicate traumatised mind.

When these thoughts and feelings threatened to overcome her, Willow tried desperately to push away these destructive thoughts. She searched deep inside of herself for a memory so pleasant that it would drown out the negative feelings. Counting to ten always helped to ease her tension.

For no apparent reason, only one pleasant memory allowed itself, to filter from the many stored memories deep within her bank of joy. It was the time that Gabriel and she walked along the towpath of the Grand Union Canal. Hand in hand, they'd walked, savouring the moment of their new-found love. A time when Willow was feeling as though she was looking at nature for the first time. She'd been in a bubble of complete happiness that day, she was euphoric and drunk on love.

Such was the emotions of this recollected time, Willow reached out to an imaginary Gabriel. She searched for his hand, his touch that evoked such intense feelings of love, it was indescribable. Willow could smell his aftershave, a mix of cologne, sandalwood and musk played with her senses. The memory, long forgotten about the heat from his body when they made love. The way it intensified the fragrance.

As the memory became more intense, she whispered words that had long since been spoken, it was as if she was back in that place. A place of peace and tranquillity beside the sparkling water of the Union Canal. She stretched her imagination to the limits, visualising the Mallard ducks and Moorhens gracefully swimming across the water and the huge white swans gliding majestically towards the pretty canal boat that was moored alongside the towpath. The swans looked so self-assured as though their place on the canal was their right, their domain and they were the rulers of their kingdom.

Without warning, dark and dangerous thoughts began to gather inside of her head once more. It was as though thunderclouds had gathered, forming a tight, constricting pressure, which suddenly released as a river of hot tears fell from her soulful sad eyes.

When the tears came, the pressure from the black clouds eased, allowing her to return to the more rational thoughts of driving home.

Willow made her way to the bathroom and rinsed her face. She slicked a touch of lipstick on her lips, placed her saviour sunglasses on and made her way into the lounge, where her parents were earnestly watching Jacob in his little car seat ready for the journey home with his mummy.

Her mum looked a little surprised when Willow entered the lounge wearing a huge pair of sunglasses and a false smile.

'Are you all right, love,' her mum inquired. 'You do know that if you want to stay over tonight, it's no trouble at all, and it will make things much easier for tomorrow, don't you think so, Tom?' Her mum looked pleadingly at Tom, who had one eye on the television watching the premier league football and the other on his grandson.

'Leave the girl be, Emma, let her make up her own mind, we've put enough pressure on our lass these past few weeks, she has a mind of her own and it's time she started using it to some good. It is true that she has had a raw deal with Gabriel, but no one could have predicted the lengths he was prepared to go to for you and Jacob. I trusted him, just as you did sweetheart, and now look, he has all but ruined you. Drove you to despair, he has, but now it's time to return to reality, Willow. Your mum and I alone cannot help you that's why it's imperative to attend the hospital appointment tomorrow, you need expert help. Someone needs to find a way of clearing out all of that flotsam and jetsam in your head and return you back to us, mended and complete.'

Willow placed Jacob's car seat into the fixed base strapped him firmly in and proceeded to make her way to the door. She felt obliged to kiss her parents on their cheek, yet truthfully, it felt insincere and more like an automatic response laid down over many years. She felt conditioned into this daughterly act of affection. The truth was that it did not feel as though it came from her heart, for that felt like a cold hard stone in the middle of her chest. Somehow, since the birth of Jacob followed by the loss of Gabriel, she'd turned into an unfeeling shadow of her former self.

Willow deliberately organised a late morning appointment at the psychiatry clinic, in order to give herself the time to bathe and feed Jacob. She needed to be super organised in preparation for taking him to her parents' home, where she knew he'd be taken care of. On arrival back home despite being tired, Willow laid everything out in readiness for the morning. She colour-coordinated Jacob's little outfit leaving it in a neat row in the order it would need to be put on. She packed the nappy bag with more than enough to last him through the visit and enough formula to cover all of his feeds. His sleep-suit and a clean set of clothes she neatly folded and placed in the bag.

Her parents did, however, persuade Willow to stay over the night following her appointment. At least on this one occasion, she'd agreed albeit reluctantly. Although they knew that Willow was besotted to the point of obsession with Jacob, her mother, in particular, was worried by her daughter's erratic behaviour, driven by her worry about Gabriel and his gambling addiction. Like most new mums, she was getting very little sleep and was already showing signs of sleep deprivation.

In addition to the preparation for Jacob, she frantically marched around the house opening and shutting cupboard doors to have a last-minute check to make sure that the contents were all neatly lined up and pushed to the far end of the cupboard, labels facing forward. Willow couldn't risk opening a cupboard and the contents falling out and hurting her precious son.

Having laid out her own colour coordinated clothes and shoes; she checked the contents of her handbag. Satisfied that everything she needed for the following day was ready.

Willow proceeded to visit every room in the house and check that the windows were closed and locked. She checked each one ten times. Then she repeated the whole process as she returned to each room and checked that the plugs were out of all the sockets and the light switches off.

Exhausted, Willow went to bed. Jacob was sleeping soundly in his cot placed close to her bed. She knew he was sleeping soundly since she'd checked the baby monitor every two minutes without fail.

Willow looked longingly at the bed but before she was able to settle for the night, there were a number of rituals she had to perform. She took off all of her clothes, folded them neatly and placed them in a pile in the laundry basket with all the edges of fabric approximately half an inch away from the laundry basket lining.

She went into the en-suite shower, placing the baby monitor on a shelf close by, but far enough away, so as not to splash it.

She washed and rinsed her hair ten times. Then, using a loafer, she scrubbed her entire body ten times. Satisfied that she was clean helped to reassure her that she couldn't be accused of being slovenly or unhygienic.

It was ten minutes past midnight when Willow finally laid her weary head on the lavender fragrance pillow. At first, she couldn't find sleep. Too many thoughts were swimming aimlessly around her mind. She ruminated on the events of the day and of future events that had not yet happened.

As a consequence, she was still awake when Jacob stirred from his sleep. At first, he made little-sucking noises, pursing his cute little rosebud lips. After the first soft mewing sound, Willow gently lifted him up and out of the cot. She swaddled him tightly in his soft night blanket and gave him his feed that she'd prepared earlier.

Jacob was a slow feeder, but this didn't bother Willow as in her mind, it decreased his risk of choking. Another thing that she was paranoid about. She was terrified of the milk going down the wrong hole and killing him. Every few minutes, she stopped the feed and sat him upright, gently tapping his back ten times, for fear of him having trapped wind. She was terrified that he may be sick and inhale the vomit. Willow had read of such things. If Gabriel was here, she knew that she'd feel safe. He would know what to do if Jacob began to choke.

It was four o'clock before she managed to return to her bed, which had now turned cold. It had taken over an hour to clear away the bottle and disinfect all the work surfaces ten times.

She managed to sleep until seven in the morning when Jacob began to cry for his morning feed.

Instinctively, Willow woke up. She felt a strange sensation in her head and a humming sound ringing in her ears. She didn't recognise the sound, which felt almost like a vibration inside of her head and was distinctively different from the sound of the loud cry, as Jacob demanded his next feed.

Her eyes seemed to resist any commands that her brain sent. She felt that her mind was awake and yet her body asleep. Despite the protests from her son, Willow was unable to move. Not a single limb responded to the commands that she willed her brain to send down the many neural pathways to trigger a response. She felt locked inside of herself, struggling to escape from some kind of trap that her own body had set.

Willow lay trapped like this, for what seemed hours. In reality, it was ten minutes, after which time, her eyelids suddenly snapped open like a doll when put into an upright position.

That ominous number ten, the bane of her life. Ten was the exact number of minutes that she remained in an almost catatonic state. Gradually, the life moved into her body. First her fingers, then spreading gradually to her upper torso and weaving down her entire body until she could unfurl her toes.

Jacob's cry was getting louder and more anxious sounding. Her son was afraid. Did he feel abandoned? She knew full well what that felt like.

With a mighty effort and injection of self-will, she raised herself from the bed and reached over into his cot, lifting Jacob into her loving arms. His cry turned into a little whimper as she gently rocked him. Willow tentatively placed her feet on the ground. Her legs felt heavy and almost numb as though all sensation had departed her. As the weight of her body pressed down on the soles of her feet, a tingling sensation rose up like a volcano gently erupting and pushing blood up through her body and into her head. It felt like electricity entering her brain and switching it on. Bright lights sparkled in her peripheral vision, thousands of tiny stars twinkled and darted about. Although frightening, it was such a surreal moment that without realising, she actually got some kind of kick and weird pleasure from the experience.

Gradually, she made her way downstairs holding Jacob firmly in her arms. There was lots to do before she could leave the house. Everywhere must be left spotlessly clean, the surfaces disinfected, all the door handles wiped down and her usual security checks repeated ten times.

The drive to the hospital after taking Jacob to her parents was a real struggle for Willow. She'd never left Jacob with anyone before and even though she knew that her parents would take good care of him, she couldn't help but feel anxious.

The traffic was worse than expected on account of the time clashing with the school run. She hadn't considered this when she asked for a morning appointment. Willow was finding it hard to concentrate on driving and be mindful as different scenarios played through her overactive mind. The same thoughts kept spinning around on repeat as though they were on a loop and playing like a disc inside of her head.

She wondered what the consultant would be like. Would he or she be sitting there in a white doctor's coat, behaving all serious and professional? How would the conversation start? In some ways, she felt embarrassed and ashamed of her predicament. How had she come to this?

A scene from *one flew over the cuckoo nest* played through her mind, driving her deeper and deeper into a dark hole.

Suddenly, she heard a car horn beeping in quick succession. While stuck at the traffic lights, she'd drifted into some kind of trance. The driver behind began to wave his hands frantically out of the window, making rude gestures with his fingers.

Jolted back to reality, Willow quickly moved forwards and immediately stalled the car. The impatient driver behind her was so close he drove straight into the back of hers. The sound of cracking glass and crumpled metal sent her into a blind panic. Her heart racing as a tsunami of sweat formed beneath her armpits, leaving two large wet patches. Once more into the breach, she thought as she buried her head in her cupped hands. The man proceeded to rage, as he approached the driver's side window. Willow buried her head in her hands. She couldn't face, eye contact with the man and had no desire to become involved in a storm of windy rhetoric. She already felt anxious and panicky, her bladder was about to dispel its content and hot acid was burning her throat.

The banging on her window was so intense that she feared the glass would surely break. Gathering on her reserves, Willow finally managed to raise her head and turn to face the window where an abnormally narrow looking man with a shrunken and shrivelled face was staring intently at her. He had a manic expression that precisely matched the way that she herself was feeling.

Behind him, a small crowd of rubberneckers had gathered, to see what all the fuss was about. Willow felt threatened, as though some posse of vigilantes had gained ground on her and were ready to hang, draw and quarter her. She quickly checked that all the doors were locked. Then proceeded to turn the radio on full volume while continuing to ignore beetle juice face outside. Time became meaningless as she sat there with her eyes closed, lost in a sensory world of music and pain. She thought that she could hear a police siren above the noise of the music, or was it part of the song. Sometimes it was hard to differentiate between fact and fiction, however, it did appear to be getting louder, which by deduction would mean it was getting closer. Suddenly, the sound of the siren stopped, once again she could concentrate on the music. Surreptitiously, Willow raised her head slightly and turned to face the passenger side window. Perhaps it had been an instinct that prompted this action. Whatever the reason, it had been a wise move on her part. A female police officer was smiling at her through the window and beckoning her to lower the electric window.

Like an obedient schoolgirl when faced with a figure of authority, she lowered the window.

'Do you require any assistance, miss? Can I call a relative or friend to come and support you? It appears that you may be experiencing a difficult time.'

Willow relaxed a little and forced a fake smile.

'Just a panic attack, officer. I'm very sorry for any inconvenience I may have caused.'

The officer reached into her top pocket and retrieved a black notebook and pen.

'We really need to get this traffic moving, miss, can you please step out of the car for a moment, so I can take a few details and I will also need to perform a breathalyser test with your permission.'

Willow nodded in agreement and reluctantly stepped outside the car. She'd never done a breathalyser test before and was surprised at the simplicity of it. She knew the test would be normal and had nothing to fear about the results. The officer took note of her contact details and said they would be in touch as needed. Satisfied with the outcome, the officer waved her on into the forward moving traffic.

She drove for ten minutes before pulling over into a lay-by, where she opened the door and vomited up the contents of her stomach. The sour taste in her mouth was foul, resulting in wave after wave of nausea rising inside of her. Her clothes were damp from the cold sweat that had enveloped her body. She could smell the acrid sweat and felt ashamed and disgusted at herself.

Willow checked the time. If she left now, there was still time to make the appointment. Her parents were adamant that she attends the hospital and she doubted that they would believe what had happened on her journey. She walked around the back of the car to check out the bumper. It was still intact with only a moderate amount of damage, just a dent and a twist to the shape. She supposed that it could be explained away and maybe a little white lie wouldn't go amiss. Resolute to get the appointment over and done with, she returned to the car and continued her journey.

As expected, the hospital car park was an absolute nightmare to find. The layout was confusing. Other drivers were in the same predicament as herself, in terms of being clueless as to which direction to head. The signposts were few and far between, with most of them obscured by overhanging trees. She knew the hospital would be busy but wasn't expecting quite so much traffic. There appeared to be some kind of event happening since she noticed a large van with the local radio logo emblazoned on both sides.

Having driven around for twenty minutes, Willow found a parking spot. It was rather a tight squeeze sandwiched between a huge Land Rover and one of the new crossover vehicles which were equal in size to the Land Rover vehicle. Having eased herself out of the driver's side door, without causing any damage, she then realised that a parking ticket was required. Willow sighed a deep, restless sigh. Her day was not going well. She had no idea how long her appointment would take, but by now she couldn't care less, so what, if she over-ran her parking ticket, she had bigger worries on her mind than a petty car park inspector. In any case, how ridiculous to pay for hospital parking, it was an absolute disgrace.

As Willow queued beside the parking metre, the sun began to emerge between the clouds, helping to warm the cool air. She welcomed the warmth on the back of her neck and shoulders, both of which felt tight and knotted.

Above her, rows of small cumulus clouds streamed out as a layer of cold air passed over the relatively warm surface of the ground. She shuddered, as a cool breeze appeared to swirl around her, adding to the feeling of ice running through her veins.

Smoothing down her hair and straightening her black pencil skirt, which had somehow twisted itself around from front to back, she entered the hospital through the electric doors. She noticed there was a lot of activity in the corridors and a buzz of excitement or maybe something else. She couldn't put her finger on it. There were several official-looking people walking about with their identity tags dangling from NHS lanyards. Most of them were carrying clipboards and were very much distracted.

Willow was embarrassed and ashamed needing to attend for a psychiatric assessment; all of these people mulling about was not helpful at all. She hadn't wanted to come and now with so many people about she began to feel paranoid that a conspiracy was going on. Perhaps her parents had somehow arranged or rented a crowd of people to report to them that their daughter had indeed turned up for her appointment. Following the signs to the psychiatric unit was challenging; she seemed to be heading away from the main hospital. It was quite a track along the cold and draughty corridors. Away from the warmth of the sun, she began to shiver. The chemical-laced air felt suffocating, she could almost taste the cleaning products. Willow didn't feel dressed appropriately, she looked too formal in her black skirt and white blouse, why hadn't she dressed in her usual comfy jeans and sweatshirt? From time to time, she looked behind her, to check that no one was following. Willow could see the security cameras dotted around, not very discreetly hidden and guessed that some kind of security officer would be checking her every movement to ensure that she arrived for her appointment and then report back to her parents.

Finally, she found the reception area for the postnatal psychosis unit. It was crammed with staff and patients. Some looked as anxious as she herself felt. Willow overheard someone talking about a cyber-attack. She knew it, she knew that she was being followed. Perhaps a drone had spotted her and was waiting for the right moment to strike. Was the hospital suddenly going to be attacked, had the enemies of the UK, decided to take action?

Willow became agitated and full of fear. An overwhelming feeling of despair overcame her, reinforced by a vacuous overriding emotion. She was ready to turn around and run away as fast as her legs could carry her. An official touched her shoulder, making Willow jump. He displayed an empty smile as though it had been painted on his face with a splash of watercolour.

'Please join the queue at the reception desk young lady and give your details if you would,' he gently requested.

Like a dutiful child, she joined the line of patients. Her neck felt hot and heavy upon her shoulders as though it had suddenly turned into a huge cannonball. Almost trance-like she stood, staring directly ahead for fear of being a victim of the cyber-attack. Willow wasn't sure what this all meant. Her day so far had been traumatic at the very least and now the situation she found herself in was surreal. She felt a strange numbness creep up through her body, her body felt empty and hollow. She began to shiver. Willow knew that she should never have come and now look what had happened. The more she thought about what may lay ahead, the more frightened she felt.

Suddenly, a large austere looking man of around forty years of age, dressed in a sharp pinstriped suit, stood directly in front of the reception desk and tapped a metal tuning fork onto the desk, drawing attention to himself.

'Can I have your attention, please everyone? I'm sorry to announce that no further appointments will take place today. We have a national emergency that has caught the NHS unaware. A global attack has rendered all of our computer systems unusable. All systems are locked, we cannot access patient records, clinical information, blood tests, or any results and reports. Please be advised that you will be offered an alternate appointment in the near future. However, we cannot at this moment in time tell you when that will be. It is likely that you will be informed by post. I apologise for any inconvenience.'

Willow froze to the spot; it was as if her brain was so overloaded it had stopped working. His words seemed to be hanging in the air as though it was a voice recording, a subliminal message of some kind. She stood motionless while the crowd of people in front and behind her in the queue dispersed in different directions. She was not aware of time or space. Her surroundings were inconsequential, her spatial awareness had closed down, and she felt oddly relaxed and calm. For a moment, Willow wondered if this was how it felt to be dead. Did death bring freedom from mental pain, was there spiritual healing when the body no longer survived. It was in the few seconds before her brain was rebooted back to life that the seeds of her plan were sown in her mind.

Slowly and deliberately, she left the hospital, returning along the same route she'd entered, almost as though she was functioning in auto-pilot mode. Willow had a plan, and nothing was going to stop her until it had been executed. She remembered the way, of course… This place was her happy place where she'd first realised that she loved Gabriel; the place where he also declared his love for her. He had held her hand as they walked along the towpath. Her hand was a perfect fit for his. He was to become her first proper lover, she'd known that for certain that day and she knew that she was ready to give herself to him, body and soul.

She parked the car in the Swan car park, hidden among the cars belonging to the families who had come out for a lunchtime treat. Calmly and serenely, Willow made her way along the towpath that wound along the Grand Union Canal. Despite the nice weather, there was no one else walking along this stretch of the union not one single dog walker in sight. If anyone was around to witness Willow in her black pencil skirt and high heels walking along the towpath, they would certainly have taken note of her inappropriate attire, which was more suitable for an office, than a hike along the towpath.

Calmly and serenely, Willow made her way along the towpath that wound along the Grand Union Canal. There was no softness of grass beneath her weary feet, just muddied soil. Her world felt soiled and dusty. There was no dew such, as she used to notice on the blades of grass when she walked this path before.

She did not notice the flowers at her feet or the incense from the fading violets covered over by the leaves. She kicked a small white pebble and for the briefest of moments, an image of Jacob fleeted through her troubled mind. This respite was quickly replaced by a tide of mental pain and torment, sweeping through her mind. It was as though she had a fire inside her head. A fire that began its life as a spark the day that she heard the judge pass sentence on her beloved husband. A fire that she knew only she could extinguish in the *Grand Union.*

She continued along the path for ten minutes before she saw the black and white markings of the Lock gate in the distance. With an unusual calmness, Willow approached the lock gates. She sat on the wide beam, swinging her legs like she did when she was a little girl on the swing which hung from a tree in their garden. Her father had spent an entire weekend making the swing for her when she was seven years old. She thought how wonderful it would be, to feel as carefree as that seven-year-old girl. She longed to switch off from everyday life and remember herself in a more tranquil, peaceful place. A place where her life was perfect, where her troubled mind was calm and free from pain. She thought of her son Jacob. His innocent sweet face. Full of love and hope.

How could she continue to sully his life, with her demons influencing his development? Her son deserved better. Willow could see no future for herself. She was unable to stretch her imagination, beyond getting through the next tormented ten minutes. She convinced herself, that Jacob would be better off without her strangling his emotional development. She had no wish to transfer her pain, and obsessive ways to her beloved son. Perhaps Gabriel would be allowed out of prison earlier than expected. Maybe even come out a better man with his addictions under control. Fundamentally, he had the right genes, he'd just lost his way that's all. Maybe the root cause was linked to one of his parents, or maybe both. She wondered if he'd married someone else, someone stronger than her, would he still have spiralled out of control with his gambling.

Willow did not want to be responsible for making any mistakes that could influence Jacob's life. Her parents would understand. She was certain that this was the only way.

She looked into the deep, murky water of the lock. Debris was floating on the top. Twigs, leaves and scum twirled around in little eddies, where the water sucked in and out of the gate paddles. She guessed that it wouldn't be long before a boat made its way up towards the lock. She could see one heading towards her, just beyond the bend, out of view for the boaters. Willow felt lightheaded, almost euphoric. She closed her eyes and listened to the wonderful sounds of nature around her. She inhaled deeply, smelling the fresh cut grass of the towpath. Nature was Willow's God. She surrendered herself to nature as she fell forwards into the grey waters of the Grand Union Canal and into the abyss.

Chapter Twenty-Eight

Emma and Tom were sitting comfortably in their cosy lounge, enjoying a cup of tea, when the news broke about the NHS cyber-attack. They had just settled Jacob for his early afternoon nap. Both feeling a little weary from the unexpected amount of energy they'd spent, looking after their grandson. Only minutes earlier, Emma had remarked to Jack that she'd forgotten how hard it was, just looking after a young baby and there wasn't any wonder that Willow was so exhausted. By all accounts, Jacob had been a good little boy, although he clearly missed his mum and was quite fretful at times. He only drank half of his milk, flatly refusing to drink all the measured amount.

Emma had spent most of the morning nursing Jacob in her arms, a task that in truth, she really enjoyed. As she rocked him, Emma reminisced about her own twin babies, Molly and Willow. Emma always felt that Molly was all around them still. In the house and garden, in her heart and mind. She never told Tom for fear of upsetting him, but sometimes she imagined Molly talking to her. Whispering in her ear. Only that morning, Molly whispered to her mum, telling her to watch over Willow. The memory of those words now reverberated in her ears. The words going around and around in a loop, buzzing and calling out to her.

It had been Tom idea to switch on the television to listen to the afternoon news. They both sat open-mouthed, as the BBC news channel announced a global attack affecting more than 200,000 victims in around 150 countries. The web had been infected by ransom ware, which they believe had possibly originated in the UK and Spain before spreading globally. As yet, nothing was proven as to the origins of the attack. The chief executive of the National Cybersecurity centre was surrounded by journalists and reporters, pressing him for information. He reported that the outbreak could continue to infect more systems and other victims may emerge also, it was indiscriminate across the public and private sectors.

Tom switched the channel over to the local news. Reports were coming in that patients were being turned away from hospitals due to the unprecedented national cyber-attack. Only immediate necessary care was being provided. Experts from the central IT department were racing to decrypt the ransom ware and attack the root cause.

Emma turned towards Tom and held out her arms to him. With tears in his weary eyes, he moved across the sofa towards her, no words needed. They both knew how much effort it had taken their daughter to even agree to attend the hospital appointment. She'd internalised the stress of recent events in her life to the point of verging on a mental breakdown and now, when she'd finally found the strength to seek out professional advice, it was likely that she'd been turned away if the news reports were anything to go by.

Chapter Twenty-Nine

A sharp, piercing pain ripped through her body as she was lifted from the water of the Union Canal. The weight of the water on her clothes threatened to suck her back under the water and into the abyss that she so longed for. Another muffled shout was followed by a further sharp pain on the opposite side of her body. Willow began to cough and retch, as she appeared to be raised up into the air. Her body felt slack and her back was arched into a position that forced her head backwards. The murky water was gurgling around at the back of her throat. Instinctively, she spat it out. As she opened her eyes and looked upwards at the sky, filled with clouds, Willow wondered if this was her journey to heaven. Suddenly, she felt her body being dragged against a slimy, stinky wall, all the time being held tightly by wooden poles and hooks.

She was barely conscious as the boater wrapped the thick black rope around her waist. He had climbed down the metal step ladders and put his own life at risk; as he reached out towards her, while she was held in place against the lock wall, by the boat hooks. Colin and Stuart were struggling to keep their ground on the bank above, as they kept the hooks into the fabric of her clothes, which about to tear apart any second.

Willow had only checked one direction before throwing herself into the lock. She'd failed to look behind her, where Colin and Stuart, two seasoned canal boaters were approaching in their own beloved boat, *Waterlily*. They had anticipated what was potentially about to happen and had quickly moored their boat a few yards from the lock, without bothering to tie it securely to the bank, such was their haste. Instinctively, they'd grabbed the boat hooks and ran towards the lock, shouting for help as they did so.

Their cries were heard by the crew on the boat approaching from the other side. The crew on *Speckled Hen* heard the frantic shouts pulsating through the quiet of the countryside. It was Michael, from *Speckled Hen* who ran up the towpath, with a lifebelt and rope. It was Michael, who pulled Willow to safety out of the lock.

Along with Colin and Stuart, they placed Willow on her side. Michael's wife arrived with blankets and informed them, that she'd contacted the emergency services.

Within minutes, an ambulance arrived. The road adjacent to the towpath was a short distance from the lock enabling the paramedics to attend to Willow. The paramedics quickly dealt with Willow and were speeding off towards the hospital just as a police car pulled up and parked in the same spot.

Colin, Stewart, Michael and his wife, Janice, were still in shock when the young police inspector, came to question them about the event. Michael and Janice suggested, they gave the report in a more comfortable environment and proposed that they go aboard their boat and have a cup of tea or something stronger, as it had been quite an ordeal.

Colin and Stewart returned to their own boat to secure it to the bank. Satisfied it was safe, they joined Michael, Janice and the police officer, aboard *Speckled Hen*. Their timing was perfect, as they walked down the steps into the boat cabin, they heard the kettle whistling. A sure sign that the tea would soon be brewed.

In typical British fashion, they sat around the table, hands wrapped around their mugs, in contemplation. The police officer introduced himself as James.

After all of the formal introductions were made and James had noted them in his report book, they each told him of their own observations of the event. It was quite clear, from their observations, that no one else was involved. The woman, who none of them recognised was most definitely alone when she threw herself into the lock. No foul play was observed from either of the witnesses. James reported that it was an attempted suicide that thankfully was avoided, by the quick actions of Michael, assisted by Stuart and Colin.

Chapter Thirty

Willow was dreaming, she was certain, for how could it be possible that Gabriel was sat beside her, holding her hand and circling his fingers in gentle movements on her palm. Perhaps it wasn't him at all, he looked like Gabriel, but his face was thinner and his beautiful eyes were deep set and dull. She knew that she must be mistaken. After all, he was still in prison. As the word prison, filled her thoughts, she felt that same wave of shame and sadness, wash over her. Her eyes refused to close, she was so intent on keeping the vision alive; for it must be a vision, one of hope and anticipation. Despite the pain behind her eyes and the intense dryness she refused to close her eyes and shut out the image of Gabriel. Willow stared straight ahead without blinking, then something in her peripheral vision caught her attention. Moving her head to one side, she continued to stare.

Then she caught sight of the uniform. A uniform she recognised from the many visits she'd made to the prison. The walk of shame was how she felt as she made her way up the prison drive to visit her husband. All of those uniformed officers, professional men and women who took a pride in their work. Just as Gabriel once did. She knew that he was a good doctor. He was loved and well respected by his patients and work colleagues alike. After the trial, this was made quite clear to her, by the practice partners. Despite their anger, they acknowledged and recognised that Gabriel had an addiction. One that lead him and his family into ruination.

A muffled sound of voices that seemed to be coming from all directions, made her feel confused. She felt strangely disorientated, almost as though she was drunk or drugged. Her thoughts were foggy and mixed up. One sound resonated above the rest and seemed to have an echo.

'Willow, Willow, please, please, wake up, wake up...wake up, wake up.'

She finally blinked her eyes as tears rolled down her cheeks. She recognised the voice now. A voice that once spoke to her of love. Her husband's voice. As she turned her head towards Gabriel, she noticed the handcuffs that stretched between him and the prison warden. Willow blinked away the tears from her eyes and tried to smile at her husband. The smile never reached her lips. She wanted it to, but somehow, the message from her brain did not reach her lips. As reality washed over her and she began to piece together the events leading to this moment. Willow began to cry. Softly at first, as though a trickle of raw emotion had just broken through. Gabriel leaned in to kiss her tear-stained cheeks. That was the moment, the spell was broken and the pain of the memory forced itself into her reality, resulting in her gasping for breath and entering into a full-blown meltdown.

The doctor was called. He gave Willow a sedative and requested for the officer to take Gabriel for a drink of tea in the staff tea room, away from the prying eyes of the public. Gabriel was glad of the offer. His guilt was consuming him. He thought when he was convicted of fraud that his shame couldn't be worse. But that was nothing compared to this. He knew that he was the sole cause of his wife's breakdown. They could dress it up as postnatal depression or psychosis all they liked. He knew that this would never have happened without him pushing her to the limit. He felt guilty as hell. He vowed to make amends for his mistakes. No matter how long it took, he planned to make things better. His wife and child needed him now, more than ever. Little Jacob must never know about his father's gambling addiction and his mother's attempted suicide. This part of their combined history will be wiped out of their story. Just has his own mother had kept the truth from Victoria and himself, so must he and Willow withhold the truth from Jacob. Theirs was a story that started out so good, but it wasn't too late for the ending to change. Gabriel would see to that, only this time not with the roll of a dice. He knew what he must do to make amends to his wife.

Twenty minutes later, still under guard of the officer, he returned to the side of his wife. Holding her hand as the cuffs rubbed and chaffed his wrists, he gently stroked her hand. With great tenderness, he leaned over and kissed her forehead.

'You will be fine,' he murmured.

'I am here for you, I am here for you both, please believe me, Willow.'

The door to the room flew open as Emma and Tom ran towards the bed, their pain visible. Gabriel instinctively stood up and moved away, head bowed in shame. Restricted and helpless, he was unable to support Emma, as she began to slide to the floor. Tom called out for assistance – a passing nurse entered the room and gently laid Emma in the recovery position. Gabriel stood by in horror – his medical training obsolete, he felt in no position to offer advice or comment on the situation. Tom looked at him with his sad weary eyes. 'Gabriel, do something. I beg you.'

Looking towards his guard, Gabriel pleaded for his cuffs to be removed. It was to no avail, the guard not aware of Gabriel's background flatly refused.

'No way, mate, what do you take me for, you will be out of here like a shot, besides there are plenty of doctors and nurses around.'

'It's not worth my job.'

As Emma began to come around, the young nurse gently assisted her to a sitting position and offered a drink of water.

'Thank you,' she responded. 'I don't know what came over me, it happened so sudden. I felt the room closing in around me and a buzzing sound in my ears – then nothing.'

Tom kneeled beside his wife enquiring if she felt strong enough to stand with assistance.

'I will fetch a wheelchair, Mr? Your wife will need to be checked over.'

'Marshall, Tom Marshall,' he answered.

The nurse returned a few moments later with a wheelchair and a nursing assistant. Together, they helped Emma into the chair.

'We are taking your wife to the emergency department, Mr Marshall, where we will do a quick ECG and blood pressure check. I think perhaps it was a simple faint, but even so, it is important that we check.'

'I will come with you, Emma. Gabriel, are you able to stay a while longer with Willow?'

The guard checked his watch and nodded his head.

'Don't be too long, as we will be leaving within the hour.'

Within minutes of her parents leaving the room, Willow began to stir from her sleep. As she focused on her surroundings once again, Willow knew for certain that her suicide attempt had failed, the realisation of the pain and distress she had caused to her loved ones hit home swift and hard. Colour rising in her cheeks, she was unable to hide her pain, it was written all over her face. Looking towards Gabriel, she saw the image of her son etched into his weary face.

'Who is taking care of Jacob?'

Truthfully, Gabriel had no idea but guessed that it must be his parents. Not wanting to distress his wife any further, he told her that Jacob was being cared for by his family. There had been no time to talk with Tom but felt sure their son would be in good hands.

'I am so sorry,' she whispered.

'Shush, it is me who should be apologising. There are no words that can ever describe how sorry and ashamed I am, Willow. The depths of my torment and self-loathing are never ending. Can you ever forgive me?'

Looking towards the prison guard, Gabriel shrugged his shoulders.

'There is so much I want to say, but now is not the time. I will serve my sentence and if you have it in your heart to forgive me, I hope that we can move on from all of this and put it where it belongs. In the past. Do we still have a future, Willow?'

She nodded her head. He read her expression and hoped to God that he was right in his interpretation of her body language.

'We both need help,' she whispered.

'I have been keeping so much from all of you. My sister Molly is in my head and although I love her, I need to let her go. Will you help me, Gabriel?'

Her pale, dry cracked lips looked, as though they may splinter and flake away any moment. The intense expression painful for him to see.

'We will find the courage to work through this, sweetheart. Jacob needs us. We need to accept our mistakes and be kinder to ourselves.'

'You know, the brain has a habit of taking us away from the sweetness of calm. The mind throws around ideas and thoughts. Little voices in our head saying negative things.'

'Can we ever get over this, Gabriel, it has been such a traumatic experience. I sometimes feel as though I am outside of my body looking at someone else's life. At times, it is as though I am watching a movie and I have the leading role.'

'We will help each other.'

'Your parents will help you to heal and maybe my sentence can be reviewed so that I can soon be home. Hang in there, sweetheart. Time is a great healer.'

Clicking his tongue and sucking in air, the guard announced it was time to leave. Gabriel was allowed to lean over to his wife and touch her hand before being led out of the hospital and back to the prison van for his journey back to serve out his sentence.

As Willow watched her husband march away shackled to the guard, she realised what a terrible thing she had attempted to do. In her mind, it was a bigger crime to attempt suicide and abandon her baby and the potential consequences far outweighed the crime that her husband had committed. Yet here she was being loved and cared for, while Gabriel was being punished. The thought of them one day in the not-too-distant future having a fresh start gave her the determination and drive to make it happen. She knew that her own recovery process would take time. Before drifting off to sleep, she whispered her final goodbye to Molly.